EX LIBRIS

VINTAGE CLASSICS

T0315619

THE CHARMERS

Stella Gibbons was born in London in 1902. She went to the North London Collegiate School and studied journalism at University College, London. She then spent ten years working for various newspapers, including the *Evening Standard*. Stella Gibbons is the author of twenty-five novels, three volumes of short stories and four volumes of poetry. Her first publication was a book of poems, *The Mountain Beast* (1930), and her first novel *Cold Comfort Farm* (1932) won the Femina Vie Heureuse Prize in 1933. Amongst her works are *Christmas at Cold Comfort Farm* (1940), *Westwood* (1946), *Conference at Cold Comfort Farm* (1959) and *Starlight* (1967). She was elected a Fellow of the Royal Society of Literature in 1950. In 1933 she married the actor and singer Allan Webb. They had one daughter. Stella Gibbons died in 1989.

ALSO BY STELLA GIBBONS

STELLA GIBBONS

The Charmers

VINTAGE BOOKS
London

Published by Vintage 2011

2 4 6 8 10 9 7 5 3 1

First published in Great Britain by Hodder & Stoughton Ltd in 1965

Vintage
Random House, 20 Vauxhall Bridge Road,
London SW1V 2SA

www.vintage-classics.info

Addresses for companies within The Random House Group
Limited can be found at: www.randomhouse.co.uk/offices.htm

The Random House Group Limited Reg. No. 954009

A CIP catalogue record for this book
is available from the British Library

ISBN 9780099560548

The Random House Group Limited supports The Forest Stewardship
Council (FSC®), the leading international forest certification organisation.
Our books carrying the FSC label are printed on FSC® certified paper.
FSC is the only forest certification scheme endorsed by the leading
environmental organisations, including Greenpeace. Our
paper procurement policy can be found at
www.randomhouse.co.uk/environment

Printed and bound in Great Britain by Clays Ltd, St Ives PLC

To Spencer without whom . . .

Chapter 1

"AND IT'S MISS SMITH, ISN'T IT? CHRISTINE SMITH. DO FORGIVE me, but we've had so many replies, and quite a lot of them were Smiths. Your letter is on that table somewhere, but—"

She glanced, rather hopelessly, across the room. "I only moved in myself three days ago, and I haven't even started to get straight."

She wore a sad-coloured dress of a material resembling sack-cloth, which was fashionable that spring, and no jewellery except an outsize brooch with a sullen look on its copper face, but the impression she conveyed was winning; her indistinctly-uttered words sounded softly, and her movements were rest-fully slow.

"Yes, I'm Christine Smith." The words were perfectly distinct and the tone bright. "Oh, I know what it is—moving. I've just been—I moved out of my old home some months ago and—"

"Yes. Well, I'd better tell you a little more about what we want."

Another glance, towards the window this time, and then, after a pause, large eyes came to rest on Christine Smith's face.

"Five of us, you see, very old friends, who've known each other for ages and ages, decided it would be cheaper and more fun to live together. So we put our money into this old place and we're having it made into four flats—no, five, with yours— Oh, and the big kitchen, and a music-room. That won't fit into anyone's flat, you see, so we're having my piano in it and we shall use it for a kind of communal sitting-room when we feel like it. We, Antonia and I, that's Miss Marriott, she lives in London, she found this place for us, decided we must have a *housekeeper*. It will be nice to have an evening meal always on tap—unless we're all out, of course. Breakfast

7

and lunch, and if anyone wants to eat things at tea—I know Diana Meredith can't live without hers—we'll do that ourselves. It's the evening meal, and getting someone in to clean the stairs and so on, and managing the house. And the catering. You see, we all do something artistic. I draw, and Miss Marriott designs clothes for Nigel Rooth's, and Clive Lennox, I expect you've heard of him, yes," (as Christine Smith vigorously nodded) "of course, he acts, so none of us want to cook in the evening. I don't quite know what Diana and James Meredith do, admire the rest of us, I suppose. Diana did do pottery at one time but she's been stuck down in the country for years and she's given it up, I think. Well, I think that's all. Six guineas a week and the flat."

She stopped abruptly, peering short-sightedly into the other's face.

The large, stately room was warmed by a stove, with a pipe which stood out from the fireplace; well-warmed, and quiet. Its windows, set in a wall papered in a design of white and blue stars on brown, overlooked a square where old white houses glimmered behind budding trees and where, at this hour in the afternoon, not much was going on.

The room was disorderly, filled with the picturesque objects that an artist—of the older generation, at least—might be assumed to have collected during a working lifetime, and the light falling into it was a pale clear orange; thin, yet serene with the promise of summer sunsets to come. A warm, quiet, oddly attractive place, and noticeably unlike the living-room at Forty-Five Mortimer Road, Crouch End, N.

Christine Smith leant slightly forward.

"Are you—offering me the job?"

Mrs. Traill nodded, looking a little bewildered, as if the situation had come to this point quicker than she had expected or meant.

"I suppose I am, really. Yes, I am. Would you like to come?"

"I'd like it very much," Miss Smith said decidedly. "But you'll want to take up references first, won't you? I did give you the name of my employers, in my letter. Lloyd and

Farmer, the big office-equipment firm on Ludgate Hill. I was with them for nearly thirty-five years."

"A long time," Mrs. Traill murmured, looking at Christine Smith, for the first time, as if she truly saw her.

"Yes. I never was in another job, went there when I was eighteen. But they were reorganizing, and couldn't fit me in."

Neatly incised in memory was Mr. Richards' face, as he sat at his desk that morning, explaining that it was really a question of her age. Very nice, he had been. He did not get on with his wife, it was rumoured. Mr. Richards.

"Mr. Richards, he's the manager, I know he would give me a reference, he said he would."

Mrs. Traill put on another kind of face from her usual one and said, "I don't like references, they seem kind of squalid, somehow. I mean, if we can't trust each other—" and she smiled. She was lovely when she smiled. Tiny lines and deep ones suddenly, fascinatingly, appeared in the porcelain of her skin, and her wide eyes grew wider.

Christine Smith said nothing. The remark seemed to her plain silly. But she had offered a reference, and if it was declined, that was her prospective employer's affair. She waited, alert and cheerful, for what was to come next.

Mrs. Traill leant forward and lightly put her hand, with its raspberry nails and faint brown blotches and another cross-looking lump of copper (a ring, this time), on hers.

"I knew, from the minute I saw you that you were *the right one*. You're so *cheerful* and *placid*. I felt at once that you're going to be the person to manage the house for us, and keep us all in order (I'm afraid we're rather scatty). Like an old-fashioned nannie."

Christine gave a little laugh. It was only slightly embarrassed, because she had expected the people who had drafted that advertisement to be unconventional—artistic types always were. But in Mortimer Road jokes about nannies had not been made, and Mortimer Road would have thought this a queer sort of interview; interviews for jobs were among the serious things of life, together with money, and domestic electrical equipment.

9

"I don't know about that," she said, "but I like the sound of the job and it will be nice to have my own place; I've been living in a bed-sitter—"

"Dreadful, so depressing. And so expensive round here." Mrs. Traill's tone was absent, for what did it matter how Christine Smith had been living when she was here, and firmly secured, in the neat black and white tweed and good walking-shoes, with her thick greying hair cut short and firmly curled about her ordinary but slightly-rosier-than-ordinary face?

That complexion must be a nuisance, get too red sometimes, mused Mrs. Traill, who had never yet conceded a physical inch to another woman in the battle of looks.

"Now, when can you come?" she said.

Miss Smith was about to reply, "Any time that suits you, I'm free now," when Mrs. Traill drifted on, "The Men are still in the house, of course. It makes everything *fearfully* messy but I rather like it, they're so *vital*. Mike, he's the fore-man, says they'll be out by the twentieth. The others are moving in on the twentieth, so—" she hesitated, gazing out of the window, as if her eye had been caught by the sunset.

"Then suppose I come on the twentieth, early," Miss Smith spoke more decidedly than usual, for being artistic was one thing and dithering was another, "and then I can get things organized a bit, before your friends come." She paused. "Would it be convenient for me to see—the flat you said I could have?"

"Of course," Mrs. Traill got up. "It's right at the top. You do sound *sensible*, Miss Smith, and that's so cosy because we're all scatty, you see, and usually thinking about our crea-tive work—I hope we shall all get on. I think we shall. I hope you don't mind stairs."

"Used to them," Christine briskly said. "Our house had fifty," and they began the climb.

Pausing when Mrs. Traill did, and looking about her, Chris-tine Smith saw peach walls, their tint deepened by the light pouring through a landing window. Three doors, opening off the little square place.

"A bedroom, and a living-room, and this is your kitchen," said Mrs. Traill, opening them one by one. Christine only glanced in, and said nothing, as each closed on a vision of plain eggshell-blue distemper and—a spiffing electric cooker, embattled with gadgets from plate-rack to horizontally-opening door. Mrs. Traill did not notice that the rosy colour in Christine Smith's cheeks had deepened to burning crimson.

"Loo and bathroom on the next floor, they're minute but yours. No room up here and it would have meant endless fuss with pipes. We rather spread ourselves on your cooker, to make up." She glanced at Christine. "Do you like it?"

"It's very nice . . . I should think you get quite a view from here, don't you?" The unnoticed blush had faded.

"Over the Square to the Heath." Mrs. Traill was leading the way down again, and was absent in her manner, as she inwardly sketched a conversation with Antonia Marriott: *Never batted an eyelid when I showed her the flat, took it entirely for granted, didn't even react to the cooker, I sometimes think some people* . . .

But Christine Smith would have agreed with Kipling's advice in *How the Rhinoceros Got His Skin*— "I shouldn't ask about the cooking-stove, if I were you"—because thirty-five years of her life had been given to people who had felt for electric cookers, and radios, and electric fires and irons and toasters, and, later on, for tape recorders and television sets, what most people feel for their families or their God.

But this, she thought, following Mrs. Traill downstairs, will be *my* cooker . . .

In the hall, Mrs. Traill paused. She was a small woman, and she now looked up thoughtfully at Christine Smith.

"That's settled then, isn't it? You'll come on the twentieth."

"Yes. At eleven if I can get the removal people to give me a definite time. There's a little place round the corner from where I'm living that does light removals."

"That's fine. Well . . . good-bye, then, until the twentieth. Oh, my 'phone number's HIG 1111. Like me to write it down?"

"Whoever could forget *that*?" cried Miss Smith, with her

first hint of a sparkle as distinct from an overall brightness, and Mrs. Traill laughed back, as she stood at the top of the steps, watching her walk away.

Down the flagged path, between the neglected beds where some greeny-yellow daffodils moved in the evening wind, out through the heavy gate of wrought-iron and into the Square, went Christine Smith. Dusk had fallen suddenly, and the old lamps, with their gentle glow, had come on, and now the five o'clock rush of traffic was in full cry. The rather sturdy figure walked briskly off in the direction of the bus-stop.

She seems a nice old thing, reflected Mrs. Traill, whose name was Fabia, beginning the climb up to her studio.

In fact, she was herself a little older than Christine Smith, but life, and travel, and being an artist, and a husband or so, and even details like her clothes, and what she ate and drank and read and listened to, had had the effect of making her seem years younger. I'm usually right about people. I think she'll do, decided Mrs. Traill.

Chapter 2

ALONE UNDER THE BENEVOLENT GLOW OF THE LAMPS, THE
rather sturdy figure opened her bag and took out a new-looking
cigarette-case and a mildly expensive lighter. The smoke went
down into her lungs with the sensation of mingled discomfort
and satisfaction that was becoming familiar. She coughed.

*Christine doesn't smoke. It's such a relief to us, when all
the girls do nowadays.*

The inward voice was old and contented. It had made that
remark for more than a quarter of a century, following it with
remarks about expense and, as time went on, about horrors
which might result from the pernicious habit.

Christine turned her mind away from the voice, and looked
down the hill in search of the bus.

It was easy to forget the kind of things Mother had said,
because her mind was full of her flat: three rooms, and Oh,
the cooker. Not all those years, during which the sight of the
newest electrical device had instantly alerted a number of
emotions, none of which were agreeable or fully acknowledged,
had been able to spoil her first sight of that cooker. I'll cook
very . . . I'll cook some . . . I'll *cook*, thought Christine Smith.

Her cigarette went out while she was on the bus, to the
amazement of the conductress who, the downward-going
vehicle being almost empty at this hour, had dared to sit down
for three minutes.

"It's gone out," she said, watching, but not believing, as
Christine ineffectually puffed. 'Cor, see mine go out. I hardly
get lit up when it's done. Want a light?"

"Oh, I've got a lighter, thanks all the same . . . I'm nearly
home when I get down, I won't bother." The bus stopped,
and she swung herself neatly off, and away across the dusky,

roaring road. The conductress rang the bell as three late, shrieking schoolgirls scrambled aboard.

"Oh I've got a *lighter*, thanks all the same," mimicked the conductress to herself. "There are some types about."

Christine left the High Street and its towering block of new offices, standing arrogantly over the derelict Victorian shops and houses, a streetful of which had been pulled down to make room for it; and made her way into the back streets.

Here, the coarse aggressive faces and the voices of almost unendurable harshness, and the glaring shops, and the reek and roar of traffic, were exchanged for a more bearable squalor, silent and almost dark. The houses were more than a hundred years old, two-storeyed, faced with grey stucco, shabby and dirty, but restored to much of their first modest domestic charm by the dimness, for most of the faint glow illuminating the street came from their windows. Halfway down, a dark passage occurred between them, running between high walls, and Christine unhesitatingly turned down it.

Her footsteps sounded loudly on the paved way, echoing back from the ancient, filthy bricks, that were scrawled in white chalk with moon-faces and the brief feuds and love-affairs of the local children. The still, sharp air smelt of soot and cats.

The street into which she came out was wider, and cleaner, and lit by a shadowless orange glare; at one end of it a high hill, black against the dimmed afterglow, unexpectedly loomed, as if the beholder had been suddenly transported to Innsbruck or Surrey. Christine gave a last glance at Parliament Hill (this was the apparition's name) as she shut her front door.

But it was not truly her front door, and in the hall she came face to face with her landlady.

Under the glare of a light with a fringed and patterned shade, on the dazzlingly-patterned linoleum, against the wall-paper crawling with what looked like stylized germs stood Mrs. Benson. The hall was bright, and gay, and challengingly clean. "Go on, dare you to find a speck of dirt," it shouted.

Mrs. Benson looked at Christine Smith from under her terrible tower of brass hair.

"How djer get on?" she demanded. She had, to do her justice, meant to say, "So you got back, then," but curiosity, which gnawed her from half-past seven in the morning until twelve at night, would have its passionate way.

'Oh . . . thank you . . . it seems very nice . . . they offered me the job and I've taken it."

"Quick work." Mrs. Benson would have preferred to hear that it was a rotten kind of job but Christine had had to take it because there didn't seem to be anything else going. "Made up your mind all of a sudden, then," she went on.

"Yes."

Christine and Mrs. Benson looked at one another.

Mrs. Benson did not like Christine, and Christine detested Mrs. Benson. Lacking the inexhaustible bank-balance of birth, she did not feel herself untouched by Mrs. Benson's curiosity, grudgingness, and spite, and she clung in Mrs. Benson's presence the more tenaciously to her own lady-like imitations of what she deeply admired. Mrs. Benson, more simply, thought that Christine was stuck-up.

But she was a little embarrassed by the naked stare of c'ear brown eyes. Such a look, who does she think she is? said Mrs. Benson's own eyes. "When you thinking of going?" she demanded. "I can let that room of yours tomorrow."

Her lodger nodded, recognizing her resentment at losing a tenant who expressed no word of regret at going.

"On the twentieth."

"You'll be going to Drake's, then. Better get round there quick, if you are. He was telling me yesterday he's that busy he don't know whether he's coming or going. I'd pop round this evening, if I was you."

Is this good-nature on Mrs. Benson's part? Or is it a lifetime's habit of arranging other people's affairs for them? We must be careful here, remembering that Mrs. Benson is not just a cow; she is a sacred one.

"Oh, tomorrow will do, I think, thanks all the same."

Christine was turning away to the door of her room when, suddenly, and with the force and colour of a vision, a picture entered her mind: with such strength and authority that afterwards she wondered if it could possibly have been a Message from Mother and Father, who perhaps Knew Better now, and wanted her to be free at last of Mortimer Road?

She saw her furniture, the pieces she had chosen before the sale, and sent away in a van to be stored at Messrs. Jeffrey's emporium somewhere out at Enfield: the Sideboard, the Dining-Room Table, her Bed, the familiar pictures no one had ever looked at, Father's Chair, and the Best Bedroom Carpet—she saw them all, in their hallowed associations and venerable comfort sitting in those three rooms with their walls of birds-egg tint in Pemberton Hall. For an instant, she experienced a pure, overwhelming feeling of repudiation. No, said her spirit.

She did not stop to think. Turning to Mrs. Benson, who had also moved away in the direction of her own quarters, she cried, rather than said, so excited and high was her voice:

"Oh—Mrs. Benson— would you like to have my furniture?"

Mrs. Benson turned, face alight with greed and suspicion.

" 'Ow do you mean, have? Store it 'ere—or buy it off of you? I can tell you here and now I've got no room for storing, in my place. And I've not money to buy second-hand stuff, neither."

"No—not store it or buy it. Have it. As . . . a present."

"I don't need anyone's old bits and pieces thank you . . . What is there, then?"

Christine rapidly ran through the list, with every second feeling more strongly impelled to get rid of it all, and with every other second crushing down the sensations of guilt.

"Quite a flatful," was Mrs. Benson's comment. "They giving you your own place, up at this place, then? I said to Stan, 'I'm sure she's got her own stuff, in store,' I said. They don't half charge you in those places neither." She paused.

Christine was now trying to work out how much of her share in the money from the sale of the house could be safely spared for new furniture . . . pale wood, against those walls . . . or . . . very dark perhaps? Second-hand 'finds', from junkshops . . . she could glue, and polish, and re-cover . . . Yes, dark would look best.

"I don't mind obliging you, if you want a home for it,"

Mrs. Benson was saying. "My sister always says I'm a fool to myself. Soft. But I'm like that. I don't mind. I'll have it."

Christine was still inexperienced in the ways of the Benson world, and she felt that she had misjudged her landlady. She did not realise that her possessions were as good as reposing in Mrs. Benson's place from the first instant that the words 'have' and 'furniture' had penetrated Mrs. Benson's consciousness.

It was arranged that the vanload from Enfield should be delivered on the afternoon of the twentieth.

Christine insisted on this, with adamant firmness. She did not want to see the Dining-Table and its attendant devoted crew being decanted into the road outside the Benson 'place', grandly unconscious of the ruthless way it had been disposed of.

Mrs. Benson agreed. If there "was some pieces that wasn't too bad" among the vanload, she did not want to have to admit as much to their donor, and thank her. Gratitude, in Mrs. Benson's view, was among the dirty words: it was as well that her tenant should leave before the furniture arrived.

Christine went into her chilly, be-patterned, too-clean bed-sitter, and cut bread and butter and boiled a kettle, and dined.

She felt tired, which was not usual with her. It had been quite an exciting afternoon, what with seeing those greeny-blue rooms and the cooker, and taking on a new job, and then giving away the furniture—actually *giving it* away, all that was left, in the material sense, of Forty-Five Mortimer Road— although, in another sense, the house and its contents and in-mates were still—could *spitefully* be the word?—alive and kicking.

They were kicking her spiritual shins, as she sat at the table drinking tea and eating bread and butter; kicking away, and muttering over and over again, *faithless, unkind, disloyal,* and plucking with the experienced hands of many years prac-tice, every muted chord of love and grief in her heart.

No, 'spitefully' was not the word, of course, what a silly idea. She must not take it all so seriously. And she even succeeded in making some timid excuses for herself after she was in bed;

thinking that, after all, no one could say she had not been a good daughter to them; and surely someone might be permitted to feel tired, and excited, when, after fifty-three years of life, of which thirty-five had been passed in earning money to buy more and more electric toasters and irons—that someone had shaken the very last survivors off the raft, and firmly kicked the raft itself off into the troubled sea, and was, for the first time, truly Leaving Home.

Chapter 3

BUT SHE AWOKE WITH THE SHOCKED REALIZATION THAT NOW she had no furniture, and, in that first moment, even considered asking it back from Mrs. Benson.

At once, she knew that this was impossible.

Encountered later, on the previous evening, Mrs. Benson had already shown an altered manner, replacing rudeness by the condescending familiarity befitting a benefactress, one who had done that soft fool, what had given all her stuff away, a good turn. Christine, no weakling, did not like to imagine the scene were she to suggest going back on her word.

She would have to go to the junk-shops. Quite an adventure, that would be.

She had glimpsed them occasionally, here and there, as she went home by bus on summer evenings, cosily peopling them with types she had read about in fiction a quarter of a century old (Christine, and Mortimer Road, did not read anything contemporary except the headlines in the papers).

A junk-shop was dark, and dirty and cavernous, with a vaguely Oriental atmosphere imparted by a gilt Buddha seated in its shadowiest corner, and some alabaster godlets with chipped noses displayed on a tray outside. Inside, there were desks and tables and chairs, decrepit but fine old pieces, of which the proprietor did not realise the value. They were, nevertheless, easily repairable by an amateur. The proprietor was male, and slightly mysterious.

The shops explored by Christine on that morning were certainly arranged to appear alluringly cavernous, but they were neither shadowy nor dirty, and in charge there was a Character, bearing small resemblance to Little Nell's Grandfather and dyed deep in the sacred consciousness of Personality.

These Characters saw slap through her or thought they did,

at the first peep; and indeed, they saw that she knew nothing about second-hand furniture, which was all that concerned them about Christine Smith, and they at once rattled off an imposing history of whatever object she happened to be looking at.

"Yes," they invariably began, "that's a . . ." and away they went; date, period, maker, type, variation if any, rarity or otherwise, had a lady in yesterday was crazy about that, and suddenly, accompanied by a holy kind of smile—wham! the Price.

Those well-informed articles in the more expensive women's papers and the informative little talks over the air had done their work. Little Nell's Grandfather knew exactly what he was selling and what the time of day was, and Christine ate her lunch at an Italian restaurant in Camden Town feeling vaguely snubbed and disappointed. But she was accustomed to both sensations and hardly noticed them.

Was it because she had made so many tiny decisions, over so many years, so carefully, that she now seemed able to make large ones casually?

Anyway, she came out of that restaurant determined not to waste any more time hunting for junk. She would buy some new furniture. Modern, perhaps, really modern.

She turned aside into the premises of a large local firm that was both old-established and progressive, and at once saw something she liked very much.

Mansfields had tried the experiment of placing an order with a Scandinavian firm, which designed and made a series of light, angular pieces in birchwood, processed to give it the silvery-pink hue associated in popular imagination with the trees, and it was this 'line', cunningly displayed against a drop-scene vaguely Northern, that had caught her eye.

She bought two chairs, and a table, a bed and a chest of drawers and a wardrobe and a bookshelf, lean and elegant, the sparry crystalline grace of the snowflake translated into wood, and they cost her three hundred pounds of her money and she came out of the department feeling rather as she used to at the Office Party every Christmas, when she had had some sherry.

On her way through the Soft Furnishings she saw a curtain material, trails of bright green ivy on a white ground, and felt that she must have it, so she bought twelve yards. That ought to be enough, and if there's any over, I'll just have cushions, thought Christine, flown with furniture and looking rather glassy about the eyes . . . Lots of cushions.

She also bought three pairs of sheets and some fluffy green-blue blankets and a saucepan or so. She ordered the curtain material to be sent to her sister's house at Edgware, and then rang her up, to announce its forthcoming arrival.

Mary Smith had early escaped from earning money to buy toasters by marrying and passing this task over to her husband. The eldest of her three clever sons had just left home and was training for a job, and she would have time to machine Christine's curtains.

She would be glad to do it, not only because she was fond of her sister, but because all the married Smiths (there were three of them) regarded Christine with suppressed and largely unconscious guilt because she had borne the heat and burden of the Forty-Five Mortimer Road day for so long. They had an uneasy feeling that they owed her something. "The same stuff for all three rooms?" asked Mary. "Even in the kitchen? I always think gingham looks nice in a kitchen. So fresh. Linda was looking at a lovely pattern of chianti bottles and French loaves the other day. Very modern. But I like gingham, myself, for a kitchen. Of course, poor Linda . . ."

Linda was betrothed to Mary's eldest son.

"How are they?" Christine, with skill born of years' practice in Mortimer Road, turned the subject aside from the desirability of gingham in the kitchen.

Mary said, Oh, they were fine. Only she did wish they had a proper home of their own to go to and not just a room and use of bath and kitchen in someone else's flat. Poor Lin, she wouldn't be having her own curtains for her kitchen, it did seem a shame . . . And then, pouncing like some mother-elephant emerging from the jungle on a point in her sister's remarks which she had only half-heard, she exclaimed with a sharpening of tone—

"Chris—this place you're going to—did you say you've got a flat?"

"Yes . . ."

". . . because is there any chance of your getting it for Lin and Michael? How big is it?"

"Yes, but Mary . . ." Christine patiently inserted her voice through the flow of excited maternal instinct, "that's quite out of the question. The flat goes with the job."

"Oh. Oh, I see. No, I suppose you couldn't . . . I was going to say, suppose Lin gave up *her* job and . . ."

"They particularly wanted someone over fifty, Mary. It said so, in their advertisement."

Mary gave a loud exasperated sigh. She longed to see Michael and Linda started off properly.

Their prospects were uncertain enough, goodness knows, what with Michael only training for his job, though it was true they were paying him well while he trained, and Linda not twenty . . . It made all the difference, having your own place. She could remember her feelings when she and Dick came back from their honeymoon in 1939; the hall at Glendene with the new hatstand gleaming, and the pretty wallpaper . . . of course, you could buy a house for next to nothing, in the days just before the war.

"It doesn't seem fair, does it?" she said, and then, for the Smiths had their gleams of sensibility and affection, "Sorry, dear, I didn't mean that. I'm glad you got such a nice job and your own place." Pause, while the sentence *Shut up all those years with Mother and Father* scurried across Mary's mind and was ignored. 'What kind of people are they?"

"Well . . . artistic, really, I suppose."

Mary said simply, Oh help, and sooner Christine than her.

"But not in a crazy kind of way. I mean, this Mrs. Traill, she was spotlessly clean, and seemed quite sensible. She draws illustrations for those stories in the women's mags: They've all known each other for years and years, she says."

"Is it a family?"

"Oh, no. Just friends, I gathered."

"Sounds weird," said Mary. "Well, I must fly, I've got masses to do. I'll send the curtains off as soon as I've got them done, Wednesday, probably. Depends when the stuff comes. Or I could . . . but you aren't on the 'phone at that place, are you?"

That place was Iver Street. She knew that her sister was not, but could not resist a sisterly dig at Christine's going to live in that awful street off the Archway.

Having promised to post off the measurements that afternoon, Christine came out of the call-box, to receive a glare from a young woman waiting outside, with hair piled into that tower which has not been seen in England for two hundred years. She gave her glare for glare, and decided to go up to Pemberton Hall and take the measurements now.

Pemberton Hall showed most of the symptoms affecting a three-hundred-year-old mansion which is having its entrails pulled about; mud, stray planks, exuberant young workmen with transistor-sets in the breast-pocket where their grandfathers would have carried a pencil, hideous distant singing, a pervading smell of putty, and slapdashery.

Christine walked in, as the front-door stood open, saying distinctly "Good-morning," with a firm nod, to a workman crouching in front of the wainscotting with a blow-lamp who said "Morning, love," with a bright upward glance out of impudent young eyes. The blowlamp hissed, the transistor wailed, and upstairs someone was banging and sawing.

Christine, taking a tape-measure out of her bag, went right up to *her* flat and shut the noise away and began measuring.

When she came down again, a big fair gentleman in sporting clothes was talking to one of the workmen in the hall. He glanced vaguely at her as she reached the lower stairs and she said, "Good-morning."

"Good-morning," said the gentleman.

"I am the housekeeper. Miss Smith," said Christine, whom thirty years of receiving customers at Lloyd and Farmer's had left without any hampering consciousness of her own personality.

23

"Oh, yes. Splendid," he exclaimed. "My name's Meredith. Very glad to . . . just having a look round. Awful mess, isn't it. But Mr. Ryan here tells me we really shall be straight by the twenty-first."

Mr. Ryan said nothing but looked sardonic.

"I was taking some measurements," said Christine. "In my flat."

Before Mr. Meredith could say more, a tallish slender woman, also wearing rather sporting clothes, came out of one of the adjoining rooms and paused, looking quickly at Christine. She was noticeably thin, and had been noticeably pretty.

"Ah, Diana—this is Miss Smith, darling, she's going to be our housekeeper. My wife, Miss Smith—Mrs. Meredith."

"We're so thankful to have got you," said Mrs. Meredith. "You mustn't be put off by the mess. It's all going to be cleared up by the end of the week. Isn't it, Mr. Ryan?"

Mr. Ryan, who was comely and carried no transistor set, began a rigmarole in an unintelligible Irish accent which gradually, for lack of hearers who could understand what he was saying, died away. He walked off, looking sarcastically at a slide-rule.

"Isn't your flat charming?" Mrs. Meredith went on, in a tone firm as Christine's own, "I'm sure you'll love it . . . so *lucky*, with accommodation in London what it is . . . I think its the nicest in the house. Two old friends of ours are mad about it—they're dying to have it."

"It is very nice," Christine said, inwardly alarmed at this news.

"When I saw that north light, in the sitting-room, I nearly decided to have it for myself—for my wheel, you know. I'm a potter."

"Oh, do you do those hand-made jugs and vases? There were some lovely ones in a shop at Lulworth, where I went on holiday last year. All black and brown, with white sort-of whirls," said Christine.

"Yes. Oh, I shall be at work again, as soon as we're settled in. Well, we mustn't keep you. We shall be seeing each other again, I expect, running in and out, before we all move in. My husband and I are staying in the village."

She smiled and nodded and turned away. Mr. Meredith smiled slightly more warmly, and did likewise.

Christine went down the steps and out past the daffodils, open now, and glowing in the sun. Not so nice as Mrs. Traill. A bit stand-offish. But a lady all right, which perhaps Mrs. Traill . . . ?

A certain kind of easiness of manner was not, for Christine, associated with birth.

But these were regions of speculation unfamiliar to her, and she put them aside with the thought that she would not be seeing much of her employers anyway, and so long as they were pleasant to her and she satisfied them, what did anything else matter?

"I don't like that woman," said Diana Meredith, the instant Christine was gone.

"Oh come, darling."

"I always know, James. I know *people*. It's my thing. I'm a natural psychologist. Not a glimmer of imagination, I should think. She just doesn't realise—or more likely won't acknowledge—her enormous luck. Typical lower-middle class. It's just like Fabia to land us with someone like that, she probably felt sorry for her."

"Oh, I don't know, darling."

"She really is an ass— I wish we'd let Amanda and Dick have it."

She turned moodily away and stared up at the chaste curve of the staircase, down which floated some masochistic transistor-plaint.

The calmness with which James Meredith heard these ominous remarks implied that he had been married to them for some time, and perhaps married as well to something loveable in the speaker. He gave her a pat on the behind, and she wheeled round with a lightning change to gaiety and they went upstairs as entwined as if they were eighteen—which, except for living in a body that had been here for some fifty years, Diana was.

25

Chapter 4

CHRISTINE SPENT MORE MONEY THAN SHE WAS PLEASED TO, during the next few days, sitting in the shops, sitting in the cinema, sitting over her lunch. Her lodgings were not a place in which anyone could sit.

Why had she gone to live there at all?

. . .

On an afternoon in January, more than a year ago now, she had happened to be on some errand which had taken her to Hampstead Village.

It had been the usual kind of Smith errand; one of the electric deities installed in the temple consecrated to their worship had turned capricious (as they all frequently did) and the shop from which this particular one had been bought was not local; Mrs Smith's infrequent excursions from beneath her own roof were usually made in search of new shops displaying gadgets, and she had found this one in Hampstead and ordered whatever-it-was to be sent home to Mortimer Road, and then, after ten days, it had Gone Wrong, and would Christine go over to Hampstead, they were sure to be open though it was a Saturday, and just ask them to pop across to Crouch End and put it right; Mrs. Smith combined an impatient belief in the power of shop-people to 'put things right' with an immediate acceptance of the fact that they usually couldn't, and would have to send the gadget back to its makers.

So Christine had uncomplainingly gone, putting aside the small tasks of interest to herself that she was leaving at home, and had enjoyed, in a mild way, the journey in a bouncing bus across the Hampstead ridge and the snowy Heath.

The shop was not easily found; it was new, and bright in a cheap way, and braving things out in a tiny back lane. The

26

young man inside it seemed at once gay and without hope—the familiar contemporary attitude—and Christine had left whatever-it-was with him and come outside again and walked off.

And then she had mislaid, rather than lost, her way for perhaps five or seven minutes, and during that time she had come upon a church, an old church, shadowed by the sweeping branches of a cedar burdened in dazzling snow. The sight of it, and the long curve of a snow-covered wall bordering the graveyard in which it stood, filled her with an unfamiliar, exquisite emotion.

Perhaps it is impossible for people who have often experienced this feeling to conceive the effect it had upon a mind stunned and dimmed for more than half a century by ugly sounds and commonplace sights, and it is true that Christine's visitor had to find its way through a thickish barrier. But it did find its way, and afterwards, for more than a year now, she had thought of the moment as 'That Day', and had wanted to have the feeling again.

Occasionally it reappeared as a kind of ghost of its self, lacking its first force, and when she had once encountered this memory-feeling in Iver Street, while taking a short cut to a bus-stop, she had associated it with the ruined grace of the old houses there and decided, in an odd, confused way that was most unlike her usual habit of mind, to look for a room there when she left Mary's, where she had gone for a few weeks after her parents' death, and go to live in one of those houses; just for a time, just until she had decided what to do about her future.

She had to admit, on reflection, that it had been a crazy thing to do.

Hadn't every action of the Smiths, ever since she could remember, been taken with the object of leaving Mrs. Benson as far behind as possible? Hadn't they scrambled up and away from her as fast and as far as they could scram, taking her position down there for granted, never mentioning her but with contempt and hatred and fear?

The Kitchen-Sink School of Drama got no support from the Smiths.

Christine's action had caused incredulity and sombre head-shakings among her family.

Willy had said that he hoped Chris was not going all funny-peculiar now that she was at a loose end, and had even considered suggesting that she should be told to go and see one of these trick-cyclists, only of course . . . anything mental . . . you never knew where you might end up . . . But Garfield, who was a bit highbrow, and interested in psychology, but nevertheless retained some Smith common-sense, said that she must naturally be psychologically disturbed by Mother and Father dying in the same week like that and losing her job and the home breaking up. So Christine had been spared the fashionable prescription for bewilderment and grief.

Mary had confined herself to marvelling at old Chris going to live in a slum, and allowing her thoughts to play not uninterestingly around the subject of her sister's age.

All were thankful that she had not suggested coming to live with any of them, for all three led lives crammed to bursting with the usual ingredients of family life, and Christine had only her share of the money from the sale of the house to live on, and was decidedly old to set about looking for a new job. There was satisfaction and relief among the Smiths when she announced that she had found employment, and they were now leaving her to get on with it. She always had.

And Christine, never having had much to tell her brothers and sister, now began to keep her affairs even more to herself.

She did not even hint to them at her early disillusionment with life in Iver Street, where she found that it was one thing to be reminded of That Day and its revelation by the exterior of the house, and another to live in one of its dark, narrow, stuffy, clean-smelling rooms, and not a word did she breathe about having given her share of the furniture to Mrs. Benson, knowing how the news of this reckless and extraordinary bestowal would be received.

She was sitting in a coffee-bar in Hampstead while thus musing over the past months. April sunlight poured through its wide windows on to the foreign cakes and the dirty English hair and beards. The place was warm and, under the serious babbling of young voices, it was quiet, and Christine was enjoying being there; the sensation of leisure was still pleasant and unfamiliar to her after some months of idleness, and even the aftertaste of a smallish gill of coffee, weak and expensive, which was a sort of döppelganger of the real thing, was agreeable.

But she could afford one-and-sixpence now, without a thought, because she was going to have a flat and six guineas a week.

Why guineas? She would have been surprised to hear that this was Antonia Marriott's idea, "because it sounded prettier." Indeed and indeed, Garfield would have found food for his psychological interpretations of human behaviour in Pemberton Hall.

Six guineas a week and that flat. Christine suddenly inwardly glowed. It was wonderful, quite wonderful, that she had really got it—especially when she remembered Mrs. Meredith's remark about those friends of hers being after it.

For the first time since the day of her engagement, she wondered why they—Mrs. Traill—had chosen her. Thirty-five years in one job had never exposed her to the chances and humiliations of looking for a new one, and, from her sheltered retreat with Messrs. Lloyd and Farmer, she had actually assumed that what was wanted was a mere capacity for hard work, and honesty (taken for granted), and experience. Only now, when she had taken in her leisure to listening to people talking at café tables and in buses, did she realise that hard work and honesty and experience were never mentioned. Age was.

Shall I go over there now? thought Christine. Straightaway, and see if my things have come? She ('She' was Mrs. Traill) is sure to have the door open.

This habit had struck Christine on her visits to the Hall because of its striking difference to that prevailing in Mortimer

Road, where you exclaimed at a knock, advanced reluctantly and suspiciously upon the front-door, and opened it four inches while putting part of your nose round it and demanding, "Yes, what is it?"

Yes, she would go. And—the disagreeable thought invaded her mind at the sight of a background figure doing something to the floor with a mop—there was the question of getting a cleaner.

The idea was so disturbing that she sat down again and resumed her thoughts.

She was completely unaccustomed to dealing with or managing them.

The late Mrs. Smith 'never would have' a cleaner, the distance which she had scrambled up from Mrs. Benson not being great enough to permit of her coping with the latter when subordinate, and, while she had the strength to flap a duster, she would do everything herself.

So Christine, unfamiliar with the notion of a Mrs. Benson in the house, quailed at the thought of employing her, and was only slightly reassured when she recalled the procession of juniors she had effortlessly controlled throughout five-and-thirty years at Lloyd and Farmer's.

Though it had to be faced that during the past five years the procession had become so outrageous in its dress (trousers to business, if you please, and the cold weather no more than an excuse—but that Mr. Richards would *not* have) and so intimidatingly casual and assured in it manner that 'effortlessly' had gradually ceased to be the word. Nevertheless, there remained the habit of mild authority, and of course the people in the house would back her up; that Mrs. Meredith wouldn't stand for any cheek or slackness, Christine was certain.

Reassured, she proceeded to the Village, and spent a few minutes there studying a board displayed in a shop. She then went into a telephone-box and dialled the number she had memorised. From where she stood, she could see Pemberton Hall, already assuming a half-inhabited air because of Mrs. Traill's curtains and the fact that the front lawn had been mown, though whether the inhabitants were coming or going it would have been difficult to decide . . . a man might be very useful . . .

"Yes?" demanded an irritable male voice.

I expect Mr. Johnson's an old-age pensioner, thought Christine, and demanded to speak to him.

"Oh yes, let 'em all come," cried the voice, derisive and affronted, and Christine hoped that Mr. Johnson was not being beseiged by prospective employers; it would make him above himself. She heard the telephone being bumped about and background noises suggesting impatient customers and temporarily postponed activities with Easter cards and cigarettes, which suggested that Mr. Johnson lived over a small newsagent-tobacconist's and at last, after a long pause, a man's voice, young and soft with a sing-song in it, said politely: "Here is Mister Johnson."

"I've seen your advert' in Ellis's, the grocers," said Christine, realising instantly from his voice that Mr. Johnson was coloured and going steadily on because for the moment she really did not know what else to do. "And I want a cleaner. For a large house in Highgate Village. To sweep the stairs down and that kind of thing—it's rather rough work." (He was a man, and young, and, of course, strong. *They* always were. He could just get on with it. Only what would they all say? A black about the place. At the thought of what they would all have all said at Mortimer Road, she really did falter in spirit. But she did not ring off.)

The pause lengthened.

"Are you there?" said Christine.

"Yes, I am here, madame. I coloured man, you know," said the voice with the faintest note of questioning.

"Oh. Yes, well," Christine liked Mr. Johnson's polite *madame* and what was the use of being, as her employers were, artistic, if you were not also broad-minded? "Of course that doesn't matter at all if you do your work properly," she went on firmly. "Now you just hold on, and I'll run across the road; the house is right opposite where I'm 'phoning from, and I'll ask . . ."

She hurried over, Mrs. Traill almost certainly wouldn't

31

mind, but Mrs. Meredith . . . Christine herself had never thought about coloured people, and there was no time to think about her views now.

By luck, Mrs. Traill was just coming down the steps, in Bedford-cord slacks and an enormous navy sweater, with her silver-gilt hair blowing about and a shopping-bag on her arm.

"Hullo," she said, waving, as Christine hurried up.

"Good-afternoon, Mrs. Traill. I've got a cleaner holding the line in the box across the road. Would you mind a black? You see I thought they're so strong; he can lift things and perhaps clean the windows. What do you think we ought to pay?"

"Oh heavens; I don't mind. I love coloured people, they're so vital. Oh . . . I don't know . . . whatever he asks . . . Good for you—quick work."

She smiled and drifted away, and Christine hurried back to the telephone.

"Yes, I still here," said Mr. Johnson, but cheerfully now. "What money you be paying you think? I must have five shillings per hour. I engineering student. Electricity."

A more experienced hirer of cleaners than Christine might have pointed out that the fact of his being a student of electrical engineering did not imply his being qualified, as a housecleaner, to demand five shillings an hour, but she was too relieved at having apparently secured a cleaner—even a black one—at all that she did not meditate pointing out anything. She did dare to say, however—

"That seems rather expensive."

"Oh, I must have five shillings per hour. Yes. I got responsibilities," was the instant reply: Mr. Johnson appeared to have soared in a remarkably short time from a humble recognition of disadvantages connected with the hue of his skin to an enviable state of self-confidence.

Christine pondered this fact, as she hung up the receiver, having arranged that he should present himself at Pemberton Hall at six o'clock on the following Monday evening. His studies at a local Polytechnic prevented his coming during the day.

"I be there. I brought up in Christian household," were

Mr. Johnson's parting words. This was more than Christine had been. If Forty-Five Mortimer Road had had a God, it was the sacred promise of coloured television in years to come.

As she walked up the steps of Pemberton Hall, Christine faced the fact that she had engaged a coloured man as a cleaner.

A *black* man. As a *cleaner*.

I must be going mental, she thought. But she also had a feeling that she was not so appalled as she should have been. He didn't sound too bad, she reflected, and anyway it will make a change.

It was not clear what she meant by this last thought, and she forgot everything when once she had reached her own landing.

Her furniture stood, lean and elegant, against the duck-egg walls, and there, in a neat large parcel on the floor, were what must be her curtains. Someone had taken them in; kind. But these people, she was sure, were kind.

Mrs. Traill, arriving half-an-hour later with the frank admission that she had come up to have a peep, stopped at the living-room door and said "Oh."

"Do ... Don't you like it?" Christine gave a small, not quite confident laugh. She was standing on a chair putting up the curtains.

"I love your furniture. And I love the curtains, too. But not with that furniture. You should have something peasanty, with scarlet and black, on very coarse white stuff ... it would look wonderful. Why not scrap these and shop around? I'll help you."

Christine's reply was to smile brightly and not answer. It was the technique perfected by years of life with Mother and Father, who had always told you, when you had made up your mind to go to Ilfracombe, that you ought to go to the Isle of Wight; you would like it better at the Isle of Wight; Mrs. Smith had a cousin who always went to the Isle of Wight and she spoke very well of it.

"But of course you know what you like and you must have it!" suddenly cried Mrs. Traill, her lovely battered face alight with the kindest of smiles. "And that very dark green does look awfully good against the greeny blue . . . well, I must fly . . . I'm in the middle of an orchid . . . very difficult to draw."

She tottered away on one of the pairs of curious Mexican or Japanese sandals which she affected, and Christine drew a stealthy breath of relief and looked affectionately at the ivy sprays.

Chapter 5

MRS. BENSON'S MANNER HAD BECOME EVER MORE CONDESCEND-
ing as the days drew on towards her lodger's departure. Such
time as she could spare from the pursuit of Bingo and harry-
ing Mr. Benson (who harried back with all his might and
main; no one need sigh for Mr. Benson) was given to the
tolerant questioning of Christine; how had she got on today,
there was always plenty to do, moving, wasn't there? Those
old places, they often had the dry rot, give her a Council
house any day—and on the last evening, as Christine was letting herself into the house about nine o'clock, she said, laughing with her head on one side: "I'll be paying you a visit one
of these days, up in your little nest, you see."

"That will be the day," Christine retorted robustly, feeling
that their mutual dislike could be brought into the open now
that they were about to part, she heartily trusted, for ever.

"Yer off tomorrow, then," Mrs. Benson said, after a pause,
shocked and surprised.

That stuck-up toffee-noses never answered back was one of
the foundations of the Benson creed. Decent pretence of
neighbourliness must always mask spite, nay, courtesies must
be exchanged, like those taking place between two knights
about to knock each other silly in a tournament.

"Yes. They'll be here in the afternoon, about three, with . . .
the . . . stuff."

"I'm sure I don't know where I'm going to put it all. I was
saying so to Stan last night. Still, I've said I'll have it and I
will. I stick by my word. My sister always says, 'Ruby'd never
let you down, she's that sort.'"

"I hope it will be . . . useful," was all that Christine could
force herself to say. The thought of the furniture had come
upon her again, in fullest force.

35

"Oh, I daresay it'll do upstairs—don't matter what you give lodgers—they're all so-and-so's." She darted a glance up the stairs. "Don't suppose we'll be here long ourselves, anyway, now. We'll be off to a Council flat. These places are coming down—hadn't you heard? Making room for one of those big blocks like they got up the Archway. Offices and that. Good thing too—dirty old holes they are—I'm sure it's not worth the trouble cleaning the place, it's as bad again in half-an-hour."

"I'm just getting out in time, then." Christine nodded and escaped to her room with "See you" shrieking in her ears.

So the graceful old row was to be demolished. The thought was painful, and linked in some way with her memory of That Day. She knew that Mrs. Benson had told her because she had divined, by the instinct that led her unerringly to any weakness in another human being, that Christine liked Iver Street, and for a moment her detestation of the woman glowed into real hatred. Oh, well. Only one more night under the same roof.

.   .   .

She left well before eleven o'clock the next morning. Mrs. Benson had rushed out on some errand, announcing that she wouldn't be half a tick, back in time to see the last of yer. But Christine, knowing that Mrs. Benson's ticks were of the expandable kind, snatched up her case and was gone for ever.

She did glance once down to the end of Iver Street. The houses, small, grubby-white, stared placidly at the sun, children skipped and shrilled, a few poor Spring flowers glowed in the little front gardens, all under the benevolent eye of old green Parliament Hill; but of the van with The Furniture, of course, there was not a sign. But, unsuspecting and complacent, The Furniture would arrive that afternoon, grandly secure in the belief that it would shortly be entering some new version of Forty-Five Mortimer Road and then . . . Bensonia. Don't be mental, thought Christine crossly, riding in the bus up to the Village. Furniture isn't like people.

"Hullo!" Mrs. Traill called gaily, through the open door of

36

Pemberton Hall, "Come on in . . . Awful news . . . Mick has just told me the boys won't be out for another week."

Mr. Ryan, who now appeared as Mick, was standing in the hall accompanied by his partner, the slide-rule. He muttered what Christine supposed was good-morning—keeping on Mrs. Traill a gaze at once sardonic and touched with proud exasperation. Look at her, it seemed to say, isn't she a wan?

Mrs. Traill said, Oh well, she supposed they would have to put up with it, and Mr. Ryan went away to drink some tea. The sunny house responded with hammering, hissing and wailing.

"They put a pipe in all wrong. A wall will have to come down," Mrs. Traill sighed. "Talking of tea, come on down to the kitchen and we'll have some. James and Diana will be here presently and Clive, I think, but Antonia isn't coming until tomorrow. This way."

The stairs, concealed behind a thick door covered with green baize ("We kept that, don't you adore the colour?" said Mrs. Traill), were so dark, steep and dangerous, and so shut away from the delicate proportions and airy grace and floods of light in the rest of the house, that Christine was almost shocked, until she remembered that they led to the part where the servants used to live. Of course, anything was good enough for Mrs. Benson.

But when, after going down a stone-floored passage, they came out into the kitchen, she forgot everything in her first sight of a Boiler.

"Isn't it fearsome?" said Mrs. Traill, noticing her fascinated stare. "And we're stuck with it for ever, because Mick says they daren't move it: it would bring both walls and the ceiling down and cost thousands."

The thing was eight feet high, made of some dirty bluish metal, with a thick rusty pipe coming out of the top and many smaller pipes, apparently made of copper, wreathing around it. The largest pipe vanished into a hole in the ceiling, now neatly squared off.

"Goodness, you don't heat the water in that?" breathed Christine.

"Of course not!" pealed Mrs. Traill. "Mick said we must never light it; I suppose he thinks we're all bonkers . . . as if anyone would dare . . . No, the boiler is in a little cellar round at the back, oil-fired, and it heats the house as well—"

"I'd noticed how warm it is."

"—and the oil is in another little cellar. There are four of them, gardening tools and things in the one near the back-door, and James has made the other one into his wine place. I'll just put the kettle on, and show you."

Christine, awed by the spectacle of the Great Boiler, had received an impression that the rest of the kitchen was equally Victorian, for the walls were papered in a shiny green-and-brown design which absorbed light, and the massive old dresser and cupboards had been retained, newly painted white.

But although this kitchen did not correspond with those Dream ones promoted by advertisers, she now saw that it was efficient. The cooker was of the newest design, and on the walls were many shining devices for unscrewing and grinding and opening. There was something else there: cosiness. As this had been the only redeeming feature of Forty-Five Mortimer Road, Christine had grown to rely upon it, and now, having missed it for some months, she welcomed it. But, because she was a Smith, she said nothing.

"Cosy, isn't it?" Mrs. Traill glanced at her. How dreary some people were. Never a word of appreciation.

"It's a bit dark, isn't it?" Christine said, and indeed she thought so, not realising that much of the cosiness was due to the dimness.

"Oh, we did that on purpose—had a dark paper, I mean. I chose it. Antonia had taken a fancy to something all over little houses. It is queer, she's so good about clothes, and has no feeling at all about that kind of thing. Let's go and see the cellars."

While they were looking round the whitewashed walls of Mr. Meredith's wine-cellar, where the racks and bins awaited their tenants, there were muffled sounds of arrival from upstairs.

"Someone's come, oh good. I'll fly up and see who it is. You make the tea," and Mrs. Traill tottered away.

Christine went back to the kitchen and made tea in an old pot of dented Victorian plate which she took from the enormous dresser. The cups and plates displayed there must belong to Mrs Traill, as the first tenant to establish herself; there were Spanish lustre saucers, grey and blue dishes from Brittany, a sea-blue jug from Bruges, some Japanese cups of eggshell fragility.

Christine turned each one upside down, curiously examining the marks on their behinds. Mrs. Traill must have Travelled. Then she set them all out on the table; people would be arriving all day, and arrivals always wanted and expected tea.

She was experiencing a faint excitement. The fear and suspicion of unknown people endemic to her home had never infected her, for she had left the nest each morning for thirty-five years to go to a job where she dealt with strangers all day. You got used to meeting people, in business.

But these people were different.

Eighteen, she had been, that first morning at Lloyd and Farmer's: with her hair—nice hair it was, she had always had a good head of hair—in a shingle, as they called it, and a hat, and gloves, and those pinky silk stockings. 1924. Seemed like another world. But she didn't feel all that different.

Voices and footsteps coming down the passage. The kitchen door opened, and Christine looked up.

"Ah—tea!" exclaimed James Meredith, "and Miss Smith —how nice to see you both." He laughed, and his wife, who, Christine saw at once, had been upset by something, gave him a resigned look. "These will come in handy, I hope."

He put a large carton, crammed with cream buns, on the table, and Diana Meredith sank into a chair, muttering to no one in particular, "Oh good heavens."

Christine now saw that someone had followed the Merediths down the passage and was standing in the doorway, surveying the room. Mrs. Traill, who was pouring tea, followed the direction of her glance.

"Clive! Darling!" she cried. "Come and have some tea . . .
Miss Smith, this is Clive Lennox . . ."

"You may have heard of him," chorused Diana and James,
as the actor came forward.

"Yes, she might just have as a schoolgirl," he said, taking
Christine's hand and gently pressing it while he gazed into her
face. "How sweet of you to come and look after us."

"Of course, I have!" Christine said eagerly. "On T.V. . . ."

"Oh he doesn't count that," cried Diana. "He doesn't count
anything really since *Mr. Melody*, do you, darling?"

"Well hardly that, dear. It would mean I hadn't worked for
fifteen years . . . Where's Antonia? Not here yet?" He sat
down, and took a cup of tea.

"She's coming tomorrow evening. She's in the country for
a few days. With . . . for a day or two." Mrs. Traill fixed an
intent gaze on the cream buns.

"I shall just gulp this and get upstairs. They'll be putting
the heavy stuff in the wrong places. James, I don't know who
you think wants to eat those things at half-past eleven in the
morning."

Diana drained her cup and turned to Christine. "You can
give us lunch today, can't you? We shall be up to our eyes."

"Yes. I'd thought of that. I'll go out and shop. Would one
o'clock be all right?" asked Christine.

"Perfect." Diana nodded, adding as if making a concession.
"It's only for today. I expect Fab—Mrs. Traill has told you
how we want—how things are to be run, hasn't she?"

"Very sketchily. But she understands. We'll work it out as
we go." Mrs. Traill smiled absently towards Christine. "None
of us are fussy about food, really. I mean, we shan't expect
marvellous menus, on the occasions when you are kind enough
to do us a meal. But—" she glanced round at the company—
"and this goes for all of us—we'd sooner have good bread and
cheese and coffee, or wine, than hot snacks or endless tea. Or
puddings."

"Here!" James Meredith looked up across his cream buns,
"Hands off puddings. I like 'em."

"We'll have puddings sometimes," Christine promised him.

James bowed, smiling, and Clive Lennox said:

"Now, James. Don't you have any of that, Miss Smith—he's only making up to you to get all the gravy. I like puddings too. I know you girls—if you're left to yourselves you'll live on wet lettuce."

"Antonia may. I like my food," said Mrs. Traill.

"Antonia has to think about her figure," said Diana.

"Oh, what nonsense, Diana. She's been 34–26–34 since she was seventeen," Mrs. Traill protested, "though personally I like something up above. It's more *feminine*," and James and Clive unsmilingly nodded.

"Work—work," exclaimed Diana, getting up. "Fabia, has Miss Smith any cash?"

"Oh—no—of course. You'd better all give her something now. We'll work out details tomorrow."

In a few moments Christine was in possession of five pounds —"one for Antonia"—and alone in the kitchen with Clive Lennox, who was unhurriedly finishing the cream buns. Mr. Meredith could be heard humming contentedly while he took a refreshing glance over his wine-cellar.

Christine, trying not to show that she was doing so, studied Mr. Lennox. It was her first opportunity to look at the celebrity in the flesh.

And after all he was only an elderly man in a shabby silver-grey suit, with a long actor's face and dark hair flecked with silver above his big, comic ears. Nothing thrilling about him.

Christine would have found it difficult to say, had she been asked, what she did find thrilling. The beautiful, debauched word meant, to her, things which she found 'far-fetched' and 'silly'; those contemptuous Smith expressions applied to suspense plays on television, and other contemporary devices for providing excitement. The thought now slipped through her mind that she had been more thrilled by That Day than by anything else in her life, and she scolded herself. What a thing to be 'thrilled' by. She *must* be going mental.

But the instant this comment from her past made itself heard, she fiercely repudiated it. Nothing—*nothing* was going to spoil the memory of That Day.

Chapter 6

SHE GLANCED UP, AND FOUND MR. LENNOX LOOKING AT HER.

"All a bit strange? You'll get used to us," he said, gaily, but gently too.

"I was in business," was all Christine could say.

"You've never done this kind of thing?" The cloud-shadow swiftness of the actor's responses can be disconcerting: he looked dismayed, but Christine's own responses were not cloud-like, and she did not notice.

"I helped my mother. I shall get on all right, I'm sure."

"Of course you will." Her firm manner and rosy, solid looks reassured him. He held out a cigarette-case which, Christine noticed, bore the sprawled engraved signature *Always—Tasha*, and she took one. He leant gracefully across the table and lit it for her.

"Aren't you going to sit down?"

"I'll just wash these up." She began to collect the cups. "I'm not used to sitting down; in business I was usually on my feet."

She began swiftly on the work. Mr. Lennox would not want to hear what went on at Lloyd and Farmer's. (The rarity of this decision, the difference it would make to social life if we all decided that no one wanted to hear about what went on at Lloyd and Farmer's, quite passed Christine by.)

Clive Lennox, who could not help caressing women with voice and manner, began to chat to her. It was an agreeable sound; his voice rose, fell, hesitated, pounced on a word, rippled. It was like listening to Semprini Serenade on the wireless, thought Christine, with an unaccustomed flight of fancy.

"I expect Fabia told you we've all known each other since the Flood? James and I were at school together, and Fabia was on tour with me between the wars—she's done a bit of everything—through her I got to know Antonia Marriott. I'd always kept up with James, he knew a couple of Fabia's husbands, too . . . But neither of 'em wanted to come here, thank God," ended Mr. Lennox with fervour.

A couple . . . ? Christine turned from the dresser to look at him.

"She's had four. But I'm gossiping. I won't say 'forget it all' because you must have a clue to us . . . Oh, you've finished! And I was so busy cackling I never offered to help you."

"That's all right," Christine said with her cheerful smile. "Talking of helping, I've got us a cleaner."

"Splendid. I'm afraid none of us is very deft with the duster."

"Er—he's black. His name's Mr. Johnson. He's coming on Monday evening."

Clive went off into a delighted peal of laughter.

"It can't be! Massa Johnson! How absolutely perfect."

"Don't you mind, then?"

"Of course not. I love nigs; my old father was so fond of nigger stories. So long as he doesn't strain the coffee through my socks . . . but I don't expect you know any of those stories, do you? Before your time. Ah, well. To work, to work."

He made an airy gesture and stolled out, leaving Christine to bustle calmly around, thinking that Mr. Lennox was nice.

They always say stage people are temperamental, she mused. But he isn't. Fancy them all being such friends . . .

Four husbands. None of these people seemed to be what you might call ordinarily married, except the Merediths, and it was plain to see, thought Christine, who wore the trousers there.

Who wore the trousers, and to what extent, had been a subject of perennial interest in Mortimer Road. Racialism might burgeon like some monstrous toadstool, earthquakes might shatter cities, newer and more appalling bombs might threaten the globe—the Smiths were more interested—and perhaps on second thoughts are they to be blamed?—in who wore the trousers.

Lunch was eaten hastily and in relays by the party, as no one

43

could leave their tasks to spend long over it, and Christine passed the rest of the day in finishing the arranging of her own flat and in shopping for the week-end.

She tramped busily about her three rooms—Christine had not a light step—aware of distant bangings and bumpings all over the house.

Furniture was gradually filling up its rooms; furniture heavy with associations and memories settling down on the uneven old floors and against the walls, curtains draping the long windows with the little panes that window-cleaners call 'postage-stamps'; an endless roll of drugget, the colour of biscuits, unrolling from Christine's landing right down the stairs to the hall, with what seems hours of hammering.

There's a deal of white paint for Mr. Johnson to keep clean, thought Christine, coming down about six o'clock to begin preparing supper.

It'll show every mark and so will the carpet, but then she thought recklessly that it all looked so nice, a bit of dirt-showing would not matter. The bareness of the walls, and the light colouring everywhere, light yet sober, was most unlike what she had all her life regarded as 'looking nice'. Yet she liked it; she liked it all, very much.

On the landing that had been allotted to Mrs. Traill, a small table, with a miniature brass fence around its top, stood outside her door, and on it was a large blue-and-white Chinese vase filled with white irises, and as she passed it, two things happened to Christine. She thought that the flowers looked as if they were going to fly away any minute, and she began to tread more lightly.

She did not know that she was doing it. It was an instinct, and she followed it so as not to disturb the quiet. For all the bumpings and bangings had ceased, and the great house was brimming with light and silence.

"Well," Christine muttered, reaching the hall, "supper."

While she was busy with her preparations, Mr. Meredith came in and began to chat, in the pauses of strolling in and out of his wine-cellar (Christine could already see that he loved that old wine-cellar).

"It's such a comfort, having enough room to keep my wine in," he confided, while she peeled potatoes. "I was brought up in the country in a draughty great place with lots of room for everything, and I've never got used to these modern hamster-hutches. My people had to go to Africa when I was about seven, and they handed me over to an old uncle with an even draughtier and larger one," laughing cheerfully, "What are you giving us? Steak? Oh splendid. We'll have a Beaune . . ." and off he went to his cellar, leaving Christine with curious thoughts about dogs.

A glance at the bottles he was carrying when he returned settled her peculiar thoughts. Beaune. So that was how you said it.

"Shall we have some light?" said he.

"A little light on the subject," said Christine, which was one of the things they had always said at home, and he laughed.

She did not know how few men there were in London, with James's background, who would have. But when he switched on the lamp standing on the big table (it really was a Victorian one, Mrs. Traill had explained, with its brass bowl and glass shade repaired and polished and wired for electricity), she did think the brilliant light showed a face lacking certain qualities that she was accustomed to seeing in the faces of the middle-aged men who came into Lloyd and Farmer's.

Mr. Richards' face had not looked like those others, either. She was still seeking a name for what was in the two faces, when Diana came in.

"Oh, Miss Smith," she began at once, huddling a stole about herself while her narrow turquoise eyes stared full at Christine. "Mrs. Traill tells me you've got a black to clean for us. How *could* you? They're as unsatisfactory as they can be—childish and dishonest and uppity—if you'd lived in Africa . . ."

Christine was not taken aback by what sounded to her like nonsense; they hadn't even seen the man yet.

"Suppose we see how he gets on," she said equably. "I know some folks don't like coloured people . . ."

"A good many folks," Diana muttered.

"—But if he's a good cleaner we shall be lucky; they're very difficult to get, these days," Christine went on, recalling various confidences from acquaintances, "and he can always keep out of your way. He'll be coming evenings, anyway."

"I did think I had seen the last of them in the house when we came Home. In Kenya you *had* to have them, of course, but I never got over feeling there was a nest of snakes in the kitchen."

"Oh, come, sweetie," said James.

"Is she carrying on about our Massa Johnson?" demanded Clive coming in. He was followed by Mrs. Traill, in a white sweater and more disgruntled jewellery, who said, "Oh, be your age, Diana. They're wonderful people, full of colour and gaiety, and so *vital*."

"You haven't lived in Africa."

"I shall soon feel I have, if I hear that again . . . I think Massa Johnson will be a nice addition to our establishment," Mrs. Traill ended gaily.

"It's ready," Christine said, and added to soothe Mrs. Meredith as she put hot plates on the table, "perhaps he won't turn up."

Her own experience of cleaners was almost confined to this fact, which she had picked up from various customers in the shop: swore she'd be there by ten sharp, knew I was desperate, seemed to take to the place: never turned up.

"Oh I do hope he will—you must have someone," Diana exclaimed, with one of her lightning changes of mood. "That would never do . . . I expect I'll get used to him." She smiled, the irritated expression fading.

"Beaune, sweetie," said James, hovering with his bottle.

"Antonia telephoned," announced Mrs. Traill, when all had been peacefully eating for some moments. "She'll be here this evening. She's got a cold."

Christine was surprised at the effect of this announcement. James whistled and appeared perturbed, Diana groaned and muttered, "Of course," and Clive Lennox said, "Poor angel." Mrs. Traill herself looked solemn, as though proclaiming some crisis of the global type.

"What time is she coming?" asked Clive next. "I might run down and meet her."

"Oh, rubbish, Peter's there, isn't he? Let him cope with her."

"He said she got no sleep last night. They ran out of petrol."

"They *what*?" Diana shrieked.

Mrs. Traill shrugged. "That's what he said. I couldn't hear properly, the line was bad."

'What I cannot stand about Antonia's colds," Diana said vigorously, "is her never getting them in the nose. Other people do, they drip and look red and sore, but not Antonia. She just caws at you attractively—like Tallulah used to. Remember Tallulah in 'Scotch Mist', Fabia?"

"Yes. But that—last night, I mean—wasn't like . . ." Mrs. Traill's sentence tailed off and she bit on a piece of toast, looking conscious. Diana just glanced at Christine.

"Where was he calling from," asked Clive, after a small silence.

"Some place on Exmoor, I gathered."

"What a fool the man is. Surely he knows by now she loathes the country," said Diana.

"There is always hope—'unfortunately', as poor Wilde said." Clive got up from the table. "I want a paper. Coming, James?"

"You may have to go down to the tube station, Mr. Meredith," warned Christine, "the paper-shops both shut at half-past five."

"Never mind, a walk will do our figures good, won't it, James?" They went out together, saying they might find a chemist's, and lay in a good stock of 'the usual things' for Antonia's cold.

"She often gets them before a show," Mrs. Traill said to Christine, when the ladies were alone and rather languidly beginning on fruit, cigarettes and coffee. ("What a trial they are, going off like that; I haven't talked to Clive for ages) And on Monday it's the Spring one."

"A dress show?" asked Christine, interested.

47

"At Nigel Rooth's, yes. Antonia usually works them out to the last tiny detail and then goes away for the week-end before the opening; Nigel R. nearly expired on the spot the first time she did it, but now he's used to it. They both say it's good for the staff, makes them responsible and so forth."

"I shouldn't feel safe, leaving it all to bits of girls," Christine said.

"Oh, Nigel R. will be very much there, don't you fret, and they aren't all girls, some of them are quite elderly."

"But if she gets this cold, worrying about it—" Christine knew about psychological ailments, thanks to many a tedious half-hour spent listening to her brother Garfield.

"Oh, she doesn't get them over *that*." Mrs. Traill's tone had become meaningful and her expression what Christine called 'kind-of-churchy'. "They're an expression of subconscious resentment. She resents her job and wants to give it up and flop on some man."

"Rubbish," said Diana, beginning to peel a plum. "This time, whatever reason she gives for catching it, we all know what she's worrying about." She looked across at Fabia and nodded. "Ferenc Briggs. Nothing subconscious about him."

Mrs. Traill sighed and looked distressed. "Poor sweetie, it is hard luck."

"Not if you're right, Fabia," Diana said, and something in the gleam of her eye and the ring in her tone caused Christine, who was listening a little bemusedly, to let her eye wander to the fast-emptying second wine bottle. "If you're right, she'll be relieved when the break comes and Ferenc's got her job. Then she can relax, and fall back into the arms of Peter—"

"He'd overbalance," gurgled Mrs. Traill, refilling her glass and her friend's.

"Well—Peter or someone. She's always got a number of them floating around."

"Clive," droned Mrs. Traill, so quietly that Christine was not quite sure she had heard the name.

48

"Don't tell me that's starting up again!" Diana said sharply, widening the turquoises.

"Oh, I think so. Didn't you notice various things this evening?"

"No, I did not. It's all your artistic imagination—I hope to God not, anyway. Shall you ever forget the time we all had? I did think—you know—when I heard he was coming here— jolly good having old Clive around, but if she's going to be here too—"

Mrs. Traill only nodded, and seemed suddenly to realise that Christine was looking from one lined, lively face to the other, as the talk went on, with the absorbed expression of a spectator at a tennis match.

"What a heavenly colour," Mrs. Traill observed, just touching the largest of the bloomy plums in their plaited wicker basket. "True amber."

"I'm glad you like them, I got them in the Village," Christine said eagerly. "Two-and-three the pound. Expensive, I know, but the flavour's good, isn't it?"

"Delicious." Diana gave a small yawn. "And so was the salad. Congratulations. Of course, you can't go wrong if you pay enough for steak."

Christine felt gratified. She dismissed the little dig by reminding herself of Mr. Lucas at Lloyd and Farmer's, for whom nothing that had ever gone right had done so because of someone's individual effort. Mrs. Meredith was going to be the one to complain, if anyone did.

Christine's salad had been chosen from a booklet called *Twenty Salads That Are Different*, given away with a woman's magazine she took in which encouraged its readers to make their cookery exciting, in face of a steely resistance from husbands who preferred it dull.

She had always enjoyed reading these recipes. At Mortimer Road, appetite had been governed by a mysterious quality called Fancy (dimly related, possibly, to what it was always telling people to do, though there was precious little Fancy flitting about those rooms) and sometimes you couldn't Fancy an apparently tasty piece of haddock or came home with a huge sickly pastry because you just Fancied it. In general, food was pushed about on plates and a surprisingly large amount of it was wasted. Tea, of course, had a place of its own; should you suffer from any minor disablement that left you without a relish for tea, this was regarded seriously— "Even tea didn't taste right."

Diana refilled their glasses, passing over Christine's at a murmur of "Oh—no more for me, thank you—I couldn't."

"That's what comes of that kind of relationship, of course," said Mrs. Traill, with her full glass held at her lips, looking pensively over the top. "Antonia and Nigel R., I mean. It's all right for twenty years because their—their individual oddities happen to fit in, and then suddenly along comes someone like Ferenc and bowls Nigel over and Antonia's had it, both as a woman and as a designer."

"I'm sure she doesn't care as a woman, Fabia. She's very fond of Nigel R. but she isn't blind to his what you call oddities; I've heard her laughing at them."

"Perhaps not, but she jolly well cares as a designer. And it's all the worse because she thinks Ferenc is a bad designer. Her pride's hurt and she's afraid of the future—she's our age remember—and I'm sure she's afraid for the House of Rooth, too. She thinks Ferenc's going to ruin it."

"He won't necessarily. I like Antonia's things, as you know, and I like Nigel's whole style. He makes clothes for ladies. But we're getting to be an extinct race." Diana refilled their glasses, "and he'll have to keep up with the times or go under. Ferenc will keep him 'with it'. I don't see why he should 'ruin' anything."

"Perhaps she'd sooner it was ruined than take second place as a designer and see Nigel Rooth's swamped by kooky clothes."

"Then she's very immature, isn't she? But, of course we both know that about our Antonia. She's very immature. I don't agree with you about her longing to retire; I think she adores it and it's her whole life—"

"And I think she won't face the fact that she's simply dying to settle down and have some man take care of her."

The last words floated rather than sounded, on the warm, drowsing air of the old room. Christine felt a faint sensation, too far-off, too slight, to be named pain. Diana was leaning back, looking thoughtfully down into her glass.

"It's just a question of finding the right man," said Mrs. Traill, wagging her head. She turned her large, now gently-swimming eyes slowly on Christine. "We don't want to make a mystery out of anything," she went on. "Darling Antonia, Miss Marriott, doesn't like being—er—married." She giggled abruptly.

Mortimer Road was for the moment completely in charge of its child, and all that Christine could offer was a small nod while she tried to keep her mouth from falling open. You read about such things, of course. But she was *Miss* Marriott. Oh, perhaps that was only the name she used in business, like Miss Owen at Lloyd and Farmer's who had really been Mrs. Jones? But how did they *know* she didn't like it? This lot seemed to know everything about each other. And who, if she was married, was she married *to*? And where was he? Or, perhaps she's divorced. That's it, Christine thought.

Mrs. Traill was sipping from her refilled glass and going on with the head-wagging.

"It's prevented her from being quite normal—"

"Everybody isn't like you, darling," Diana struck in, on a note of pure—could it be spite? Christine stared at her. "I still think a lot of it's due to that ghastly mother of hers."

"Oh now, Diana. I've always rather liked Mrs. Marriott."

"She encourages people to be shallow and frivolous—"

"Hark who's talking! Who won't even *discuss* apartheid?"

"I won't discuss it because there's nothing to discuss. Unless you've actually *lived* in Africa . . ."

      .   .   .

Suddenly there sounded a long peal on the front-door bell, conveying an immediate impression of urgency and despair. Mrs. Traill started, spilling her wine, and said resignedly, "There she is."

"You gave her a key, surely? She is an old ass."

"She'll have lost it." Mrs. Traill was beginning hastily to carve slices of the big tinned tongue that Christine had laid in as a week-end standby.

"And that's a waste of time," Diana pointed out. "She'll only want hot rum."

"Is there any?"

"How should I know?" She shrugged. "Sure to be, I should think—James brought some of everything that's bottled, for that place of his."

Christine now looked with interest towards the door. Through it, after a prelude of slow steps descending stairs, came, in a touching procession—Clive, James, a youngish-elderly man with a silly pink face, and a tall shape wrapped in glorious mink, diffusing an aroma of eucalyptus from a huge paper handkerchief held to its nose.

"Here she is," James proclaimed tenderly.

The youngish elderly man leapt a little way in the air and made exuberant gestures of greeting towards Mrs. Traill and Mrs. Meredith, which they returned with an air of being used to him and not all that glad to see him. There now settled over the kitchen an atmosphere suggesting that some-one desperately ill had arrived at a log-cabin in the middle of a blizzard.

"Darling!" cried Mrs. Traill softly, "what appalling luck! Is it one of your very bad ones?"

The handkerchief oscillated, as the head, covered in big loops of ashy-glittering hair, feebly nodded. Clive, guiding her by an arm encircling the mink, settled her in a chair.

"James, is there any rum?" he asked importantly.

"Rum . . ." breathed a husky voice ". . . best thing."

"Yes, darling, right now . . . Christine, the kettle . . . Clive, take off her coat, she mustn't get over-heated."

Seated, and with her coat whisked away by tender hands, Miss Marriott at last removed the hankerchief and revealed a face of purest 1906 Chocolate-Box—Gabrielle Ray and Evelyn Laye and Phyllis Dare—graced by swooning false eyelashes. "She looked, perhaps, if you wished to be ill-natured, eight-

and-twenty," as Ouida said of her Russian princess in *Moths*, and wore a skirt and sweater of the same colour as the plums on the table; the eyelashes were a perfect match to both.

She blinked round on the circle of anxious, affectionate faces, while Christine, standing by the Aga to remove the kettle the second it boiled, looked at her curiously and thought that she was so like a big doll she hardly seemed real.

"Divine to be here at last," Miss Marriott sighed. "How adorable it all looks. How are you all, dears?" smiling wanly round.

"Rather flat out with settling in," Diana said. "When did all this start?"

"Oh . . ." Antonia made a pettish gesture, and the man with the pink face said eagerly, "It's all my fault. We ran out of petrol near Ferrow Ley, it's a tiny place, not more than a crossroads and two cottages, one empty, really, and would you credit me, when I did get to the nearest garage, it was shut. She had to sit in the car for nearly two hours—"

"Freezing. Heater flaked out," Antonia murmured with closed eyes.

". . . until I found an A.A. box . . ."

The recital continued, the pink one delivering it in a deprecating tone revealing his deep sense of guilt, while Mrs. Traill listened with a grave, judicial expression and Clive and James hovering, darting off to fetch aspirins, or administering sips of rum.

". . . only hope to God she'll be up to it tomorrow," and Peter's tale wavered off into silence, with an anxious glance at his love. She was sucking down the boiling concoction with an air of weary endurance but instantly sat upright and announced in a voice ringing with energy—

"Of course I'll be all right. I daren't be ill with that little swine getting his foot in whenever there's half an inch . . . Don't be silly,' with a crushing look at Peter.

He instantly said, well, he must be pushing, and she wailed, "Oh don't get all hurt now, please. You must have some dinner." She turned to Mrs. Traill. "He can have some tongue, can't he?"

Peter, however, earnestly persisted in his intention of pushing, and was at length languidly waved off by Antonia and seen out by James. He retreated in a diminuendo of apologies, still explaining that it had all been his fault.

No one said anything when James reappeared, but Mrs. Traill drew the biscuits towards her and Clive leant over the table to cut himself a wedge of cheese.

"Antonia, darling, this is our Miss Smith—she's going to look after us," Diana said, in a moment, and Christine exchanged smiles with Miss Marriott. There was something likeable, something immediately winning, about her; Christine felt that she would not hurt a fly. She also felt that she was rather wet.

The party stayed long over the supper-table that first evening; at half-past ten, Christine stopped trying to tidy up and went off to bed, dismissed with absent, flashing smiles from her absorbedly gossiping employers.

Someone called Amanda was providing the laughter: she seemed to have had a stormy time of it following her second divorce and the attempts of her discarded first husband to get back jewellery that had belonged to his mother. In every country in Europe. And then, of course, there was Dick. Christine went out with her ears full of the gurgling, affectionately-malicious voices—Oh, you know Amanda, that's typical Amanda—he couldn't have, Fabia; you're embroidering. Miss Marriott's cold seemed to be better.

Slowly, as she climbed the long flights of stairs, she entered into a realm of silence and peace, while the laughter and voices from the kitchen grew fainter and fainter until she heard it no more.

Stars looked in at landing windows, lamplight shone through the branches of a flowering tree in the Square, making every blossom and leaf into some fantastic tropical butterfly. Distant traffic droned, paused, droned on again, as it climbed Highgate Hill. My flat, thought Christine, pausing to look out of her landing window over dark sleeping roofs and the rounded masses of sleeping trees, my home. Mine.

Cries about hot-water bottles, Vick, boiling baths, that

wonderful stuff that man in Paris put Fabia on to, and a final landing colloquy between Fabia and James about the pathetic and extraordinary behaviour of that poor ass, Peter, floated up to her until past midnight, breaking in on a wakefulness due to the excitement that she had felt, and controlled, throughout the day. Into the small hours, it seemed to her between waking and sleeping, she heard the light gay murmur of their voices and, surely once there was singing, and a scatter of applause. They keep all hours, she thought drowsily, as she at last fell asleep.

Chapter 7

MISS MARRIOTT REMAINED INVISIBLE THROUGHOUT THE QUIET Sunday that followed. But on Monday morning she appeared in the kitchen at nine o'clock, looking dewy, fresh and coldless.

"Is there any coffee?" she asked, smiling a little at Christine.

"I have got it all ready to make. But I was just wondering who would be coming down . . . Mrs. Traill said would I give you all breakfast for the next few days, just while you're settling in . . ."

"Divine," Miss Marriott said lifelessly, sitting down at the table and beginning to fidget with the cups. 'Oh, I think everybody'll want coffee."

Christine was about to measure the powder from a tin into the first cup when there came a low shriek and an arresting hand.

"Not that muck out of a tin! Haven't we any real coffee?" Enormous sapphire eyes swept the kitchen distractedly, coming to rest on Christine's face.

"There is half a pound. I did get some. Mrs. Traill said to get it but I thought it'ud save time." Christine was slightly flustered and thinking that she had excuse to be.

"And don't boil the milk. Scald it. It spoils the flavour to boil it. And sugar. Yes, sugar—two teaspoonfuls—for once." Miss Marriott sighed and her voice died away.

Nervy, thought Christine, piecing together the fragments of gossip overheard, and shovelling coffee beans into the patent grinder fixed to the wall. Looks older by daylight, too. She concentrated on the grinding, resisting a temptation to count the strings of pink beads that filled the scooped-out neck of Miss Marriott's black suit. Her eyelashes were black this morning, as well.

"Hullo, darling. Better?" Clive Lennox came in, smiling absently at Christine while bending over Miss Marriott. She opened her eyes long enough to rub her cheek against his, then shut them again, and Christine approached with a cup, saying, "Your coffee, Miss Marriott," with an intonation unconsciously modelled on that of a butler she had seen in some film. Antonia groped for it, and drank.

"Oh . . ." she sighed, cradling improbably long fingers about the cup, "that's good . . . that's very good," nodding at Christine. "Yes, I'm better . . . I hope I'll be better still at five this evening, when that little bastard's numbers are out of the way."

"The first-night feeling. Don't I know it," Clive muttered.

"No. No, it isn't like that now, Clive. It used to be, but at least then I did know I had a clear field; some numbers would just be more of a hit than others. But this time—that little so-and-so's first show, and sharing it with him—it's all so muddly. I do loathe him so, and his horrible little jackets all over pearly-king buttons."

She waved away the bread which Christine was holding towards her and rested her head on her hand.

"Better eat something. Can't face up to things on an empty stomach," said James Meredith, who came in humming and was the first to give Christine what she called 'a proper good-morning'.

"James, I couldn't. I'm having milk and sugar in my coffee, that will have to do. You're both being so sweet, but honestly this morning it will just have to do."

James shook his head.

"Bacon and egg, Mr. Meredith?" Christine enquired, feeling sure of her ground this time, and having received a beam and a silent and definitely conspiratorial nod in answer, set to work.

"I'll take some coffee to the girls to wake them up," he said in a moment, and while Antonia slowly drank her coffee and was persuaded by Clive to try a piece of toast, Christine made two trays ready.

She hoped that there wouldn't be this fuss every morning,

57

meals on trays, and people sitting about half-crying. Still, she hadn't got to take anything upstairs and yesterday no one had come down to breakfast at all.

James went out, having deftly put everything onto one tray.

". . . and his frightful, frightful old mum," Antonia was sighing, "all bursting out of black satin and her shoes three sizes too small and short sleeves. Her huge arms make me feel quite ill—and Nigel said she was 'wonderful'. Wonderful! I used to think Nigel had taste."

Clive confined himself to fondling her long limp hand.

"She keeps hinting that one of us might be trying to marry him. As if we would, or he could. I really don't think she knows anything about . . . anything," glancing sideways under the eyelashes towards Christine. "She was one of those Ivor-worshippers—well, we all know what a darling Ivor could be—I'm not blaming the boy for his name—but—"

She got up slowly, a long, black, immoderately-slender shape topped with loops of hair neither silver nor gold, pressing distraught hands against the barely visible, scrupulously creamed wrinkles on her forehead.

"I want to see him design a suit. That's all I want," she sighed. "One suit—the kind of thing you wear to go shopping in, and put something on it if you go on to lunch with people. Lunch!" The hands came down, dropping to her sides. "All he's ever heard of is high tea—with chips."

Clive sat looking up at her, with distress and one or two other feelings gliding cloudily over his face.

"Nigel says—and I know it's true, in a way—his name and his mum and that waify look and his accent are just handed to us on a platter so far as publicity goes—but when did Nigel Rooth's want that kind of publicity or need it? 'Beautiful clothes for gentlewomen'. Yes, I know it sounds corny now. Twenty years ago it didn't."

She gave a last gusty sigh, then glanced at the clock and uttered one of her subdued shrieks.

"I'll only take twenty minutes, the worst rush is over," said Clive soothingly.

"You are sweet. They said they'd only keep mine a week, and it's already ten days, blast them. Thank you, love," as she slipped her arms into the coat he held out.

"'Couldn't let you go off without a word," croaked Mrs. Traill, hobbling in on a pair of sandals that looked vaguely Javanese and carrying an empty cup. "Best of luck, honey."

"Oh, I shall need it—" she shook her head at them despairingly.

"Bear up," said Diana, following, and also carrying one. "All the luck in the world, pet."

They called it after her affectionately, heartily, as she went out supported by Clive; then they sat down and pushed the cups hopefully at Christine and began to nibble fruit and toast. Both wore exotic and becoming dressing-gowns.

"It would be this week of all weeks, her car being laid up," Mrs. Meredith said. "It must be the last straw."

"Now, Diana! You know she welcomes any chance to flop on to Clive."

Mrs. Meredith shrugged and did not answer, but James shook his head as he sat behind *The Times*.

"This psychological approach . . . now I should have said his driving her down was just a convenient arrangement with an old friend."

"No, James. It goes deeper, and you have to look for the *hidden motive*," Mrs. Traill said severely.

"Well, I'm going upstairs to look at my *Times*," and with a cheerful laugh he went out.

Christine was sorry. She had already responded to the un-Mortimer-like atmosphere of Pemberton Hall sufficiently to admit to herself that she preferred the company of its gentlemen to that of its ladies; they were less critical, she felt, more ready to be pleased with what she did. At Mortimer Road you always expressed thankfulness when no men were about, and must tell yourself you meant it.

"Antonia always has been crazy about clothes." Mrs. Meredith said musingly, "Remembering her drawing 'fashion ladies' when she was seven, Fabia, and designing frocks with longish skirts well before anyone would look at them, in the

59

late 'twenties? You know," with a vivid transformation of tone and expression, "I'd give my ears for her job, Ferenc or no Ferenc, but all she does is grizzle."

"P'raps she doesn't like going out to work any more?" put in Christine, rinsing cups; continually, during the past three days, she had thought of all those years at Lloyd and Farmer's and wondered how she had endured them. The relaxed atmosphere in the room invited her to join in the conversation.

Diana just glanced at her.

"Oh bosh, she adores it. That's why there's all this fuss about Ferenc. She's terrified she'll have to resign, just to save her face, if he gets made top designer, or whatever Nigel calls it. I think it would be more dignified if she retired now, before she has to. She can afford it—she must have thousands put away, she's been earning a great deal of money for over fifteen years."

"It's not that simple," said Mrs. Traill.

"It never is, bless your neurotic old heart . . . Well, this won't do, I must go out and buy a hat," and Diana sauntered off.

Mrs. Traill shook her silvery fleece. "Diana and her hats— so *ageing*," she said, following her friend out of the kitchen.

Christine began to make her plans for the evening. Her employers could look after themselves; they would understand that she must be on hand, with a new cleaner arriving and black at that; and she herself would eat something later, when Mr. Johnson's capacities had been proved and her mind was at rest—or not, perhaps.

It would be better, she decided, to have them all downstairs at supper when he arrived and not wandering around the house, for Mrs. Meredith had made it plain that she would hate the sight of him, and Mrs. Traill—well, she might get too friendly with him: for I'm sure, thought Christine, that she likes men, black or white.

She saw none of them all that day, and greatly enjoyed pottering about her flat and cautiously cooking her lunch. By six, when Mr. Johnson was expected, she had assembled an attractive-looking cold meal in the kitchen.

Six o'clock struck.

She drew herself up, and prepared to meet her ebony Mrs. Benson.

. . .

Punctually at a quarter to seven, there was a by-no-means hesitant knock, followed by a peal on the bell.

"You're three-quarters of an hour late," accused Christine, jerking the door open with no wavering hand.

Mr. Johnson, who looked about nineteen and was having trouble with a voluminous scarf and the evening breeze, gave a loud cheerful laugh.

"Oh, yes. I know I late. I couldn't help. I got responsibilities. You got a very big house. This all your house?" He followed her into the hall, looking around with smiling curiosity.

"No, it isn't. I'm the housekeeper. It belongs to some ladies and gentlemen who've bought it. Come this way."

She led him down the stairs. Instinct told her to talk to him as if he were a child, and a child who must be kept in order. *Begin*, decided Christine, *as you mean to go on; I* can see he's the kind who'll be sitting about drinking coffee and asking questions all the evening if he gets half a chance.

"Long way down," observed Mr. Johnson. Christine did not answer. A slight initial liking for Mr. Johnson's young face, and his smiles, she ignored.

Outside the kitchen door she had arranged some cleaning materials.

"That a broom," said Mr. Johnson, pointing with an air of pleased recognition, "and that a brush. What that red thing?"

"That's a dust-pan."

"Dust-pan. Pan. What you use it for?"

"What—good gracious, haven't you ever seen a dust-pan before? That's to put the dirt in, when you sweep down the stairs."

"I live in dirty house, now," said Mr. Johnson, smiling more brightly. "Dirty peoples. I brought up in Christian household; we have broom, and dust. Maybe we have dust-pan. Long time ago, I forget."

"Yes, well, you'll soon learn," Christine said firmly. "Now, I'll take you up to the top of the house."

She led him all the way up the stairs again, up and up, to the landing below her own. (Up there, she was not having him).

"Now," she said, as they paused, Mr. Johnson standing on the stair below her laden with brush and duster and pan and smiling hopefully, "I want you to sweep the stair-carpet and rub the paint at the sides with the duster, and dust between the banisters. I'll show you, and then you can get on by yourself."

She showed him. He did not receive instruction as she would have wished, continually interrupting with impatience —"Yes, I understand. That easy. I know now."—and gazing around him while she was demonstrating. But she was not going to waste his time—at five shillings an hour, indeed, and hurried through her task.

"I never done cleaning work before," he remarked, as she was going downstairs again, "except maybe when I a little kid in Christian household. But I soon learn. I intelligent."

She went down, accompanied by the not-reassuring sound of a brush banging smartly against fresh paint.

She arranged things a little more to her satisfaction in the kitchen and presently the household began to drift in: first James Meredith, who almost at once went out to get the appropriate wine from his cellar, having first asked her what they were going to eat; and then Mrs. Traill, smilingly confessing that she had talked to Mr. Johnson on the stairs and he seemed an utter lamb, and then Diana, poising her new hat on one finger.

"Thought I'd like your verdict on it," she said.

Mrs. Traill said that she disliked hats and never wore them; they put years on to your age; they kept the sun from your hair—

"I don't want the sun on my hair."

—They were always such conventional shapes; she used to make her own at one time; pick up a Mexican or Chinese straw, the peasants had wonderful ones—

"I dare say. I got this at Harrods. Like it?"

The two of them looked at half a yard of violet net and six or seven little violet velvet bows in silence.

"Very smart," James said at last, in a tone suggesting to Christine that he had said the same thing many times before; but at that moment in swept Antonia, preceded by a faint disturbance that was not exactly a rustle, and a waft of *Amour-Amour*, and followed by Clive Lennox.

"Angel of a hat. Exactly right for you. Lots of them about, of course, but what does that matter if it's Good Fashion," she said, falling into a chair. She was white with tiredness, and Clive at once set about getting her a drink. James indicated the wine; Clive shook his head and mouthed *Whisky* and went off, followed by James, to the cellar.

"Well, how did it go?" asked Diana, turning a jug upside down on the dresser and setting the hat on it.

"Oh, my things did very well, better than I expected. I knew I'd got one or two good numbers but I've been so fussed about that little tick I didn't realise *how* good, and one in particular, *Fall Folly*, stopped the show. That's being photographed for *Harpers*. They do keep some sense of proportion and occasionally show their readers clothes that haven't gone mad . . . and my others did well, too."

"Of course you must still have a lot of fans from just after the war. I know they're getting old," Diana said, "but—"

"Meaning that it was applause from old-hat people for old-hat numbers? Thank you."

"Don't be so touchy, darling. I was going on to say that I expect they've trained their daughters to like your kind of clothes; you'll have a new generation growing up, all adoring you."

Antonia shut her eyes. "Nigel's pleased," she said, "and that's something, nowadays."

Christine listened with divided attention to all this because she was expecting any moment to hear the banging of Mr. Johnson's brush as he came down the kitchen stairs. But she could not hear it, even in the distance, and presently she slipped out of the room.

63

All was quiet as she hastened up to the hall, her mind full of forebodings not unconnected with the colour of Mr. Johnson's skin which her common-sense instantly checked. And sure enough he was not sacrificing a white cockerel in the Merediths' bathroom or sticking pins into an image of herself.

But she did find him sitting on the top step of the kitchen flight, silent, seeming suddenly older, all his smiles gone and his hands drooping dejectedly between his knees in some way that brought out in them a simian look.

"Hullo—what's the matter? Aren't you feeling well?" Christine demanded briskly.

He slowly moved his eyes until he was looking at her, without lifting his head, and shook it.

"Can't you get on?"

Mr. Johnson slowly waved his hand over the dust-pan, the brush, and the duster and broom, all of which, she saw, had accompanied him as he made his way down the stairs.

"This," he said, in an immensely deep and sad voice, "woman's work."

"Well, you should have though of that before, shouldn't you?" said Christine, marshalling the considerable, though largely unconscious, forces of Mortimer Road. "I think it all works out nicely. I want a bit of help, you need the money, what does it matter if it is woman's work, as you call it?"

"I a man," he said sorrowfully.

"Well, it's too late to do anything about that now," Christine retorted briskly. "I wouldn't think about whose work it is. You just get on with it. When you get to the bottom there'll be a nice cup of tea. That'll cheer you up."

Mr. Johnson looked more cheerful immediately, and even laid a languid hand on the brush.

"Is true, about what you say. Is just work, for money. I got responsibilities. I like two cups tea, with plenty sugar. Also sandwich."

"There won't be sandwich." She was annoyed to find his way of talking infectious. "Sandwiches, I mean, but I daresay I could find you a biscuit—"

64

"Slice of cake," said Mr. Johnson eagerly.

Christine laughed. Really, he was just a great child.

"Perhaps. Now you get on with your job."

She left him, and in a moment heard the brush banging against the banisters again, and also a deep buzzing noise, not musical by any standards of her own, but pleasant to hear. Mr. Johnson was humming "There is a green hill far away," and even Christine Smith knew that tune.

"Is that our Massa Johnson? How's he shaping?" asked Clive, as the banging and buzzing became faintly audible in the kitchen.

"I don't know yet. He's got a lot to learn—"

"I hope,' interrupted Mrs. Traill, "I do hope you won't spoil him, Christine—"

"How do you mean?—spoil him, Mrs. Traill? I certainly shan't let him take any liberties."

"I didn't mean that kind of thing. We've got to treat him like a *friend*, and not ruin all that grand *warmth* and *vitality* and *joy of life*."

"So long as he does his work properly and isn't nearly an hour late every time, like he was this evening, I shan't take over-much notice of him. He seems nothing but a great child, anyway," Christine said.

"Bless him," carolled Mrs. Traill.

These remarks, admirably in the spirit of togetherness as they were, only reinforced her decision to keep Mr. Johnson as much as possible out of Mrs. Traill's way.

She sat down, and began to eat her interrupted supper.

Antonia seemed to have revived under the stimulus of food and drink.

"Nigel was all out. He'd been up all night, of course, and then this morning he had a terrible turn-up with Ferenc because the little brute wouldn't wash or shave before the show. It really was frightful. You could hear them screaming at each other all over the house. Some of the girls were crying, they all adore Nigel, of course, and would like to murder Ferenc. You could hear every word they said, Nigel shouting that he didn't make clothes for the kind of women who liked dirty unshaven little boys and Ferenc shrieking they were a lot of old trouts and better dead . . . It really was so ugly . . . I was shaking all over."

"What happened?" James asked, as Antonia paused; he had been listening with an expression of disbelief. "Has Nigel gone off his head? He was all through the War. Didn't he get a D.S.O.?"

"Oh, lord, yes. With bar. I don't know. It's all . . . it's just ugly."

Christine ventured to ask a question. She was so interested in the story that her desire to know the end of it overcame shyness.

"And did he get him to wash and shave?" she asked.

Antonia turned and looked at her; perhaps it was the appearance of a new listener, to whom all this was as interesting as it was to herself, that gave the first touch of warmth to her manner.

"Oh, yes, in the end. Nigel usually gets what he wants; he isn't at all a weak person, or he wouldn't be where he is. Ferenc went out and had a Turkish bath."

"I should hope so," said Christine, satisfied with this happy ending. "I should think you all never heard of such a thing—a smart Dress Show, and one of the designers dirty and not shaved."

"You're quite right—we never did," said Antonia, laughing hysterically, "but the world's getting to be a very funny place." She pushed her empty glass towards Clive.

"Was his mum there? I must say I like the sound of her," said Mrs. Traill.

"Oh, God, yes, in a sort of plum cocktail dress—a horror if ever there was one—Madame Netté of Wood Green High Street, I should think—and short sleeves, of course. How can you like the sound of her, Fabia? She's quite dreadful."

"You know I adore vital people."

"She's vital all right. You can have her. Every time one of his glitter-and-sparkles jobs came on she stood up to clap. No one in the audience minded, of course. I think they all thought she was rather sweet. I wouldn't mind her so much

66

myself, if she and Ferenc between them weren't ruining Nigel Rooth's as fast as they can ruin."

"Perhaps, he *won't last*," said Mrs. Traill thoughtfully. "Everyone can't always be wanting to wear glitter and sparkles."

"I wish I could believe it. But don't you worry, he'll learn. He'll learn, the little louse. I've said I just want to see him design one wearable suit, but the day he does design it, it'll be all up with me."

"Nigel would never let you resign, Antonia. He really does love you."

Antonia said something about 'infatuation' that Christine, who was busy for a moment at the dresser, did not catch; then turned to Clive, saying, "Well, darling? How did yours go?"

Christine then learned that Mr. Lennox had been up that morning for an audition for 'the new Noël', and had got the part. She listened with such interest, while grinding the beans that had replaced her despised tin of coffee powder, that she did not realise Miss Marriott's absorption in her own affairs, and her account of them, had crowded out the announcement of his news until this moment.

But it did strike her that everyone, even Miss Marriott, seemed more pleased about this than they had been about the success of *Fall Folly*. James slapped him on the back, Mrs. Traill and Diana kissed him, and Antonia herself sat on his knee and gave him sips of the champagne James had at once gone to fetch.

What a house it was—Dress Shows, and auditions for new musicals, and champagne! And everybody so charming, so good to look at and leading such interesting lives. Christine could hardly believe her luck in coming to live here; Mortimer Road, Lloyd and Farmer's, her family living and dead, seemed far away.

Chapter 8

THE LONG DAYS FULL OF QUIET OCCUPATION, THE PEACEFUL nights, and the awakenings unrasped by any thoughts of having to hurry up because that Number 127a never stops a second longer than it need—they began to flow past, and in no time, it seemed to Christine, she had been at Pemberton Hall a month.

Mr. Johnson continued to arrive on Monday and Thursday evenings, sometimes he was very late and sometimes he was just late. He was never punctual or early, but he soon acquired competence, if not enthusiasm or skill, in his tasks, and gradually—but not so gradually that Christine Smith was not aware of what was going on—he began to have a couple of sandwiches with his evening cup of tea.

He came down into the kitchen for this 'little break' as he called it; and sat at the table in his thick sensible clothes to have it. Christine did not know even that she liked to look at him, much less that the reason for her liking was the gracefulness of his young body.

"Sometimes they are very graceful. They fall into marvellous poses," Mrs. Traill had remarked, having (unfortunately, in Christine's opinion) strayed into the kitchen one evening while Mr. Johnson was having his break. She did not say this while he was actually there, though Christine had a secret conviction that she would have been capable of it. "It's his blackness, you know. It defines the pose, just as a silhouette defines shape."

Yes. Christine thought a little about this, after Mr. Johnson had returned to his work and Mrs. Traill had gone upstairs. I can see what she means—in a kind of way.

But her chief feelings were those of relief: that Mr. Johnson had showed no tendency to respond to Mrs. Traill's rather caressing manner, and also that he was sensible about his clothes; wearing strong thick shoes and sweaters all through that bitter spring, and even now only beginning to emerge cautiously into open-necked shirts. She felt a bit responsible for him, so black and young as he was, and would not have liked to see him shivering in a thin suit.

Her own relationship with him remained precisely what it had been on the first evening; a firm, sensible attitude on her part meeting occasional childish moodiness on his. But although this capriciousness was tiresome, Christine preferred Mr. Johnson, whom she could manage perfectly, to any of your Mrs. Bensons whom she was quite sure she could not.

She had never seen Mrs. Benson since the day when she had left Iver Street for ever. But she had not forgotten her.

Iver Street had gone. London was changing so quickly that someone born before 1914 could hardly realise the rate at which old houses were being torn down and massive, whitish blocks of flats and offices going up; and when Christine happened one day to go down to the Archway Road, she actually gasped to see, where the gardens and little cream-coloured façades of Iver Street had faced the sun, a gap that must have been all of two hundred yards long and a hundred wide. On its far perimeter were a few old houses, looking shaky and forlorn as if their turn were coming next, and already a new building had been run up, an arrogant, dazzling white oblong with hundreds of windows suggesting supercilious eyes. Two great machines, trembling and rumbling about like prehistoric monsters, were clawing out giant lumps of brick and earth under a smiling blue sky.

Christine stood watching for a while, feeling oddly sad, and wondering where Mrs. Benson had gone, and hoping it was out of the neighbourhood.

In her light summer coat, with a new scarf tucked in at her neck, and her hair kept neatly in place by one of the new chemical sprays, she stood watching the scene and thinking, now, of That Day.

It was four months since she had seen or heard anything that reminded her of That Day, and now it was only a memory of Iver Street that did: Iver Street, existing no more except as a kind of ghost street, a picture in some people's minds. Something in the memory of those lost cream façades that used to look so modestly at the sun reminded her of it.

Sighing, and feeling that it was foolish to sigh, she turned away.

.   .   .

The Long Room, the one overlooking the Square, where the piano stood in its glossy, quiet blackness against the white-rose walls, was the one room in Pemberton Hall into which Christine did not think she would be invited.

She had been shown over the rooms of all her fellow-tenants; usually about six in the evening, when they assembled in someone's flat for a drink; and she went into the Long Room almost daily to dust it and to replace faded or dead flowers. But she had supposed that its true use would be for parties, to which she would not go; it had been nice of them to show her their flats; they had wanted to make her feel at home, she supposed; but parties were another matter.

One afternoon she was dusting the piano, Mr. Johnson's cloth having left broad expanses untouched, when Mrs. Traill put her head round the door and invited her to come and see her latest drawing. She had just finished it, she said, and wanted an audience's opinion.

Christine, interested and flattered, followed her into the big room full of sun, where the picture, pretty in the anaemic, shapeless contemporary fashion of prettiness, stood amidst the clutter on Mrs. Traill's long working-table.

"It's for a story called *Nevermore, Beloved*," remarked the artist, bending forward to scrawl a more delicate tip to the nose of the unmistakably feminine shape entwined with a squarer male one. "Terrible tripe, of course . . ."

"I think it's wonderful, I can't think how you do it," Christine marvelled. "Oh, I like some of those stories, I think they're lovely. I take in *Homemaker*."

"There was a Talk on the Third Programme some weeks ago about them," Mrs. Traill went on. "This man—he was very clever, with several degrees—he said they were really harmful, they gave girls a wrong idea about Life."

"Well, I expect they'll learn soon enough," Christine said comfortably, still admiring the picture. "And do they just tell you what they want you to draw, and then you draw it?"

"I have to read the story, of course."

"Well, I think it's wonderful, I do really, Mrs. Traill."

"I wish you would call me Fabia," Mrs. Traill said, smiling up at her. " 'Mrs. Traill' sounds so formal."

"Oh I couldn't do that, thank you all the same for thinking of it," Christine said decidedly. "I expect it's being in business all those years. I never could get used to it. Some of those bits of girls took to calling Mr. Richards—he was our manager—Tom, if you please. Not to his face, of course, but I thought it was shocking—so disrespectful."

"But friendlier, don't you think?" said Mrs. Traill. "You don't mind my calling you 'Christine', do you?"

"Oh, no, I like it," hastily, "but that's different."

Mrs. Traill laughed and they went back to their separate occupations.

Crossing the landing, Christine was thinking that Mrs. Traill couldn't know much about the homes some of the girls came from, those girls who spoke of Mr. Richards as 'Tom' and read the stories she had called 'terrible tripe'. Christine herself did not know much. But she did know that anything giving them nice ideas about Life was all to the good.

Nice ideas about Life, reflected Christine, putting out a hand to push open the door of the Long Room, could never do anyone harm. Because sometimes in the papers—and even on television . . . but it didn't do to think about such things, as Mother always used to say.

Suddenly, while her hand was on the door, it swung wide open revealing the room's entire impressive length of warm white wall and shining, polished, narrow-planked floor. A vase of Spring flowers stood on a table by the window, and petals blew off in a shower, scattering along the dim blue and purple carpet.

That's the second time that door's done that. I'll have to

speak to them about it and get it seen to, thought Christine, it must be loose on the hinges or something, because it isn't all that windy today.

.   .   .

Christine's family had been quite content to let her settle into her new life without telephoning or visiting them. They had been mildly uneasy about her, what with her rushing off to live in that run-down place and then going to work for artists, but the news that she would have a flat set their minds at rest; it was her first home of her own, she would have more than enough to do, and could be left alone until some family occasion demanded her presence.

One now presented itself; the wedding of that Michael who was the son of Christine's sister Mary; and Mary wrote to her sister, enclosing an invitation and asking at the end of her note how Christine was getting along?

Christine was too much her family's product not to answer almost immediately, but she confined her reply to the casual question in a couple of lines, saying she was getting along all right: she wanted, very much, to avoid hinting at the new world that was opening before her.

She did not miss her family. She had always felt herself to be the odd-woman-out in the home circle, the one who was unlikely to marry, and could be relied upon to look after Mother and Father and keep them supplied with electric kettles and toasters until they subsided into their graves; and her new employers were the last kind of people to arouse family memories or domestic reveries. They none of them seemed to have any family, except Miss Marriott, whose mother, it appeared, wrote a gossip column in one of the high-class magazines.

"Awful snobbish nonsense, of course," Mrs. Traill had observed to Christine, when this lady's name had come up in conversation during one of the communal meals, and Christine had afterwards ventured some interested questions. "All about the Hon. This and Lady the Other and the Biggleton-Buswaites . . . She's getting on now, of course, she's like the chicken in that nigger-story of Clive's—'litle, but dam' ole' but she still gets around—Bermuda, Fez, everywhere. Like me. Diana can't stand her, says she's ruined Antonia's life."

This was purest Romance to Christine. Again and again, she marvelled at her luck in finding a home amongst such glamorous people.

She gathered from remarks dropped between the friends that Mrs. Traill had been too busy travelling all over the world, marrying her husbands and buying her Mexican sandals and Javanese pottery, even to pause and have a baby. Mr. Lennox did have this daughter, Glynis, who was only seventeen and had recently got herself accepted at some school for training actresses where it was very difficult to get in. But the Merediths, who were just the kind of people you might expect to have grown-up, even married, sons and daughters, apparently had none, and Miss Marriott—well, there were mysteries about her. Christine found this family-less state unusual, and far more interesting than the stifling family-atmosphere she had all her life been used to.

*   *   *

The wedding-day was bright and fair, and the ceremony was held—in a church, of course—at a suburb near Hendon.

Most of the large Smith family into which Christine had been born was there, and a number of their very old friends. The bride looked sweet and the bridegroom looked a fool, which is what Smiths expect and like at weddings.

Christine's thoughts about Mortimer Road had become increasingly clear—and resentful—during her time at Pemberton Hall. Once or twice she found the words *wasted my life in that place* going through her head. But, although she compared her new employers with the Smiths gathered at the wedding, and even found the words *nicer and more kind of intelligent* to describe the former, and even though they seemed in some way closer to That Day than Smiths, she came away from the reception feeling cheerful, and fond of them all.

73

It was the cosy Smith atmosphere. Once your feet had been caught in it, perhaps you never quite got them free.

Having briskly declined the offer of a lift from some cousins, she set out on an enjoyable homeward journey by bus; through roads of newish houses where many trees, and small gardens filled with brilliant flowers surrounding tiny lawns, gave an agreeable, and quite false, rural impression. The warm wind blew in through the windows, the sky was all blue except for swathes of ravelled white cloud floating high, and on the horizon dark trees, gathered together by distance, might have been a real forest.

The bus stopped—at a Request, Christine noticed, because this was the kind of thing she did notice (she would have made a first-class witness)—and some people came up the stairs and one of them was Mr. Richards, from the office; from Lloyd and Farmer's.

Christine was so surprised that she felt quite a shock. It was Mr. Richards, she never had an instant's doubt. But he did look pale and tired. Perhaps he had been ill.

She was sitting in the back seat near the stairs, and when he half-turned to make certain of catching the conductor's eye and hand him the fare—that was like him, he was always a one for quiet efficiency—he saw Christine.

He looked surprised, and he smiled and raised his hat (Mr. Richards had the habits of one over fifty years old) but he finished giving his fare, and getting his change, and counting it, and putting it away in a small purse, before he spoke to her.

"Miss Smith! What are you doing here? Do you live in this part of the world?"

"No, I've been to my nephew's wedding. Do you live near here, Mr. Richards?"

"No, I'm staying with some relations . . . er . . ." At this moment the man sitting next to Christine got up and went down the stairs and Mr. Richards said masterfully, "I'll come and sit next to you . . ." and moved adroitly into the place, adding with a laugh, "that is . . . if I may?"

Christine laughed too. But she thought that this had not

been the way of Mr. Richards in the office. Kind he always had been, especially on that morning when he had had to break the news to her. But not one for jokes.

"And what are you doing?" he went on. "I don't expect you had any difficulty about getting another job."

This was part of the kindness, because he must have known, better than most, that women over fifty did not find it easy to get another job. But she could answer cheerfully, and did, explaining what she was doing and where, and adding that Pemberton Hall was a fine old place.

Then she said, after he had commented that it all sounded satisfactory and he was glad she was well placed . . . "And how is Lloyd and Farmer's?"

She spoke with a playfulness which she would never have permitted herself in the office. But the day was so fine and she felt affectionate towards her family again after months of un-acknowledged estrangement, and she was quite pleased to see Mr. Richards.

He said abruptly, "I'm not with them any more."

"Oh, I am sorry," said Christine. "They must miss you . . . it wouldn't seem the same there without you."

Mr. Richards smiled. It was not a real smile.

"I don't think they miss me much," he said. "There were big changes after you left, Miss Smith. Many changes. I'm not sorry to be out of it." Then after a pause he added, looking out of the window, "You knew my wife died?"

"No. No, I didn't know that. Oh. I am sorry . . . you have had some bad luck, haven't you, Mr. Richards."

They said no more for a little while. It did not occur to Christine that one does not refer to the death of a man's wife as bad luck, because she was eager to show her sympathy, but afterwards she remembered office gossip about his not getting on with the dead one, and did wonder if it was all bad luck?

The small silence was broken by some remark from Mr. Richards, and after that they got on nicely until the bus was approaching a stop where he said that he must get off. Christine was preparing a remark about its having been nice to see him, when she saw him taking out a little notebook.

"Now if you will let me have your telephone number," he said, "I should like to ring you up one day soon and see if you would be free one afternoon to come and have a cup of tea with me."

"It's Highgate 1111," said Christine, very surprised. "Thanks, it's very nice of you."

She had accepted the invitation unhesitatingly. After he had gone down the steps at the next stop, she continued to look ahead, deliberately not glancing down to see if he were waving.

The bus moved on, and she experienced a slight sensation of relief. Out to tea with Mr. Richards. Well. Also Fancy.

Chapter 9

CHRISTINE'S LIFE HAD NOT BEEN ONE IN WHICH THE SENTENCE *he had not telephoned* had played the part it does in the lives of most women. She had known one or two men for a couple of months and been out with them to a cinema or for a walk, and 'nothing had come of it'.

Smiths expect something to come of it, and that something is what they call wedding bells.

None of these men had aroused any feelings in her, beyond a conviction that they were not the same to get along with, somehow, as women; and, when ten days passed and Mr. Richards had not telephoned, she only thought, 'Oh well, I expect he will, some time', and the matter began to drift out of her mind.

One evening while she was going out to the garden to water some zinnias which Mrs. Traill had bought "because those gorgeous colours remind me of Txlculpa," Miss Marriot spoke to her.

"We want to have a party on Sunday evening, Christine, for Clive's daughter—you know she's just got into this school. Can you arrange it? Glasses, and a few bits to eat, and so forth. It won't be many—just us, and Glynis, and my mother, and one or two people Clive knows and Mr. Rooth. James will see to the drinks. And, of course, you'll come, won't you?"

Looking like an angel burdened with some troubling secret, she stood at the foot of the stairs in her dark suit, the jewel on her lapel flashing in the dusk, and smiled—absently, as usual. She always seemed, Christine thought, to be thinking about something else when she spoke to you.

"Oh, thank you, Miss Marriott, I'd love to come. Er—those little biscuits, shall I get? And put cheese on them and those olives? Things like that? I would offer to make you a cake—but I'm still only learning, really—"

"Oh, God, no. Not cake. Ask Fabia, she'll know. That's lovely, then." She nodded and drifted away.

This was exciting news. Christine was to meet a gossip-writer and a dress-designer, and no doubt the ladies would be wearing lovely clothes. She would have liked to see them all eating a cake baked and iced by herself, but it wasn't wanted, and anyway she could not have made one yet.

Mrs. Traill was helpful. She took over the catering, saying that she had to go into Soho anyway on the Saturday and would buy some snazzy biscuits. And Nigel Rooth adored caviare, they must have some caviare.

"They won't want much. It's at half-past eight—most people will have had dinner. It's just an excuse for us all to get together, really, and I think Clive has some sort of a dim feeling it might do that little Glynis good to see a bit of formal entertaining—he's given her some money to have the kind of party she'll really enjoy with all her weirdy beardy friends. Of course she won't *enjoy* coming to us. But we really couldn't face having all the noise and the mess here. She'll just have to put up with nothing but conversation, for once."

Even Christine could feel that this was hardly the spirit in which you gave a party for someone, and experienced a little sympathy for this Glynis.

"Is she pretty, Mrs. Traill?" she asked.

"Oh, I wouldn't say pretty. Mostly mouth and eyes, like they all manage to be, nowadays. She's very *unfeminine*. Too thin, and her hair always needs brushing. And you simply cannot get anywhere with her. I think it's one's *duty* to know the young, and realise what goes on in their heads and usually I'm pretty good with them but honestly she won't let you in an inch. I expect it will be a flop. I can't bear conventional parties; when we lived in Esthonia we always had them on the shore. Baked our own fish. Caught it, and then baked it on stones. Delicious. But Diana and Antonia are both *deadly* conventional about entertaining."

It had struck Christine before now that so far as Mrs. Traill was concerned there was only one way of living, and looking, and thinking, and that was Mrs. Traill's.

She condemned in others what she approved in herself; rebuking the yet-unseen Glynis for thinness, for example, while keeping the severest watch on her own exiguous waist and hips, and wagging her head dolorously if, at the end of each week's ritual weighing, she had put on an ounce. And what could be less feminine than her trousers, and her sombrely-hued old men's shirts, and her jerkins embroidered by peasants in whom the traditional merriment had died some collective death?

Yet she had had four husbands. There must be *something* that attracted them, thought Christine, who described as *not exactly pretty* Mrs. Traill's face, with its brown bulging brow, and heavy-lidded grey eyes and mouth shaped like a bow, unpainted and serene, all framed in the fleece of wanton silver hair.

When Christine came into the Long Room about nine o'clock on Sunday evening, her first thought was one of self-congratulation.

Under protest, she had spent the larger part of the day polishing, and dusting, and arranging the claw-legged table with its load of bottles and what to her seemed a thin display of tiny biscuits and scraps of strongly-flavoured foods. But there were flowers and flowers. She had spent three hours, picking and arranging them; and gleams from burnished silver here and there, and a warm apricot light from many little lamps lying along the walls. The long curtains at the windows were not drawn.

She had remained upstairs, changing her dress, while the company arrived. There were only five of them, beside her employers, and everybody was sitting in an informal circle before the fireplace hidden in lilac and young fern; there was a scent from the lilac, and the light rise and fall of voices, and laughter.

Christine sidled in, so far as a large person could sidle, and,

79

excited and full of pleasant anticipation, took a chair next to a wall slightly outside the circle. A large dark man in evening-dress with a red carnation in his buttonhole at once turned his head to stare at her, with a look of open interest.

"Ah . . ." said Clive Lennox, in a tone that welcomed her pleasantly, and turning from where he stood pouring out something beside the table to smile at her, "here's Christine . . . she's kind enough to look after us all."

"Keeps us in order, don't you, Christine."

"Won't stand any nonsense," said Diana Meredith, winking.

"It's utter bliss, we never have to think about a thing," muttered Antonia mechanically; she was almost lying on the sofa beside the dark man who had stared at Christine, with his fingers just touching her wrist.

"Now, dear, what will you drink?' asked Clive.

Christine said in her usual clear voice that she would like a gin and orange, please, and Clive poured it out and handed it to one of the guests, a man whom Christine thought looked like an actor, to pass to her.

She did not, now, feel as confident as she had sounded, for the friendly murmurs that had followed her general introduction had been pierced on their conclusion by one sharp little voice. It suggested the yap of a Pekinese, and what it had said was: "How do you do, Miss Smith." It came from a small shape in a light dress who sat on the other side of Antonia.

Near the fireplace, on a tuffet, sat another shape, consisting chiefly of long, long dark boots and long, long dark hair. The boots were drawn up almost to its chin. The eyes were cast down. The hands were clasped between the knees and the whole pose suggested suffering mutely borne.

Christine sat sipping her gin and orange, which Clive had made enjoyably strong, and found to her satisfaction that she could stare as much as she liked, because no one now was looking at her or taking any notice of her.

They were talking about Noël Coward.

"Surely by now he doesn't care what the critics say? People will go to see him anyway; our generation because we adore him and he talks our language and the young ones—those of them who care about the theatre—because he's becoming a classic," said Diana.

"No one likes bad notices," said another man who also diffused an atmosphere of the stage; that is to say, he was livelier and better-groomed and handled his voice in a way that was different from most people's. "When you're in something by Noël, it's those catty remarks sending up the book."

"Have you much to do in it, darling? I've been in such a rush, I've never taken it all in," sighed Antonia, turning to Clive.

"Only second-lead, dear," he said mildly. But Christine noticed that his eyes wandered always back to her; away to his daughter, then moving from one guest to another to make sure everyone's glass was full, but always back to Antonia, in her black chiffon sheath that broke into a mermaid's tail of frills just below her knees.

"I did tell you," he murmured, and she turned to him with a remorseful smile.

"Always so good, isn't he, to people who've been in his shows before," said Diana.

"Well, thank you, love, I was hoping I'd got the job on my merits—poor things, but mine own," Clive said.

"Don't be so touchy, darling!" suddenly cried Antonia ringingly. "Peter, get me a drink, I'm as dry as bones."

Yes. Peter was there, pink in white tie and tails, sitting rather out of the circle, just as Christine was, and doing more listening and looking than talking. They hadn't even troubled to let her know that he was coming, and they were always making fun of him, he was one of their perpetual jokes, like Amanda and her mother-in-law. But Christine, without any reason, liked him.

He now got up and went across to the table and competently prepared the drink which Antonia instructed him about in the same carrying, impatient voice.

"Well mixed, brother," said James.

"Ha, that's experience," said Peter, carrying the full glass deftly across the room. "I usually end up doing this at parties.

Often thought if that lot gets in and taxes us out of existence in the autumn, I'll get a job as a barman."

"Think they will?"

"Get in? Haven't a clue. Hope to God not, anyway." He sat down in his corner and began again to look at Antonia.

She, sipping at her glass, had turned away from the party and was listening to the little woman next to her, who, Christine supposed, must be the famous Mrs. Marriott, the gossip-writer.

She not only sounded like a Pekinese but looked rather like one, with her short, round-eyed, snub-nosed face, if a Pekinese can be imagined wearing a shift-dress of oatmeal-tinted brocade and a gauze scarf. Her hair was dressed in frizzy blue curls and there were six rows of pearls clasped tightly about her neck. That's to hide it, thought Christine, she must be getting on. But she's ever so smart.

The conversation was absorbingly interesting to her.

". . . the Braithewaites, and Colonel Lester (their girl's just off to the Sorbonne). Then on Wednesday I flew up to Gailglass for young Hugh's twenty-first, fireworks and a barbecue with a whole sheep and Games the next day. And we danced till four, then back here for Lady Muir's dance for Katherine, and Susan Gillespie . . ."

It sounded an unbelievable kind of life, flying off to parties in grand houses and writing about them afterwards.

The two actors and Clive were talking in a group by themselves—animatedly and with frequent bursts of laughter, and Mrs. Traill, who this evening wore a drab hessian shift with buttons like pebbles and more pebbles in her ears, after listening smilingly to their talk for a little while, joined them, and the laughter became more frequent; Christine remembered Clive saying that Mrs. Traill had been on tour with him "between the wars"; the group would have something in common.

Diana and James had drawn Peter from his corner and were talking with him about cars; only she, and Glynis, and the big dark man next to Antonia, were out of it for a brief moment; silent, not laughing.

"The flowers are simply delicious," he suddenly called across to her. "Who arranged them? You?"

Christine smiled and nodded.

"At least . . ." he edged a little nearer to her, lessening the distance, "they aren't arranged at all; they're divinely natural. Of course, you've never been to one of those awful places where they teach you to bunch up chicken-wire and 'balance values', have you?"

"Oh no. I just—but I've always thought it would be nice to understand how to arrange them properly," said Christine, glowing under the interest in the heavy dark face and the kindness in the pouched, bloodshot eyes. He threw up his hands.

"Oh, my God. Now promise me you'll never have any lessons. If you knew how refreshing those great country bunches are—and the grass, the grass was an inspiration, I wish you could come down to my showrooms and arrange the flowers for me, the people who do it never seem to get them quite right . . . promise me you won't waste your money on lessons," he implored, leaning towards her. She almost felt the faint heat from his thick body, coming at her across the gap that separated them, and was a little embarrassed by his intense manner.

"All right," she said, laughing, "I won't."

"Darling . . ." said Antonia, turning her head, "what are you going on at Christine about . . . the flowers? Aren't they lovely, she's our clever girl, aren't you?" smiling at Christine. He had taken out a flat gold watch and was looking at it. "And you can put that away, Nigel. It isn't ten yet."

"I know, darling, I'm desolate at having to, but honestly I must. You know what he's like if one's late. So *touchy*. I sometimes feel if I have to take one more scene I shall quietly *die*."

This conversation went on in a rapid undertone, while the two pairs of eyes, the large sapphire ones and those small and richly grey as water-rinsed pebbles stared into each other and painfully smiled.

"Why take them at all?"

"Now, darling . . . How many more times have we got to have this one out?"

"Well at least say something to the child. It's supposed to be her party."

He glanced across the room to where Glynis Lennox, roused from apparent dozing by the conversation between Mrs. Traill and the three actors, was now sitting upright on her tuffet and listening with a solemn expression.

"Why in God's name does she dress like that? It's an outrage. She's exactly like that early photograph of Mrs. Pat that used to be in my mother's sitting-room. She could look wonderful."

"Go and tell her so. Clive adores her but I can't get near her; those clothes put me off so."

"All right. But then I really must run."

He got up heavily—Christine's first thought about him had been that here was a man giving much time and planning to not looking elderly—and went across the room to Glynis and squatted in front of her. Her enormous dark eyes flew round and fitted themselves, startled, on his face.

"Have you ever heard of an actress called Mrs. Pat Campbell?" he demanded.

"Of course. Paula Tanqueray." Glynis retorted, so clearly that most people stopped talking and turned towards them.

"You're exactly like her. But exactly. My mother had a big photograph of her in her sitting-room and I used to worship it when I was six . . . Now if I make you a red dress, very dark red, and give it you for a present, will you burn those truly terrible boots and wear it?"

"Yes, I will. And thank you very much," she said, keeping her eyes on his face. Her tone was rather cold.

"I should like to make it à la princesse. But if I did I suppose you wouldn't have the guts to wear it. Or would you?"

"Yes, I would," she said.

"Without knowing what à la princesse means?" beginning to smile.

For the first time, Glynis's composure wavered slightly. "I—

isn't it fitting to the body, without a join at the waist?" she asked, also beginning to smile.

"That's right, put briefly." He struggled up; the squatting position had been trying. "It's a romantic fashion; and you'll look as if you were in fancy dress. But you'll also look like Mrs. Pat come to life again . . . I'll put ruching at the neck, a low neck, and elbow sleeves, very puffed . . . and you'll wear it? Promise?"

She nodded, laughing. Everybody had crowded round them, and someone started to clap. Rooth bowed ironically. "Thank you, thank you one and all, ladies and gentlemen, and good-night. Sweet Antonia, sweet Fabia, sweet Diana, thank you for a lovely party. Good-night, young Stella," to Glynis.

Smiling regally, he walked out of the room with Antonia. Christine was a little disappointed that he went past without looking at her or saying anything.

"Thank God," a man's voice muttered: Christine could not be quite sure whose it was.

"Oh, I think he's ever so charming," she said ardently, to Clive, who stood near her.

"Yes. He's not a bad chap," Clive said, and though dampened by his moderate tone she told herself that he couldn't have made that remark. "A bit trying sometimes, but aren't we all?"

Mrs. Traill was saying kindly, "There, Glynis. Aren't you lucky! A frock from the House of Rooth."

"One of the last sane ones it's likely to make," said Diana, "and therefore will have scarcity value—if any of us care."

"Oh, come," one of the actors said.

"Well, he sickens me. Keeping Antonia on a string." Diana sank her voice to a hurried drone, so that Mrs. Marriott, who was being given a fresh drink, could not possibly hear. "She isn't in love with him, of course. I doubt if she could be with anyone. She's a darling but nothing but a clothes-horse, but she wouldn't at all mind marrying him. They've been great and good friends for years and I think he's often hinted at it. But now he's besotted with some little cockney boy who designs for him, and heaven knows how it'll end."

85

"Well—it'll end," said the actor.

He turned to Glynis. "So you're going to start taking the bread out of our mouths in a year or two, are you?" She nodded, sparkling up at him silently with a complete change of personality: she never *intended* to come to life only when men spoke to her; she knew that it was bad policy and bad manners; but it happened in the same way that she breathed. They were beginning to chat, when—

"Are you interested in clothes, Glynis?" Mrs. Marriott asked across the room, in a voice that sounded remote, as if relayed from some mountain sanctuary.

"No, I'm not, Mrs. Marriott. I hate them," Glynis said, looking straight at her.

Antonia, who had just come back into the room, started violently. Clive's sensitive face managed to look anxious and amused, and proud, all at once; everyone had reseated themselves on the departure of the celebrity, and there was the slightest sensation of relaxation.

Chapter 10

"WELL, IF YOU'RE GOING TO WEAR A 'PRINCESSE' DRESS, YOU'LL have to put on some weight," Mrs. Traill said. "No, I mean it, Glynis. I'm speaking now as an artist. You need it here," she sketched a movement about her own slight bosom. "It's more feminine."

"Bustiness is no advantage to a serious actress. But I can always put it on if I have to, for a part. I put it on easily."

"You see—dedicated," Clive said gravely aside to James, who also looked very serious.

"You don't eat enough, I'm sure," said Mrs. Marriott, arranging the silver gauze stole and still speaking in the detached voice that seemed to be laying down, not unkindly, some universal law, "I was talking to Lucy Verinder this morning—you remember Lucy, Antonia, we used to stay at her palazzo in Istria when you were a little thing—her youngest girl is sharing a flat with three others in Chelsea somewhere, and she seems to live on those tins of spaghetti I'm told you can buy for sixpence—marvellous value, I suppose, but they cannot be nourishing at that price and it's so worrying for poor Lucy." She looked across the room at Glynis. "Now tell us about yourself, my dear—what are your hobbies? Polly, this child who's sharing the flat in Chelsea, is studying the History of Art at the Guggenheim Institute."

"I haven't any hobbies. I only care about acting, and that isn't a hobby, it's my life," Glynis said.

"Well, well," Mrs. Marriott said indulgently. Her flat yellowish-grey eye lingered on the boots.

"Oh, Glynis—" Mrs. Traill put her head on one side, "with so much going on in the world . . . At your age you *ought* to *feel* about these things. They don't matter to people like me, who've opted out and live in a private world of our own, but you ought to *feel*. You, at you age, ought to be *burning* about these great questions . . ."

Glynis's voice seemed to have the power of making the room fall quiet; it was not only its youth, contrasting with all the forty and fifty-year-old tones, but the latent power in it, hinting that it could, if she were aroused, shriek with pain or croon with love or chant in triumph. So far, too, she had had the good sense to leave it natural; it was highly unelocutionary.

So, when she stirred on her tuffet and lifted her head and looked across the room at Mrs. Traill and said: "I do think about those things. Of course I think about them," another silence followed. This time, the voice was not quite steady.

She deliberately swept the groups of faces with her thickly-lashed eyes, and began to speak.

And then and there, into the Long Room filled with flowers and soft light and complex and tired, but still eagerly living, elderly people, stomped The Problems; a global one, a racial one, and two or three of the comparatively minor ones which are nevertheless lashingly active. Round and round, up and down, backwards and forwards they marched, and no one but Glynis uttered a word; not even Mrs. Marriott, who was the only person to make a slight movement of the lips once or twice or start with a "But—" that got no further. And it went on for nearly ten minutes.

Glynis stopped talking abruptly. She took a biscuit off a plate and sipped her wine and was silent, staring into the distance, and her silence had the quality of more, and yet more, apocalyptic speech.

James, who was hospitably suspending a bottle over her glass, caught a tiny shake of the head from her father and unobtrusively set it down again.

The silence—not an impressed one, Glynis felt—was broken by Mrs. Marriott. She adjusted the silver gauze, and said equably:

"Really, my dear—I know your father will understand this and forgive me if I speak frankly—do you realise that if you—er—go on like that no one who is anybody will ever ask you anywhere? You cannot possibly have any idea of how it sounds to someone of my generation. All the time you were talking I was wondering what old Lady Clontarf (though she is very old she still takes an active interest in her Lepers and her Deprived Children) would have said to a girl of your age dominating the conversation in a roomful of grown-up people—well, of course, in her day such a thing could never have happened. It would have been unthinkable. She was the finest hostess of her generation and she set the model for thousands of women who could never, of course, have afforded her beautiful house or her men-servants, but who liked to keep up a standard. I am sure she would be really shocked. World affairs! What can a girl of your age know of such things? (It was different for Margot Asquith, of course; she grew up among clever men who ran the country.) What can you possibly know about the difficulties of such men, many of whom are old enough to be your grandfather who are giving their lives, and in some cases their health, to try and settle these—er —terrible questions? I advise you to concentrate on your acting. If you really get on, you will give a lot of harmless pleasure to hard-working people. I am very fond of a good play myself. James, may I have some more of your delicious brandy?"

Glynis, after exchanging a long look with her mentor, slowly lowered her face on to her knees until it was hidden. Its expression, before it disappeared in hair and dusty leather, was one of stony calm.

Clive went across to Mrs. Marriott with the decanter, with all kinds of expressions on his own face. As he refilled her glass she looked up at him, smiling, and murmured, "You and I are such old friends, I am sure you will forgive me for my little lecture. She's an attractive child—but really those boots are only fit for the hunting-field—if that. Someone had to do it."

Clive, looking slightly hunted himself, muttered something friendly, and then Antonia, holding out a beseeching hand, said softly: "Won't you sing for us?"

"Ah, yes," and "Do," said everybody, and he went to the piano. Mrs. Marriott lit herself a cigarette and leant back, with a polite expectation on her withered pekinese's face.

Christine was divided between sympathy for Glynis and

89

excitement at the immediately forthcoming treat. Poor kid—getting her on to that Bomb-sitting, it was too bad—it was supposed to be her party, wasn't it?—and suddenly with a murmured, "Excuse me, please," she got up from her place in the modest corner and, pushing her way carefully past Antonia (who looked up with an irritated surprise that made Christine wish she could sink through the carpet) crossed over to Glynis and sat down by her.

But she had not the nerve to speak. She wondered if the poor kid was crying? It was what she, Christine, would have felt like doing if anyone had gone for her like that. Not but what she did not (this was how Christine put it to herself, never having become self-conscious about double negatives) agree with Mrs. Marriott. A bit of a girl, carrying on like that! And what nice home *would* want her? In those boots, and reminding everybody of all those awful things?—at a party, too!

Then she forgot Glynis, because, out of a ripple of runs and deep chords, the theme of *Lost Moonlight* came up, and took possession of the audience and the room.

You probably know *Lost Moonlight,* and if you are over forty you are fond of it. It was loved during the last war. The theme of the lyric is not original, something of the same kind having been said by Sappho about three thousand years ago, but somehow it goes on being topical. Clive had an unusually pleasing light baritone, apparently untouched by the years, and of course he could put it over to the last nuance. Christine listened in a trance of pleasure, while the young man, and the girl, and the summer moonlight of their lost happiness floated vaguely before her inward eye. Lovely, she thought as she listened, lovely. Yet the delight was not the delight of That Day.

She became aware of movement beside her; Glynis was lifting her head. Cautiously, afraid to break the spell, Christine glanced at her. Now she was sitting upright, and Christine saw that her eyes were fixed on her father, while a tiny smile of purest pleasure and pride transformed her face—the smile of a little girl who has been allowed to sit up past her bedtime

to hear 'Daddy's song'. She looked younger even than seventeen.

A light chord sounded, a last prolonged ripple went up and
out into the summer night. Clive looked round, and smiled.

They were all clapping and calling affectionately—"Thank
you, darling." "Oh, beautiful." "You're better than ever." And
as if breaking out irrepressibly, from Diana—"Oh, if only
Maurice were here!"

There was a pause, a kind of wavering silence, and a sound
not quite a sigh, from the whole room. "Ah, yes," someone
murmured.

"Those rotten 'adapted' and 'arranged' versions—it must be
years since I've heard it sung what you'd call 'straight'," James
Meredith said.

"Who composed it?" Christine turned to Glynis. "Your
father?"

"Daddy! No, he can only sing, bless him. Maurice Condron, a friend of Daddy's—of all of them. He was killed at
Calais, in the war. They gave him a posthumous V.C."

"After he had passed on?" asked Christine, with a dim
idea of the long word's meaning.

"Yes. He really was—a hero. I never knew him, of course."

She pressed her lips together suddenly, and got up and went
over to the piano, where her father was vamping a gay little
air.

"Daddy, I must go. I'm sorry, but I'm meeting somebody."

"Must you, dear? Well—I'll see you to the bus."

"No, it doesn't matter. I'm being met—thank you all the
same." She turned to Antonia, who was leaning far over the
piano picking out 'I Could Have Danced All Night' with one
improbably long finger. The pose revealed her slight breasts,
delicately lapped by the black chiffon and suggesting two
flowers, rather than a part of the human body meant to feed
a child. "I say—did he mean that about the dress?"

"Of course. Nigel always does what he says he's going to."
Antonia looked up under her brows.

"Then what'll I do about it? I mean, when do you think
it will be ready?"

"I simply can't say, Glynis. You'll have to be measured and have at least two fittings. And I'll bring it back here, and put it on you, and show you how to wear it."

"Well . . ." Glynis suddenly smiled broadly, "that's kind of you . . . But what is there to show? It's just putting it on, isn't it? Do you think it'll fall off me or something? And how about this 'measuring'?"

"I'll get that done. Look in at Randolph Square one afternoon next week."

"I can't. I've got classes until five, every day."

"Come in later, when you've finished. We're there till all hours, a dress-house isn't like some fiddly little office."

"Oh, all right. Such a fuss . . . it's only a dress." But her tone was good-tempered.

"You won't think that when once I've put it on you," Antonia said. "Nigel is one of the great ones, you know. He set the fashion all over the world, just after the war, for season after season. He and Dior."

"But he's on his way out now, isn't he? His things are old hat."

"His 'things' are classic. They'll last. Now you run along to your date, I'll see to everything."

While these arrangements were being made Glynis had been reaching into the gap behind a sofa, and now fished up a leather jacket, suggesting in its grim blackness and numerous buckles some form of armour, which she slung on. She then faced the company and made a brief speech thanking them for a delightful evening, finishing up by turning and confronting Mrs. Marriott—whose eyes were fixed upon the jacket.

"I expect I was a bore," said Glynis, "talking so much, I mean. But it was implied that I take no interest in world affairs and it was my duty to say what I did. I daresay there may be something in what you said. I might think about it. Good-night." With which, she walked out—beautifully.

When Clive came back from seeing her out of the house he found them still laughing; even Mrs. Marriott was smiling, though far from broadly, down into her brandy glass.

"Isn't it funny—" Antonia was saying, "you can tell she's

an actress? She hasn't even started training—but you can tell.
I'll bet you," turning to Clive, "that in five years her name'll
be up in those little bright lights." She lifted her glass. "Congratulations, papa."

Christine, who was watching sympathetically, saw him give
her a glance that was startling. Why, he loves her! she
thought, at once looking away from the two; I can see it; he
loves her.

What an evening it was being!

Clive began to laugh with them, looking round at their
laughing faces.

"What a child it is . . . but you can see, can't you? She's got
it, hasn't she? Hasn't she got it?"

Tenderly, warmly, they told him over and over again that
she had.

Glynis, charging across the square in the dim light, crashed
into a young man who was coming to meet her, with enough
force to have sent most young men off their feet. But this one
was stocky and strong; he seized her, swung her up, and
nuzzled her soft face with his bearded one, she returning the
nuzzling with slightly less ardour. Oh, it was well that old
Lady Clontarf could not see those boots waving slowly in the
air.

He set her down again, thrust a paperback into his pocket,
shoved his arm through hers, and began to march her down
the hill.

"How was it? I thought you were stuck there for the night."

"It's only eleven." (She did not add I hope you haven't been
waiting long.) "Oh, it was all rather pathetic, really. None of
them are real—except Daddy, of course. Fabia Traill said I
wasn't feminine."

"Ho! ho! that really is a good one!" he said.

She glanced at him. "She meant I wasn't fat."

"What on earth were you doing, all those hours?"

"Oh, sitting around. Not what you and I would call talking,

it was conversation, I suppose. Nigel Rooth is going to make me a dress."

"The homo designer? I say, is he having a change of heart or something?"

"Tom," said Glynis, after a pause while they walked down the hill in silence. "You say all the things everyone else does."

"Well, isn't he a homo?"

"I don't know. I thought he was charming."

"They often are, we all know that. Anyway I hope we shan't see you becoming sweet and suburban. I shan't like it, even if I do say all the things everyone else does."

"I shall wear it to parties. I'm tired of being scruffy anyway, it's a bore remembering to be. I've got to learn to wear clothes and make up my face, I may as well start now."

"They've been corrupting you! I can feel it."

"Oh don't be so—so raw. The only person who did anything like get at me was old Mrs. Marriott, Antonia's mother. She delivered a speech at me. No one would ask me anywhere if I talked about—you-know-what."

"Did you talk about it? Good on you, flea." He pressed her arm against his side.

"They seemed to want me to, so I did."

"I expect the subject has a morbid fascination for them. Most of them have no imagination and their minds are hopelessly set in the past. They think it would be like 1939."

"Don't . . . it wasn't too bad, really, only it all seemed so unreal and there was nothing to eat but horrible little biscuits tasting of pepper. Daddy did sing his song."

"Oh, God. 'Lost Moo-o-nlight'," he mimicked.

"Belt up," said Glynis distinctly, and dragged away her arm.

"What's up? What have I done now?"

"They may be unreal, and smug, but I've known most of them all my life and—they aren't so bad. They can't help being old. And, anyway, Daddy's going to be in the new Noël Coward."

"Good heavens—do you expect me to congratulate you? I should think you'd keep *that* piece of good news to yourself."

"It is good news. He likes it, anyway, it's good news for him.

You really have less imagination than anyone I ever met—talk about *them* having none."

"I have no imagination! *I*, who find it almost impossible to get through my life because I've got so much imagination! That—really—is—rich."

"I didn't mean you haven't *any*, flea. But you can't get inside other people's minds unless they're a bit like yourself."

"Do you realise what you've just said? I'm going to write novels—you've practically told me that I've been born without the equipment to do it."

"Oh, don't take it so seriously. All I meant was"—her voice began to quaver maddeningly—"you know how I get worked up about The Bomb and of course I don't like that old woman saying no one's ever going to ask me anywhere or like me—what about *audiences*, I was thinking all the time she was talking—what about *audiences*. And you know I love that song. Dearly," she added more decidedly, the quaver having been mastered. "So will you kindly—not—say—that kind of thing."

Silence. "I'm sorry, flea," he said at last. She put her arm through his again. "That's all right, flea."

"Say it, flea. Say 'I love you'. Please."

Glynis shook her head, looking straight down the hill to the lights glittering in the valley; she did not slide her large dark glance round on him, nor was there a trace of coquetry in the smile that curved her unpainted lips. Her steps rang as if in some triumphal march.

"Now be quiet, flea. You know I never will say it, it's too serious. Let's go somewhere and eat. After those beastly peppery biscuits, I'm starving."

"All right, where would you like to go?" he asked eagerly. "I haven't much on me . . ."

Boots twinkling, voices now rising and falling amicably, they went on down the hill into London.

Chapter 11

"I EXPECT YOU'VE BEEN WONDERING WHY GLYNIS IS SO UTTERLY different from her father," began Mrs. Traill, one morning some days after the party.

"You'll need that all dug over; it hasn't been touched for years," said Christine; she had heard what was said, but was more interested in the flower-bed in the garden at the back of the house which she and Mrs. Traill were inspecting.

'You see he married somebody very *tense*, for his first wife, she was always making scenes (yes, it will need doing, won't it; I wish we could get hold of a man) and Glynis is like her."

"That's like Mr. Meredith, he always says 'get a man, get a man.' But they aren't so easy to get, these days. I saw in the paper gardeners were getting a pound an hour, somewhere down Kensington way."

"It's strange, isn't it; you would think the peace and primitive joy in handling growing things would make them more or less indifferent to money . . ." murmured Mrs. Traill, whose remarks made Christine understand why Diana could occasionally be overheard declaring, "Fabia is bonkers, and we have to face it."

"I suppose they have to live," she said briskly. "There's a lovely rose," lifting the heavy crimson head to sniff it. "Considering nothing's been done to the garden, it looks quite nice."

"Yes, but a bit desolate, don't you think? . . . He could paint the shed for Diana, too."

"The shed for her pottery?"

"Yes." They both turned to look at the shed. "She won't get a single pot made," said Mrs. Traill. "She *talks* about it, but never a pot shall we see. She's like that. What she *truly* likes is more and more hats. She's got fifteen already . . . But if

James likes to buy her a wheel, and pamper her, that's his business . . . Do you think Mr. Johnson would dig the garden for us?"

"I could ask him," said Christine doubtfully, "But I hae ma doots . . . he's been rather funny, lately."

"Oh, you don't think someone's got hold of him and made him politically conscious? That child-like, innocent-type is quite unfitted for political maturity."

"I shouldn't think he'd understand if they had. No, it's this other job he's got, somewhere in Hampstead. He seems to be always over there, these days."

"I expect they pay him more. We could manage that, if he asks about it."

"I don't think it's the money, Mrs. Traill. He seems to like going there. When he comes on to us, afterwards, he's full of giggles, and singing, and ever so cheerful. I think it's more the job and the people, really."

"Oh well, we must hope for the best . . . look at that rose. How funny."

"What?" Christine stared through the clear summer air towards the bush, and was just in time to see the rose she had admired swaying as if in a stiff breeze. It came gently into position again, with languorously drooping head.

"You do get the odd draught in this garden; I was noticing the other day," she said.

Mrs. Traill sauntered back to the house, her prevailing mood of dreaminess having apparently replaced the mood of energy which had caused her to suggest an inspection of the garden. She alternated thus; Christine had noticed it, and had some time ago decided that if she wanted anything accomplished with Mrs. Traill's help, she would have to do it herself. She did not mind; she felt cheerful, and content, and had many small interesting plans of her own which were only occasionally dimly shadowed by thoughts of Mr. Richards and his threatened tea-drinking.

She had already done one or two unadventurous jobs in the garden; planted some stock seedlings, and several times cut the grass, which grew fast in spite of the prevailing shade.

But the narrow, green-lawned, quiet place—with its view of distant churches and the white blocks of new flats and that great American hotel and featureless grey vistas, all framed in the high brown brick walls of two neighbouring houses—seemed to be silently but actively resisting alteration. Seedlings might be put in, a shrub pruned here, the grass might be kept featly short—but the garden had looked like this for two hundred years, and it was not going to be changed. It was so quiet! The singing of birds echoed there. Christine drew one of the three or four sighs of pleasure she had breathed in her life as she stood looking at it.

.　　　　　.　　　　　.

Later that afternoon, Diana Meredith and Mrs. Traill sat gossiping in the former's flat. Christine Smith, surprisingly, was the subject of tongues usually busy with more colourful personalities.

"I bet you—if I took her out into the garden this evening and showed her those lights, she'd simply say 'very nice', or something of that sort. I'm almost certain she's all of a piece, right through," Diana said.

Mrs. Traill had taken refuge in waggings of her head and murmurings about never knowing ourselves or anyone else.

"Bosh. I know James and he knows me . . . Well, will you have a little bet?"

"No, Diana. I don't think it would be kind . . . and there's almost no one left in England, now, like Christine Smith—"

"What nonsense—Oxford Street is full of her . . ."

". . . and if you scare her off or upset her we shall be sunk."

"We shall be sunk anyway if those swine get in in the autumn." Diana said viciously, lighting her cigarette.

"Well perhaps they won't . . . How boring it all is. As if anything mattered but Art and Love!"

Diana, leaning back in her chair, blew out smoke, shook her head, and surveyed her friend affectionately for some seconds in silence.

"Well, are you on?" she asked at last. "I'm only going to show her the lights of London. Half-a-crown, then. Done?"

"Oh, all right. But I do think it's cruel and unfair . . . Do you still dislike her?"

"Our Christine? Did I dislike her? Oh yes—I believe I did, just at first. I thought she was typical lower-middle class which is absolutely the type I loathe most, timid and narrow and inhibited, but now I'm not so sure . . . and she *is* efficient. It's because I'm not so sure that I want to try this experiment with the lights. No, I don't dislike her, now."

So, that evening after they had finished supper, Diana suggested that she and Christine should go out and look at the lights because it was a wonderful evening, so clear.

Christine followed her, out into the chilly dusk. She was a little surprised by the invitation but was accustomed, by now, to Mrs. Meredith's moods.

"It's too small, of course," Diana said over her shoulder. Country gardens spoil you for town ones . . . There . . .just look at that."

A faint glow, neither green nor yellow, lingered in the garden, as if contained by the walls, and through it the flowers that were white or yellow still glimmered. At the end of the long dim lawn there was the low wall, and beyond it a mighty, sparkling, glittering, twinkling cloud, like the *diamanté* bosom of some colossal meretricious sorceress—orange, white-gold, silver, and a cold, decadent mauve; alluring, far off—quite, quite unreal. Oh, come on down, said the sorceress, do.

"Very nice," said Christine, after a pause, and Diana thought, *what did I tell you? Half-a-crown, please.*

Chilled, and mildly irritated, she turned away from the astonishing spectacle.

"Isn't it strange, this light?" she said, feeling that it was only fair to Mrs. Traill give Christine another chance. "A friend of ours, Maurice Condron, said once that it was like the taste of lemons."

"Is that the one who wrote that song, who was . . . He passed over at Calais?"

Diana had shuddered—perhaps at a memory, or at Christine's phrase. "Yes. (Let's go in, it's getting cold.) He was the most wonderful person—nobody could make one laugh as

Maurice could—except Dick Keiler, perhaps . . . but not like Maurice."

Christine heard her sigh.

She had only asked the question about this Maurice, of whom she had already heard something from Glynis Lennox, and in whom she wasn't much interested, from a sudden fierce instinct of self-defence.

She had wanted to hide from Diana the quick, intense joy that had come upon her at the sight of the afterglow in the garden. Immediately recognized, transforming herself and everything she was conscious of, and welcomed with as near as Christine could aproach to rapture, it was the very emotion of That Day, belonging—but she did not know this—neither to heart nor to senses but to the spirit that had been starved into numbness for nearly half a century.

It lasted for perhaps a few seconds—she did not know how long. Then it had gone, and she was following Mrs. Meredith back to the house and wondering aloud whether they should ask Mr. Johnson to dig the garden? She only hoped, Christine said sensibly, that he had not seen that piece in the papers about those gardeners in Kensington earning a pound an hour.

Yes, it had gone again, just as it had gone when she had seen the snow-laden cedar tree in Hampstead. She turned to take a last look; the light lingered yet, the flowers glimmered through its aquamarine dusk, but where was the delight? She could only remember it; she could no longer feel it.

But it did come, she thought, following the now silent and withdrawn Diana down the stone-paved passage. That's the second time. It could come again. It's always there, somewhere, waiting.

Where?

She put the thought from her mind and went back to the kitchen and began on the washing-up.

.   .   .

There was really nothing to think over.

It had come again, and that was a wonderful thing to have happened. She would have liked a walk by herself, over the

100

Heath, just to think about it; but it would have been only daydreaming; there was nothing to do, or to decide; that was the delight, but also the strangeness, about this fleeting feeling; she could neither command it to come nor use it in any way when it did.

But she would have liked her solitary walk, and what prevented her from having it was the fact that she was meeting Mr. Richards outside the bus-stop for Kenwood House at three. He had telephoned about nine on the previous evening and made the arrangement.

Across the Square, in her summer coat, hatless, with a white cotton flower in her lapel, carrying her white bag and gloves, she went. It was a fine day and the outing would 'make a break'. But Mortimer Road was not completely easy in its mind about Mr. Richards. It sensed, from afar, Change, possibly Bother, looming up on some yet distant horizon.

Mr. Richards was at the bus-stop, also hatless—which made him look younger—and wearing a nice grey suit. Christine was pleased to have such an escort; she liked a man to dress well. But she did just wonder what they would find to talk about.

She need not have; Mr. Richards had already been to the house and secured a guide-book and as they walked on under the trees, he gave her an outline of its history. She listened, but with half her mind wondered what he did with himself all day, if he had time to wander round getting guide-books before meeting her at three? He must be still out of a job.

The big, cool house was crowded with visitors, moving slowly past the smiling or pensive Gainsborough beauties and the gleaming furniture; the occasion was not quite so novel to Christine as it would have been six months ago, because she herself now lived in a house with gleaming furniture and beauties, but it was full of interest, and she was enjoying it.

Mr. Richards was easy to get on with, mingling his attention to what there was to see with pleasant general remarks, and while she half-listened to him, she concentrated the other part of her mind on really studying what the girls in the paintings wore. Those corsets! And their shoes looked too tight. But lovely materials. She had always had a secret wish to wear a sash.

"Tired?" asked Mr. Richards, as they paused before Lord Leighton's 'Orphans', the little girl in the Kate Greenaway frock nursing an infant rabbit.

"Poor little mite, she does look sad, what a pity he couldn't have painted her smiling. Not a bit. But I could do with a cup of tea."

"If he had, there wouldn't have been any point in the title . . . and how could he have got the rabbit to smile, anyway?" Mr. Richards was teasing her, and she smiled back at him. "How about going along, then? It's early, but it won't be so crowded."

He gently steered her by her elbow, which she found slightly irritating.

"Now you wait here, Christine, and I'll go and forage."

He arranged her at a table, and hastened away. She sat there, staring down at her gloves. 'Christine'. Fancy . . . and this was only the first time they had been out. H'm . . .

The table was one of those set around a small walled garden at the side of the house's stables. Here a number of people were already drinking tea and eating sausage rolls and fruit salad and watching other people doing the same—with every excuse, for this little garden is a favourite resort of the lively German-Jewish families that live in West Hampstead and Golders Green, and every table had its private operetta.

She took away her fascinated stare from a wonderfully wrinkled face, topped with marigold curls, which was changing its expression every three seconds, and saw Mr. Richards coming across the grass with a laden tray.

"You're going to call me Tom, aren't you?" he said, smiling and setting it down. "I've already taken the bull by the horns and called you 'Christine'. Now—will you do the honours, please?"

She had a confused feeling of relief that he had not said *will you be mother* . . . It would have been . . . Here, what *is* all this? It's only because I'm not used to going about with a

man, she told herself sensibly, and smiled at Mr. Richards—
Tom, then—across the teacups.

"I hope you like buns, Christine, buns and butter? Most
of the cakes looked rather richer than I thought you would
care for. But buns haven't changed much these forty years.
No, they haven't been able to do much to buns. I'm very
partial to a bun and butter."

So was Christine, and so much better for you than those
sickly cakes. Good, hot, strong tea. And then cigarettes.

She listened while he talked.

She had a feeling, as his talk went on, that he was not used
to being listened to, because every now and then he stopped,
and looked—sort of defiantly—at her. But she did not interrupt, or even comment, but sat opposite to him looking into
his eyes with her own cheerful brown ones, and saying nothing.

What came up from Mr. Richards'—Tom's—talk was a
feeling of disapproval—rather bitter, really—about what they
had been doing these last years to everything except buns; and
a dislike of change, especially change in business methods; and
a strong pull backwards towards the world before the war,
when times were much harder of course—but money was
worth more, and things were more, well, solid.

He had a lot to say about social conditions, then and now,
and Christine's thoughts began to wander, and she had to
concentrate so as not to miss any remarks that might reveal
what he himself was doing nowadays? (As if anyone cared
about the coal-miners in 1937.)

He paused, and drank some tea.

"I was wondering—have you retired completely, then?"
asked Christine.

Curiosity impelled her, and the dead hand of Mortimer
Road was growing less strong every day.

Mortimer Road would have thought twice about asking that
question. It would have been dying to know, oh, yes, and why
shouldn't it know, it would have demanded? But it would
have felt that such a question, from an unmarried 'girl' to a

widower, might warn him that she was trying to find out *how the land lay*, and so forth.

But Christine thought that he seemed pleased at her taking an interest.

"No, Christine. I'm working four days a week at a business supplies firm at Bow, supervising, and doing some accounting work. It's quite interesting . . . The journey across London is terrible, of course, that's the chief disadvantage—public transport nowadays . . ."

He was off again. They had done things to public transport.

He grumbles, Mr. Richards—Tom—does, was Christine's discovery of the afternoon. But she let him go on, feeling that he needed to; also, she was sorry for him. Sorry for Mr. Richards. I never thought I should be that, thought Christine. It just shows.

After what seemed a long time, he calmed down, spoke more quietly, and seemed in better spirits. Got it off his chest, thought Christine—let's hope. For she quite expected that he was going to ask her out again, and she did not want 'all this' every time she sacrificed an afternoon in her dear flat to spend it with him.

"Well! I must have been boring you. It's too bad—you'll have to forgive me," he said, smiling at her. "The fact is I've had rather a packet in the last eight months—resigning from the firm, and then my wife . . . I think everything's rather got on top of me."

"I don't mind. A bit of a grumble does us all good now and then. I know I often have one."

"I don't believe you do, Christine. I believe you're one of the rare ones who are always on top of things. But it doesn't make you unsympathetic. You're a good listener."

Christine glanced across at the nearest German-Jewish face which was being thrust into that of a neighbour at the same table with every appearance of a lifelong hatred about to explode in violence, then down at her gloves.

"I'm naturally strong, I expect. Mother always said I had a very good constitution." (Yes, and had not Mother also said *you must be imagining it*, if one complained of anything wrong anywhere? Luckily, one had never had anything seriously wrong anywhere, and perhaps Mother's attitude was better than pampering. Perhaps.)

He laughed, and glanced at his watch. He looked younger and more cheerful.

"I don't want to break up the party, Christine, I should like to sit here talking all evening but my sister has got some friends coming in this evening, and I promised I would be there."

"Are you living with her, then?" Christine asked another of those unconsciously leading questions, as they got up from the table.

"With her and her family, yes. Just until I get a place of my own again. I sold the house, when my wife died . . . It's comfortable enough there, but too full of noisy teenagers for my taste . . . I'm not used to young people, she has a boy and a girl and the house is always full of their friends."

The face at the next table now had its arm round its friend's neck and was calling everybody to witness that Leni was vonderful. Christine glanced at them in mild wonder as she went by.

Evening shadows were stretching themselves under the beeches that shelter the little old red-and-gold caravan outside Kenwood House, as they walked up towards the bus-stop. The distant grassy slopes looked larger and more golden in that light than they were; almost majestic, and as if in the real country.

Mr. Richards suddenly took Christine's arm.

"I've enjoyed our afternoon," he said, "very much. We must do it again, Christine."

"Yes, thank you, I've enjoyed it too. It's been very nice."

Nicer if you hadn't kept on about those miners, though. Christine allowed her arm to hang rather slackly; she seemed to be getting on with Mr. Richards—Tom—quicker than she liked or wanted.

"I'll 'phone you, then, Christine." Could that be a gentle pressure on her arm?

It could; it was repeated as he helped her on to the bus, on which—and Christine was not sorry—there was room for only one.

"In you get—no, I'll get the next one—I'll be all right—Good-bye, Christine, or rather, au revoir."

She wished that he would not do what she thought of as *Christine-ing me all over the place.* She looked down at her gloves; good, they were clean enough to serve for a second time. Then she glanced back. He was standing there, gazing after the bus, and waving. She did remember to smile and wave in return but she did not feel like smiling; was Mr. Richards—Tom then—going to be a nuisance?

Chapter 12

CHRISTINE THOUGHT OFTEN ABOUT THIS OUTING AND TWO others which took place during the next ten days or so; and she would have liked to talk to someone about what might become a problem.

This was a wish almost unprecedented, with her. At home, no one had shown much interest in what she had to say or listened for long if she had begun hesitatingly to confide any of her small private worries, few as they were, because her brothers and sister were all livelier and a little more articulate. They were also more positive and more demanding, with opinions which they believed to be their own, and they got themselves listened to.

Slightly more attention had been paid to Christine between the age of seventeen and twenty-seven. But as it gradually became clear that she was not going to marry, the family, also gradually, ceased to take much notice of what she said. As to what she may have been thinking or feeling . . . in that house, thoughts and feelings came a bad second, as we know, to electric toasters.

Now, of course, she could not have talked to any of her family, and did not want to. There might, she knew, have been a show of real interest if they had thought that this renewed acquaintance with Mr. Richards was going to 'lead to any-thing', but she did not want to talk to anyone who would think in that way; in spite of beginning to fear, rather than to hope—as the days went on and there was more than one longish telephone chat with Tom—that 'something might be brewing'.

She needed to talk to someone more intelligent. That was how she put it to herself. Yet although she felt certain her employers were just that, every instinct warned her—and shyness was there, too—against talking to any of them (well, it could only have been Mrs. Traill: she was still slightly nervous of the other four). Of them all, she was most drawn to Mr. Meredith. But one didn't confide in men about that kind of thing. Men were there to be asked about mending fuses or getting cars to go when they stuck, and, besides, it would have been quite out of the question.

She was also prevented from even considering confiding in her employers because of what they might immediately think.

They might suppose that she was going to get engaged right away 'or some such rubbish', and begin looking around for . . . other tenants . . . She had never quite forgotten that the frequently-mentioned and always laughter-inducing Dick and Amanda had been 'mad about it and dying to have it'.

No: she would have to think things out for herself, as she always had and as, she supposed, she always would. On my lonesome, as usual, thought Christine.

After all, was there so much to think out? There was no more than a strong suspicion that later on she might have to make up her mind about something important.

Well—she could always say 'No'.

But she felt cross, and embarrassed, and afraid of looking a fool, at her age, and sometimes she wished she had never come across Mr. Richards again on the top of that bus. She had liked seeing him every day at Lloyd and Farmer's; looked up to him, somehow; she knew that, now. She had not wanted to be taken out to tea and to hear about all those problems and coal-miners.

If you had asked her, Christine would have said it was all a bit of a bother.

But there was always plenty to take her mind off it; the care of her flat, the household shopping, the preparation of the evening meal which they all found enjoyable at the end of those days which, Christine still could not help feeling, were a bit aimless and idle.

True, three of them worked. Miss Marriott worked hard; she did not leave in the morning until after the horror of the rush-hour had slackened, but she never got home until nearly eight in the evening and always looked white and drained when she did. Mr. Lennox was rehearsing hard; he slept late, left the house at a quarter to ten, and often wasn't back until the small hours; Christine would often hear his little red Mini-minor drawing up in the Square after two in the morning. Gay, sweet to everybody, he dashed in and out wearing a light overcoat and frequently bringing large bunches of carnations to adorn the hall.

Christine sometimes compared him with Tom. Never a word from Mr. Lennox about those old Problems; all he cared about was the Stage. She thought of him as a perfect gentleman.

Mrs. Traill worked, too; she was perpetually gently occupied, drawing her pictures in her big sunny studio and then "beetling off" as she called it, to Fleet Street with her wares; but so unhurriedly, so driftingly, that her activities scarcely seemed to deserve the name *work*, which for Christine had all her life been associated with dullness and pressure and a certain numbing monotony.

When she had been with them three months she discovered one day that what made her employers' work different from the work done outside the tranced circle of Pemberton Hall, was the fact that they enjoyed it; even Miss Marriott, driven, exasperated, often calling upon Heaven to witness that one day she would resign, would say now and then that she adored her job: as the summer went on, Christine heard her say it less.

Mr. Meredith was as regular in his habits as if he went out to business, Christine thought. His bath-water running, the slight sounds as he moved about taking tea in to his wife, then his descent to the hall for his *Times* and a lordly slam of the front-door, followed by the long quietness while they breakfasted—these were repeated every day at precisely the same times.

He had his sherry at eleven, with Mrs. Meredith if she had not gone down into London, sometimes in their flat and sometimes—under protest, Christine knew, because she had heard him—in that shed which got the morning sun, where Mrs. Meredith was one day going to make her pottery. Most afternoons he went off to watch the cricket; sometimes he was out all day watching it, and during the Test Matches the wireless in his flat could be heard, muffled by distance, giving out descriptions of play and scores.

There was not one television set in all the five flats.

Mrs. Traill had spoken to Christine about this after she had been there for some weeks.

"We thought we'd wait until we saw whether you were the kind of person who would like one," she said candidly. "You see, if we'd said in our advertisement that there was one in your flat, we might have got the kind of person we didn't want."

Christine was looking at her intently.

"Would you like one?" Mrs. Traill went on, and Christine started slightly and said, colouring deeply and with actual agitation in her unually placid voice—"No, Oh, no—thank you, Mrs. Traill, but I don't want it at all. I . . . I don't care for it."

"Really can't stand it, can't you?" Mrs. Traill was looking at her curiously, but her eyes were kind.

"I don't mind it all that much; I think it's very nice for the old folks and for people who can't get about, but I would never want one. Thank you all the same," she added.

"All right, then. I can't stick it myself, all bluey-mauve and wobbling up and down and sideways, and mostly sheer rubbish . . . All right then, we'll just forget about it."

But while Mrs. Traill went off on one of her excursions to look at people in streets and parks who might act as unconscious models, Christine could not, all day, forget that conversation.

She to want a television! She who had lived for years with people who cared so much more for television than they did for human beings, or for anything that might faintly suggest the feeling of That Day! The mere idea of a television, with its small cold face, in *her* flat made her feel faintly sick.

She told herself not to be so silly. She told herself all the arguments in favour of the invention, and how educational it was, and what a blessing to those in hospital, and so on.

It was useless. She passionately did not want one.

Because, behind the surely harmless toy, there were ranged like little implacable sightless ghosts, all the devices—the heaters and the hair-dryers and the toasters and the blankets and the kettles—to buy which she had worked for thirty-five years at Lloyd and Farmer's.

I was—half-starved, that's what I was she thought, standing at the window above the Square and looking out unseeingly at life going quietly on there.

I didn't know it, but I was. All that electric stuff . . . so expensive . . . and always going wrong. Catch *me* having a television.

I might have been asleep, all those years, for all I heard, or felt, or saw.

She continued to stand there, looking out with resentful eyes at the quiet trees, and gradually a voice inside herself began telling her that there was no need to feel resentful. *You need not have one; no one is making you; there is no danger,* the voice said. *You can go on doing what you like, without any of the people in the house wanting to stop you.*

I am lucky, thought Christine, It's true, I can. And slowly her thoughts became calm again.

       ·   ·   ·

It seemed to her that Diana Meredith did nothing but go down into London every day.

"She's getting her bearings," Mrs. Traill had once remarked. "After being stuck in Africa, longing to be back, she feels stunned, I really do believe, at having got here at last. She's had about thirty years of longing to be Home. So you can understand that she feels a bit stunned."

Christine now looked with mingled curiosity and sympathy at Mrs. Meredith. She was beginning to understand what it was to long to be Home; though where Home exactly was, she had not even dimly decided.

Diana would get back about six o'clock, fagged and flushed,

and laden with paper bags printed with the names and devices of all the most elegant London shops. Most of them bore the sober greenish-grey, and the restrained design, of the great building that houses Harrods.

"Oh, that place!" Diana once sighed out one evening on her return from one of these forays. "Sometimes I think I'd like to go there when I die."

She was lying back, exhausted, in a long chair in the garden, where Mrs. Traill was enjoying the end of a hot day in an exiguous sun-dress, and Christine was watering some seedlings.

"The last shop," Diana went on, "the very last shop left in London, where you never see too much of anything, or a bad design, or anything that's bad quality, or hear an ugly noise. You can forget that London's changed since 1932—and yet the place is completely 'with it.' I'd like to go and live there. If they had a flat to let up in their top storey, I'd move in tonight."

"I expect you do see a lot of changes, having lived abroad so long," Christine said placidly. She looked across at Diana from her place on the lawn, where she was kneeling, with earth-covered fingers, on a piece of sacking.

She was learning that some Smith remarks could be offered to these people who were in almost every way so different from Smiths. Some, yes; but Smith pop-eyedness at different behaviour, Smith envious disapproval of other people's possessions, these fell into a silence.

If she could have said *They're stinking rich* or *Oh well, everyone to his taste* or uttered one of the airy obscenities that commonly dismissed such goings-on as did not appeal to her employers, she could have taken a more active part in the gossip at the evening meal. But she could neither get used to its tone nor imitate it, though it continued to fascinate her.

"Changes!" Diana now said deeply. "It's heartbreaking. I can hardly bear it. All round Warren Street it looks as if there'd been atomic war. It was no beauty spot, heaven knows, thirty years ago, but need they have been quite so wholesale?"

"You can't expect people to put up with dirt and overcrowding and no room to drive properly just because you enjoy looking at the picturesque," said Mrs. Traill.

"I don't expect them to put up with it. All I'm saying is, I miss my old London, the one I was young in."

"You have to have progress." Christine got up and dusted her skirt. "Well, I must go and get supper."

"*That* is what sends me clawing up the wall about her," Diana said vigorously in a moment. "'You *have* to have progress' . . . all these clichés. I damned well know you have to have it, it's like some horrible natural law. I know you have to have it, all right, I just wish it was different."

"At least we can lie up here in the garden and hear ourselves speak and smell the wallflowers," said Mrs. Traill. "If we had to live down there, you might long and yearn for progress."

"I know all that, my girl, as well as you do . . . Do you see any signs of her mind getting wider?"

"From time to time. But only a very little. She is quite shockingly indifferent to what's going on in the rest of the world. The whole of India could starve to death this week-end, for all she cares."

"I don't care much myself."

"I know you don't but at least you do feel guilty . . . "

"Who says I do?" Diana sat up and began to collect her parcels. "I can't do anything about it. And as for Africa, South, East, North and the Congo, it can tear itself to pieces so far as I am concerned. As soon as James retired I gave up feeling the slightest interest in any of them . . . except that it infuriates me to see the way they're spoiled and pampered over here. What they need is a touch of the whip."

Mrs. Traill shook her head.

"They do, Fabia. You haven't lived among them . . . I don't think anyone has the slightest right to judge the South Africans who hasn't actually lived among blacks."

"Most of them over here are Jamaicans . . . "

"The colour's the same, isn't it?"

She went into the house, leaving behind her a trail of some scent that was a blend of pepper and violets.

Christine had had more than one lecture from Mrs. Meredith about 'training' Mr. Johnson. Diana herself put the word in inverted commas.

"Now, you've got to get one thing, and really it's only one because everything else depends on it—into your head: *firmness*. If you're lucky enough to get a good one they make wonderful servants—more the kind to please Mrs. Traill than me, too much of this famous 'gaiety' and treating you like their mother and so on— and they're marvellous with children, being nothing but children themselves. They're natural thieves and liars and you mustn't take too much notice of it. But it just isn't fair to them to treat that boy as you would a white person. You must show him how things have got to be done, and keep on showing him."

"I do, Mrs. Meredith. But he always says 'Yes, I know that, yes, I know that.'"

"Oh, they all think they know everything. That's their inferiority complex . . . You must just ignore it."

"Mrs. Meredith, I've been meaning to speak to you about this—he's gone mad about this other place he goes to in Hampstead. He says he can't come to us twice a week now, because he must go to them. They want him to go and live in, if you please. Quite condescending he was. I thought I'd just mention it."

"What's the attraction there?" Diana asked languidly. "More money?"

"Well, would you believe it, only three-and-six the hour! I was surprised. He let it slip last week."

"Can't be the money, then. I expect they spoil him and flatter him. You'd better talk to Mrs. Traill about it. If this were Africa I could soon tell you what to do. But it isn't."

Christine had been annoyed by this gradual revelation of Mr. Johnson's growing allegiance to another household. It seemed to her both a slight to Pemberton Hall and a threat to herself; later on, she might have to descend into the Hades of Bensonia to look for another cleaner.

And he continued to arrive just before seven, instead of at six o'clock, as the original arrangement between them had said.

One evening, she opened the door to him at five to seven as usual, and, having had to toil up from the pleasant supper-table and leave an interesting discussion between the ladies about Glynis Lennox's clothes, to say nothing of a plateful of supper she considered she had earned, Christinne was rightfully annoyed.

"I wish you could be on time," she said sharply. "Look at that clock. Just on seven."

Mr. Johnson rolled his eyes towards the dial of the grandfather clock, decorated with faded wreaths of flowers in pink and blue, that stood in the hall. His round head was bare to the summer breeze and his clean shirt open at the throat. A pair of slight grey trousers, apparently insecurely anchored, barely veiled his legs. He took no notice of what she had said, but, as if he were listening to some other sound, stood with head slightly bent, smiling. Then he looked up at her in the way he had that used, at first, to make her wonder a little what was coming; with eyes very white and very dark under his low brows.

"House say 'happy welcome'," he murmured.

"What?" Christine said, staring.

"House say that when I come in. Every time, I hear that. It is a kind and a gracious feeling, madame."

"Yes . . . well . . . " Christine did not know quite what to say. If this was a way of turning off her rebuke—but she was not certain that it was—what a disarming one!

She said no more, but glanced round uncertainly, as if suddenly conscious of the house's silence and the fading sunny light; behind Mr. Johnson's pensively-lowered head, she saw the houses in the Square, and above them, clear depths of turquoise sky; the old trees looked heavy and richly green. It was very quiet; a quiet summer evening.

She looked at him again; it was true, there was just that feeling in the hall; it did say 'happy welcome', but she had a confused impression that something more than flowers and shining wood and clear walls was saying it.

"Yes . . . well," she said again at last, in a tone less sure of itself, "you'd better get on now, everything's ready for you."

"I have my tea, two cup, and my sandwich about half-past eight," instructed Mr. Johnson, hauling up the slight grey garments in preparation for his duties.

Christine's retort, "We'll see about that," did not reach her lips. She went downstairs feeling confused, and the next thing she saw was Mr. Meredith smilingly refilling her glass.

"I wish she hadn't said that about hating clothes," Antonia Marriott was saying earnestly, "it's quite serious, you know. Not now, I don't mean now. Few people under thirty can wear their things, anyway, unless they've been trained. I mean later on. A lot of people of her age feel like that. They see divine clothes and they feel sort of helpless. You know—*Oh, I could never wear that*, and it makes them despairing and they think they hate them. Then they go on looking quite awful for years, and when the time comes, and they *realize*, it's probably *too late*." She paused, with eyes like blue saucers, and stared tragically at her friends.

"We all know clothes are your religion," said Diana. "Everybody isn't like that."

Antonia just let the saucers sweep over the lines of Diana's dress. Diana laughed.

"I know, darling, I know. The shoulders don't quite fit and the waist's wrong somewhere. I bought it in a hurry."

"I'll do it for you," Miss Marriott said eagerly, "I've half-an-hour to spare."

"You can't possibly do it in half-an-hour."

"I could just pin it . . . "

"You're not going to just pin it. Your Mr. Herz would be delighted to get here and find you on your knees with your mouth full of pins."

"He wouldn't mind. He knows all about pins and things; he made his little money in the rag trade."

"Going to marry him, Antonia?" James asked amiably.

"I might." Antonia got up from the table, not looking at anybody. "I don't know what it is, I just seem to get tireder and tireder and tireder."

She suddenly put her hands up to her face, and stood there. There was a short silence, then Mrs. Traill soothingly said that she would be better after her holiday, adding that she supposed she would go to that heavenly place in Bermuda where her mother would be staying?

116

"Well, I think it would be better if she went somewhere quite by herself," Diana said firmly, ignoring a shake of the head from Mrs. Traill; Antonia took her hands down from her face, smiled dewily round on everyone, and remarked that she must go up and do things to her face.

"Sorry," she called over her shoulder as she undulated out of the room.

"Diana, why must you always try to put her off being with her mother?" demanded Mrs. Traill.

"Because I think she's a pernicious influence. She wants to keep her as the beautifully-dressed little girl who's grown up just enough to hold down a marvellous job."

"I'm sure you're absolutely wrong. She's been encouraging her to marry for years."

"Precious lot there is to encourage! She'll never marry anyone—why should she?"

"I think she might, Diana, if she could find someone who'd agree to a mariage blanc."

"I suppose you think Mr. Herz might?"

While Mrs. Traill was pondering this with a dubious pursing of the lips, James got up and went out with a remark about the heavyweight match being on in three minutes.

"I don't, somehow, think he would . . ."

"Fabia, it was a joke, my girl—J-O-K-E, you know. What people laugh at."

"Often people are very sensitive under that rather worldly exterior. We can't ever really know people . . ."

"Oh, for Pete's sake . . . come out and look at the lights."

"I will when I've finished this." Mrs. Traill held up her glass. "Have some more . . . Had it occurred to you that Clive might?"

"Might what? Mariage blanc? No, it had not. He's a perfectly ordinary sweet human person. No nonsense of that kind about him."

"He does still—" Mrs. Traill glanced at Christine, who was unobtrusively beginning to clear the table—"Haven't you noticed?"

"I have indeed. I'm only so surprised that I can't believe

117

it—after all these years. I thought it would wear off after a few weeks but it doesn't seem to have. Of course, I never have understood why Antonia gets them the way she does. She's very unvital—and that's old hat, if you like—and she's frigid. Can you imagine anything less attractive?

"Oh, outside of the raw thing, you can never tell what's going to get them. One noticeable thing about Antonia is, you'd be sure she'd never give any trouble or be bitchy. She's sweet, and she's placid. And so pretty, Diana. It's an old-fashioned type but she *is* pretty."

"She hasn't been placid lately. I've never seen anyone so changed. I admit she used to be."

"It's since this Ferenc business. It must be frightful for her. I think she'd been relying for years on marrying Nigel and retiring."

Diana made a face.

"It wouldn't suit you or me, of course. I'd rather—well, there are a whole heap of things I'd rather do. But she's been living in that world ever since she was nineteen, remember, and she's rather forgotten what the real world's like, I sometimes think. And though he's a bit odd in some ways—"

Diana gave a small shout of hard laughter.

"Well," Mrs. Traill, colouring, looked almost angry. "I like to give people the benefit of the doubt. This Ferenc business is the first bit of serious trouble there's been. I don't think she loves Nigel in the ordinary sense of the word but I think she's awfully fond of him, and she was relying on him for her old age, and her pride's hurt and she feels miserable and lost. They've always got on so well together, and I think he's genuinely fond of her."

"A pair of freaks," was what Diana said, leaning forward to stub out her cigarette.

"Sometimes you can be so stupid and hard, I wonder we haven't split up years ago." Mrs. Traill said, with none of her usual indistinct articulation or dreamy manner, and Diana looked a little taken aback.

"Yes . . . I'm sorry," she said in a moment, "that was bitchy. But though I'm not one of your children-and-marriage worshippers, I do like normal people. I suppose the fact is I'm fond of Antonia, and she maddens me. I'd like to see her settled and happy, and she wobbles and drifts about until I could hit her."

"She's got herself into this situation and ther's no one to get her out of it, that's the trouble. She's never got over that disastrous time with Clive in Italy—"

But what happened in Italy was never revealed to Christine, who for some time had been listening with all her ears, for both ladies, absently gathering up their bags and cigarettes, drifted out of the room and up to the Long Room, whence she presently heard tunes loved in the thirties being played, and laughter.

She continued tidying the kitchen. Her hope of picking up some hint, some revelation about the behaviour of men and women in their relation as wooer and wooed, which might help her inexperience in her own situation, had been disappointed.

She would also liked to have known why that time in Italy had been disastrous.

Really . . . Christine scrubbed vigorously at a stain on a tea-towel . . . they were funny people. They were charming, and kind, though not what you would call really friendly, and ever so interesting, but some of their talk and ideas made her think of those plays Tom had taken her to.

Tom was fond of going to the theatre. Much of Christine's pleasure in the thought of tickets for the new Noël Coward, which Mr. Lennox had promised her ("Always provided we get a run, gallant laughter") had been marred by the thought that there were sure to be two, and she would have to invite Tom, and she felt sure he would not enjoy it.

She was growing to like their outings; her first irritation—which had been largely shyness—at his attentiveness had vanished, and she had come to look for the guiding hand on her elbow and the little compliments. "Got to take care of you, haven't we? Mustn't lose a good thing when we've got it"—small, stiff jokes.

But how he did like talking!

It seemed that he could not have enough of sitting at some table with Christine, drinking tea and eating those buttered buns he was so wild about, and talk, talk, talk about the state the world was in, and how much better the state was that it used to be in, and what he would do about it if he was in charge.

Christine listened. Oh, yes, she listened; she even heard what he was saying and tried to think about it. But she would have preferred just an occasional remark about the Chinese geese on the pond, or the weather, or merely sitting and enjoying the buns and tea and the sunshine and saying nothing.

In the museums and art galleries he still found what she thought of as 'plenty to say,' and here it was pleasanter, because there was always something to look at, though often Christine did not care for what they were looking at; some old Roman thing, for instance, or some ugly great muddle of a picture.

Tom said that it was their duty to keep up with the times: "get with it," he said playfully; there was no reason why they should be old-fashioned because they were middle-aged; hence these excursions to galleries and jazz concerts (though here Christine did put her foot down; one visit to one of those, and she told him flatly that she would never go to one again. "The noise," she said, "was enough to deafen you."

Tom, after muttering that it could be a new and vitalizing experience, gave in and said that in fact he agreed with her. Christine added that she supposed it was all right for teenagers, but he did not answer.)

So, having also firmly dealt with suggestions that they should go to more of a certain kind of play to which he had twice taken her, she felt that, if she had not succeeded in guaranteeing the kind of enjoyment she liked from their outings, she had at least quashed his attempts to let her in for a series of thoroughly disagreeable occasions. Those plays had been nothing but a waste of her time and his money—and I'm sure, she thought, that he's not all that comfortably off.

Chapter 13

THERE WERE BOTHER AND CHANGE, PERHAPS, BUT THEY WERE A long way off on the horizon, and perhaps would not come any nearer. The roses came out, and Christine bought a second pair of white gloves.

June was marked by great activity on the part of Mrs. Meredith.

Having wearied of her daily visit to London because everything was so changed and the traffic was appalling and the petrol fumes sickened her and the streets were crammed with foreigners, she took to staying at home. Almost at once she was making plans for transforming the garden shed into her workshop.

"It's nothing but a pipe-dream," Mrs. Traill confided to Christine. "She used to make pots when we were all young, before, she went off to Africa with James, and Maurice encouraged her, and told her she had talent, as he told poor Dick he could write.

(He encouraged me, too, but I really do have it). And now she thinks she'd like to take it up again and make a few what she calls 'pennies'. As if anyone would want to buy the kind of thing she'll make! She's got quite a good bit of money of her own and James has a good pension; they don't need 'pennies'! It's all an excruciating bore, and we shall never hear the end of it."

The first sign that Diana's plans were beginning to take shape was her appearance in a series of becoming overalls, in lilac or blue or pink, and made of the newest materials that almost take care of themselves, so washable and dryable and uncreasable and generally biddable are they. Very elegant she looked in these loose, flower-hued garments, with her dark hair newly and expertly cut so as to bring out its streaks of silver, and what Christine thought of as 'a kind of French fringe'.

"Real artists don't get themselves up in special clothes," Mrs. Traill said scornfully, one afternoon when Diana had gone humming down the garden to inspect the proposed workshop, wearing one of these creations. "They're much too busy thinking about their work. You don't see me," she enlarged, "buying clothes to draw in."

"Well, no, Mrs. Traill, but I would say you have your own definite style."

"One works it out over the years," murmured Mrs. Traill, pleased, "but with me it's been more or less unconscious. I've never been a clothes-horse, and I could never stick those 'lons and 'lenes she's so sold on, I must have natural materials. It's nothing but subconscious laziness, you know, really, liking all these materials that practically wash and dry themselves. That khaki shift of mine takes three days to dry properly."

Christine was tactfully silent. The gloomy garment in question seemed to her much less desirable than Diana's airy new acquisitions; she had been quite depressed by it, hanging on the line for the three days, dripping, and slowly swinging its mud-coloured scanty folds in the breeze.

"There is no substitute for wool! as the adverts. say," she contributed at last, with a little laugh.

"Well, it's quite true, for once. And it's so dotty, because all those pinks and blues will only get all over clay . . . It's a waste of 'pennies' . . . but they're her 'pennies' and if she likes to waste them . . . I'd better go and see what she's up to, I suppose."

She wandered away, and Christine knew that she would give advice, and point out the advantages and disadvantages of the shed, in the kindest way.

She had learned that the criticisms of one another made by Mrs. Traill and Mrs. Meredith, often in strong terms, did not mean that they did not like one another, nor, when they groaned in concert about Miss Marriott, deploring her mismanagement of her affairs, did it mean that they would offer her anything but eager sympathy and affection when the opportunity came.

Miss Marriott herself greeted any statement of strong opinion on the part of Diana with the muttered, "She's bonkers and we have to face it," which Christine had first heard Diana herself mutter about Mrs. Traill.

Mr. Lennox and Mr. Meredith did not criticize one another to her, nor did they comment upon the behaviour of the ladies unless everyone was gathered together round the supper-table or in the Long Room. Then their judgements or criticisms were delivered so that everyone could hear them, and were often emphasized with a wave of James's cigar or Clive's long double-jointed finger.

Christine had come to the conclusion, after some vague thoughts, that in Mortimer Road you were always running people down and didn't really like them though you were nice to their face, and in Pemberton Hall you ran people down and weren't always nice to their faces but you did like them.

The next thing that happened was Diana announcing that she had been over to Hampstead enquiring about paint and whitewash and brushes, and was going to do up the shed herself.

"You can't," Mrs. Traill said flatly. "You're no good at that kind of thing. Remember the time we had that room in Swiss Cottage, and we thought we'd do it up ourselves because the landlord was such a swine about repairs, and the mess you made of the ceiling?"

"Well, ceilings! I'm not proposing to do the ceiling. Of course I shall get a man in to do that."

"Why not get a man in to do the lot?" James suggested, who, Christine could see, was dismayed at this plan. (Mr. Meredith was the kind of gentleman, she thought, who believed that Men, respectful, able-bodied and willing, still lived just round the corner and could be 'got in'.)

"Actually I can't remember the ceiling," said Diana. "It isn't the ordinary kind, anyway."

"It's beams," said Mrs. Traill, "quite old beams. You could scrape them down and wax them and they would look very good."

"I am *not* waxing beams, Fabia. Good heavens, there's no need to tart the place up—I only want a shed to work in."

"What are the walls?" Antonia enquired languidly.

"Brick. They're filthy. If you had them washed down and re-whitewashed, with the beams waxed, they'd look very good indeed." Mrs. Traill's eye was sparkling.

"Pink would look heavenly," said Antonia. "Rather Spanish."

"*I don't want it to look Spanish or anything else*: it isn't going to be a show-place."

"We could have tea in there on wet days," put in Clive; he and James were laughing.

Diana put her head in her hands.

"I wish I'd never mentioned the damned place . . . just leave me alone to get on with it in my own way, will you, please?"

Someone changed the subject. The next afternoon Christine, coming out to hang tea-towels in the little yard immediately beyond James's wine-cellar, saw, down at the end of the garden, Mrs. Traill's trousered form standing by the shed, serenely removing its one small window.

"She'll need more light," she called, "she's gone over to the Arrchway to buy a frame . . . I hope she won't make a muddle of the measurements."

"Can you do all that? Fancy," marvelled Christine, coming to stand by her and watch for a moment the skilled use of the chisel.

"One of my husbands taught me. He carved," Mrs. Traill answered. "I enjoy it."

"And can you put the new window in and everything?"

"Oh yes."

"The glass too?"

"Oh yes. I like doing it."

And, Diana reappearing at this moment followed by a largish Scout earning his Bob-a-Job by carrying the window-frame, Christine went back to the house, followed by Diana's favourable comments on the parking facilities in Archway as compared with those of Knightsbridge. (Christine knew that, after her first attempts, she had given up taking the Mini-minor they had bought down into London; it was permanently sitting outside Pemberton Hall in the Square, and was used only as a local runabout and for very occasional drives out into what Diana, emphatically said, were the "hopelessly spoiled Home Counties.")

By the evening the window was installed, and Mrs. Traill was carefully polishing a large single pane that flung back the late sun.

"Queer how they had no idea in those days of letting in light," she commented to Christine, who had strolled out to gaze and admire. "You'd think they were afraid of it."

"I don't like too much glare, myself," said Christine, and Mrs. Traill turned and looked at her as she said, "Oh, I adore light. I can't have too much of it."

"It does fade the carpets," Christine said; she sometimes had a sensation as if every tradition she had ever held was being swept away in a great flood of novelty, that, though it usually carried her along willingly and even pleasurably, must sometimes be resisted if she were not to feel entirely without roots.

And it did fade the carpets.

"Blow the carpets," said Mrs. Traill absently, and then Diana came out of the shed, where she had been dabbing ineffectually at a wall with a broom, and sighed that the glare in there was unbearable and she would never be able to see.

"I'll fix you up a blind, blast you," Mrs. Traill promised, with no lessening of amiability.

Christine, after this, expected to see Mrs. Traill take over the transformation of the shed entirely, and that was what happened. Diana was told to concentrate on finding herself a suitable wheel and buying all the other things that she would require, and Mrs. Traill neglected possible commissions for drawings by abandoning her visits to editors and telephone talks with her contacts, while contentedly scraping and distemper-ing and waxing from early in the morning until dusk.

The beams disappointed her by turning out to be of some inferior wood, instead of the oak for which she had hoped. But when they were well-scraped, and painstakingly oiled, and she had given herself what she said might be "my strained heart come back again" by reaching up to polish them during the whole of one very hot day, they did look clean.

But Christine's opinion was that you could say no more than that for them. A white ply-board ceiling put up by a handyman, she thought, would have been easier, and would have looked twice as nice.

"Well, I can't help it if she is worn to a frazzle coping with my beams," Diana said, coming out of Mrs. Traill's bedroom, where the latter was extended prone. "I told her I didn't care how they looked . . . now we shall never hear the end of it, I suppose, because they don't look as good as oak would have."

"Isn't she coming down to supper?" Christine asked.

"No . . . I'm going to make her one of my special cold soups . . . is there any sherry open?"

Restored by the soup and a night's sleep, Mrs. Traill was at work again the next morning, fixing up the blind to meet Diana's complaint of glare; lavishing delicate care and ferocious energy on rotting brick and worm-eaten wood, and Diana alternately grumbling at her for being an ass and cherishing her with nourishing recipes when she fell exhausted on her bed. Sometimes she did both at once, offering the tray laden with egg-nog while telling Mrs. Traill that she was bonkers and they had to face it.

When, after fourteen days concentrated labour, the shed was finally painted a greenish-blue carefully mixed by Mrs. Traill herself, and its floor had been covered with Japanese matting, and she announced that it was finished, Christine felt that everything seemed flat; she had been unconsciously looking forward to some kind of climax at the end of all the activity. She ventured to ask if they were going to have a house-warming?

"Who for? The wheel?" Diana asked smartly.

"No, Mrs. Meredith, but people do, don't they? When they move in, and it is a kind of moving in, if you're going to be working there most days."

"We'll see. Mr. Lennox's first night is coming off in about three weeks, I might ask some people in, if I can get enough stuff done to show them, and we could sit up and wait for the notices to come in—I hope those swine of critics will lush themselves well up beforehand, or they'll be bitchy about it . . . I'll talk to the others."

Apparently the others agreed because, later that day, Christine found Mrs. Traill fallen into a fever of longing for pink and orange Chinese lanterns to hang from the trees in the garden, where the party was to be held. Dressed in her oldest and toughest trousers and an ancient sleeveless blouse, she descended next day into London in search of them.

"That's it, you see," Diana observed to Christine while they were drinking coffee in the garden after her departure. "If you ever wonder why she's had four husbands and got through them all, that's the answer. She gets these *ideés fixes* about things, absolute obsessive compulsions, and everything has to go overboard until she's worked through them. Husbands and all. I know, I've seen her at it, for getting on for forty years . . . Men just will not stand it. Of course," she went on absently, "she didn't wear out all four of them; she was married the first time at eighteen, that gives her about nine years with each of them—not so startling. And the first one died. But it always came to the same thing with the others. Off she had to go, to Mexico or Turkey or somewhere. Even Dick couldn't put up with it in the end, he was the last one—and he's by no means a conventional type. It's a good thing she never had any children."

"Haven't any of you, all you great friends, I mean—got any family?" Was this the same Dick who had been crazy about her, Christine's flat? At least they'd never think of having him and his Amanda here, if he'd once been married to Mrs. Traill. Christine felt a little satisfaction at thus neatly summing up the relationship of her employers—*all you great friends*.

"We belong to the first generation that didn't *like* it's family," Diana said hardly, "and was too busy having a good time after the First War to want brats . . . Glynis was a mistake. Clive adores her now, of course, but when he knew Tasha was going to have her, neither of them was delighted, I can tell you."

Christine was silent, listening to the Two Voices which, increasingly as the weeks went on, lifted themselves up within her mind. *I do think it's sad when a little one isn't wanted,* said Mortimer Road. *They're a terrible nuisance and there's no peace,* crisply retorted the voice of Pemberton Hall.

Only That Day was silent. She did not know, she had not the dimmest, faintest idea, of what That Day would say, or how its voice would sound. Had it a voice—That Day?

I must be going crackers, she thought, recalling herself with a start and looking quickly at Mrs. Meredith.

"When I see the way the world's going, I'm damned glad *I* never slipped up," Diana was saying.

But here Christine said that it was time she did some shopping and went.

Chapter 14

A new note had been struck in the rhythm of her life by the butting-in—she thought of it as a butting-in—of Tom's sister Moira.

Moira was Mrs. Rusting, and she lived in one of the older suburbs north of London, where a few streets of pleasant old brown brick Edwardian houses—Smith houses—were being hemmed in at a voracious rate of consumption of the few remaining open fields, by well-planned blocks of two-storey houses, with sinks under the kitchen windows. Lately Tom had been talking of Christine's going to tea there.

"I've been thinking for some time that you and she ought to get together," he would say. "She'd love to meet you, she's always so interested in people."

The word 'nosey' would lodge itself in Christine's mind. And then, when she took a plunge and confided to Tom her suspicion that Mr. Johnson was about to desert them for the attractive family in Hampstead, he said, "Moira could help you there. She doesn't have a cleaner herself, they're too expensive these days, and Anne, that's my niece, helps in the house of course, but Moira might just know of someone."

Christine's satisfaction at Tom's having understood her terror of bringing Mrs. Benson into Pemberton Hall was marred by this patronizing suggestion. Just as she had decided that although he might be full of his miners and all those Problems, he completely understood and sympathized about having Mrs. Benson in your home, out he came with his old Moira again.

She made a sound which was intended to convey gratitude but gratitude was the last emotion she felt. A cleaner recommended by Moira Rusting, perhaps on chatty terms with Moira Rusting, and reporting back to Moira Rusting all that went on at Pemberton Hall—no, thank you.

Moira was certain to think that Christine's employers were 'funny'. And Christine did not want this. She liked it at Pemberton Hall; she liked her employers; she was having what she liked for the first time in half a century, and she wanted no criticism from anyone.

"We really must fix up this tea-party," he would say. "I know you'll like her. Only we'll have to give at least a week's notice. She'll want to make one of her special cakes and they take three days."

Christine did not mind the week's notice; of course you let people know well in advance when you were coming to tea, but—three days to make a cake! Moira must be one of those cushion-straighteners, ash-tray-whisker-away, mind-the-lino-leum types, of which she had had a lifetime's surfeit in her own family; Auntie Beryl, she would be like Auntie Beryl, Christine was sure. Auntie Beryl was a wonderful cook.

She had so far imbibed the manners of Pemberton Hall as to think Strewth, which was one of Diana Meredith's expressions, but her face, now deeply rosed by hatless days in the sunniest part of the garden, expressed only the amiable interest of a prospective guest.

Nearly six months ago, that face had almost shown what its owner was: her true nature had been so deeply overlaid by the habits acquired in years of monotony and lovelessness that never a hint of it had showed in her firm, well-moulded lips and candid eyes; and the expression had been nearly unchanging in its cheerful alertness. But now it was a mask: a rosy, polite, attentive mask . . . and Christine Smith was becoming accustomed to wearing it.

But it was not easy to wear it when she realised that the visit to Tom's sister must be followed by an invitation from herself to tea in her flat. She contrived to keep it on, but—she'll get no cakes that take three days from me, thought Christine.

.   .   .

Mrs. Traill's pursuit of the Chinese lanterns and Mr. Johnson's growing lateness in arrival and slackness in his work seemed to be the chief topics discussed during the next week, though there was an increasing sense of slightly anxious excitement about the first night of what Christine called "Mr. Lennox's show."

She had gathered, from remarks dropped by the friends, that while it would not matter to Mr. Coward what the brutes of critics said, it would matter to Mr. Lennox, because he had not yet been on the stage long enough—only about thirty years—to establish him as an Old Favourite, and until you were an Old Favourite, you were never safe from the critics.

And even Agatha Christie, Mr. Meredith said, had come in for a slating from them over the past few years; presumably because she had made a fortune out of not writing plays about The Problems. The sight of a tennis-racquet on the stage, said James with an unaccustomed flight of fancy, threw those chaps into the sort of state other chaps got into about blood sports or hanging.

Christine had cautiously sounded Tom on his views about the forthcoming production, and from his replies, had most reluctantly decided that she *would* have to ask him to go with her. He had said that that kind of show did no harm, and then added the ominous remark that he wouldn't mind seeing it himself.

What with Moira, and the threat of her visit to Mr. Lennox's show being spoiled, Christine's new assumption that life would go on steadily getting pleasanter was slightly checked during the month of June—and then Mr. Johnson 'turned traitor', very suddenly.

That was how his behaviour would have been described by Mortimer Road. Smiths are not much good at nursing injuries and betrayals which have occurred on a large scale; they quickly forget what the Germans are, keeping their long memories for that red-haired assistant in Miller's who was always so impatient with poor Flo, and they accept astounding changes with a placid "Fancy" or "Whatever will they think up next." But just occasionally, confronted by what strikes them as some flagrant breach of contract or human decency, they come out with the deep organ-note of the melodrama popular throughout the fifty or so Victorian years during which the Smiths were England. Christine used this note now, and thought of Mr. Johnson as a *traitor*.

Mr. Meredith and Mrs. Traill had come out from the shed, where they had been making final preparations for the potter's wheel which was to arrive later that week, and were strolling towards the house, gossiping, when they heard a voice, raised in annoyance outside the lower garden door. Christine was addressing the slight black form, drawn up close to the wall, and looking fixedly down into the bucket of rubbish it carried.

"Well, I must say you might have given us warning. Going off at a moment's notice like this. You know perfectly well I can't get anybody else outside two or three weeks, if that. You've been well paid here, Mr. Johnson" (the title was spoken with sarcastic emphasis) "and I think it's too bad of you."

Her firm tone faltered a little as the two ladies came up, for she did not want them to hear her rebuking the traitor to Pemberton Hall whom her own rashness and inexperience was responsible for bringing there. They would think she was inefficient, and easily taken in, and—alarming thought—not fit to be trusted with the running of the place.

"What's the trouble?" Mrs. Traill enquired easily, pausing, while Diana stared coldly at Mr. Johnson's down-bent wool. "Mr. Johnson thinking of leaving us?"

"Thinking!" Christine's indignation and alarm gave fresh force to her tone. "He's going off this very evening—going to live in, in that place in Hampstead. I've just been telling him, I think it's too bad."

"Why are you going there?" Diana shot out. "Come on, now, you tell us. And look at me while you're talking."

It was the first time that Christine had heard her address him in the weeks that he had been working there, and the note in her voice and the transformation of her personality contrasted so extraordinarily with the evening quiet of the garden that she stared at her in something like consternation.

"Come on, now," she repeated. "You tell."

There was a pause. Then he slowly lifted his head and looked at her, fixing his jetty eyes on hers in a stare that was only solemn, neither resentful nor timid.

"Is a good place there, madame," he answered. "They give me my own room and a television set just for me and two pounds ten shilling per week." He bent, and picked up the bucket. "So I finish my work this evening and I go off there," He sidled past them, almost whispering, "Pardon, madame, excuse," and disappeared along the passage before any of the three could say a word.

Diana surprised Christine by suddenly laughing.

"Oh—let him get on with it," she said. "What else did we expect? At least you," to Mrs. Traill, "needn't fret your social conscience over him . . . He's going to be what the good Lord intended him to be . . . a slave."

Mrs. Traill was smiling. "I don't think it's only the room and the television set . . . didn't he say something once about there being children there? They're always wonderful with children—I think that's the attraction. It's rather sweet."

Christine did not think it rather sweet. The words 'sly' and 'feathering his nest' occurred to her whenever, during the evening, she heard Mr. Johnson's brush rattling for the last time against the banisters, and she could not see why a black, however clean and decent, should have a television set all to himself. It was the last thing, as we know, that she would have wanted, and what had Mr. Johnson done to deserve this contemporary blessing?

It did not occur to her that slaves nowadays are at the very top of a sellers' market.

· · ·

Mrs. Traill was coming down the stairs on her way to post a letter about ten that evening, when she was surprised to see Mr. Johnson in the hall. He was seldom in the house as late as this, adding to his habit of arriving nearer seven than six that of invariably leaving nearer a quarter to nine than nine o'clock, and this evening he must have kept himself out of the occupants' way while finishing up some small tasks or putting an extra sheen on the surface of Antonia's bath (which, James

Meredith swore, he must clean with her toothbrush if one judged by the time he spent in there). Mrs. Traill liked, as she was fond of saying, to think the best of people and to give them the benefit of the doubt, and she believed that Mr. Johnson felt pangs of conscience, and had been working them out by a final, more scrupulous, attention to his duties.

"Hullo, Johnnie—" she said ('Mr. Johnson' had always seemed rather absurd, to her) "just off? You're late this evening."

"Yes. I wash all the broom, the stair brushes, the dustpan, all," said he. "Clean for the woman that come. I think you have a woman the next time. This woman's work, I tell Miss Smith so."

"Well, never mind, you're going off to a new place . . . I hope you'll be happy." She studied him in the faint light from the afterglow that filled the hall; let people say what they would, the jet skin and the shining obsidian eye, rimmed by a blue paler than the hottest sky of his native island, did veil him with a mystery that was impenetrable. He was a young male creature, gentle as some gazelle or lemur that had never tasted any food but fruits, thought Mrs. Traill, but that was all you could tell.

A kind old lady, thought Mr. Johnson, and speaks softly to me. He smiled broadly at her.

"I been happy here, madame, is a happy house. I told Miss Smith, when I come into this house it say *happy welcome*. But in *that* house where I go to live, there three little boys, and when I go to the door I say 'Yoo-hoo' through letter-box and they all shouting 'Johnnie, Johnnie,' and when they open the door the littlest boy he jump up in my arms and kiss me. That better for me, I think. So I go. Good-night, madame."

He bowed and opened the door and went out, shutting it noiselessly.

Mrs. Traill stood for a moment, surprised. It was true, the hall did say *happy welcome*. Though the summer dusk and the quiet could have seemed sad, the faint light coming through the landing windows was not melancholy, the silence was not dead; the shapes of the furniture and colour of the flowers all silently breathed the same message, *Happy welcome*. Maurice! she thought suddenly, where are you, and shall we ever all be together again? And that was strange, because she had not been thinking of him, she had not been thinking of him at all. Yet—if his spirit still existed, wouldn't it love this house where five of his oldest friends lived together? Wouldn't he want to be with them?

And then she remembered how he could always make them laugh, all of them, even Dick and Amanda at their worst—dear Maurice. She went quietly back to her studio, thinking of him. In what unimaginable country was he now?

Chapter 15

Christine's fear of descending into Bensonia and hunting in its chip-scented shades for a cleaner had scarcely turned into a dread before Antonia Marriott rescued her.

Miss Marriott had taken to walking on Hampstead Heath.

She looked out of place there, Christine was sure; her height, and her perfect grooming and her exotic necklaces did not seem to fit in among shabby hazel bushes and trodden grass and old trees. But she went, and on the increasingly rare occasions when Clive Lennox was not rehearsing, he went with her.

A few days after the traitorous defection of Mr. Johnson, while Christine was still telling herself that tomorrow she would put an advertisement on that board outside the Post Office, she was coming in from shopping—and from failure to put any advertisement on the board, no advertisement was yet written—when she met them at the gate.

"I hear we've lost our Massa Johnson," said Clive, as they all paused together; Miss Marriot was untying a chiffon scarf from under her chin.

"Yes, Mr. Lennox, he went off the other night, without so much as a by-your-leave," answered Christine. "It's cured me of having blacks as cleaners, anyway," she went on, encouraged by their interested expression to confess those misgivings which had so recently been justified. "I didn't like the idea, right from the start, but I hadn't had much experience with cleaners, I don't mind saying so now. And sure enough, off he went."

" 'He was a good cleaner, as cleaners go, and as cleaners go, he went'," Clive murmured, and Antonia uttered an absent laugh; she was resettling a loop of hair, peering into a little mirror. "Not to worry," she said, "I know a girl who runs one of those domestic bureaux, she'll fix us up."

She took from her great handbag a notebook bound in olive leather and stamped with her initials in gilt, and scribbled in it. "My secretary will ring her tomorrow. Happy now?"

When she ceased to look preoccupied and worried, her smile was very sweet. Christine could understand why a man should look at her as Mr. Lennox was looking.

"Thank you, it's ever so kind of you. The only thing is—what are they asking?"

"What are—Oh, how much an hour you mean. I don't know exactly, but I do know that it's under two pounds for the afternoon, because Mary told me. Quite cheap."

So long as you think so, thought Mortimer Road.

"Well, thank you ever so much, Miss Marriott. I don't mind telling you, I was a bit worried about getting the right kind of person for us . . . then someone will just come along?"

"Positive to. (A man, incidentally. Mary doesn't have women.). Tomorrow, probably . . . "

She smiled again, as she went up the stairs before Christine, Clive standing aside to let them pass. Christine heard them muttering something about a drink as they went into his flat.

The right kind of person for us. Yes, Christine could think of them, all six, as *us* now. They had their own 'ways', as a household, and she enjoyed thinking about her position as their housekeeper. She felt herself to be fully and firmly established, in a job with very nice, refined people . . . at least, in some ways they were refined.

.   .   .

When someone known and loved for years is seen again after a long absence, there is a shock; the familiar face has grown older. This was expected by the reason but not by the heart, and it is the heart that takes the impact. Then the weeks pass, and the well-known face becomes entirely the heart's again, and the change is accepted.

Clive had not seen Antonia for some years when they met again just before the household assembled in Pemberton Hall, and he had been startled by the change in her; thinner, so fine drawn, her huge eyes and delicate nose and wistful mouth and long neck all older—older—older: Antonia, who he unconsciously thought of as personifying *Lost Moonlight,* and the Thirties, and a certain kind of dancing. He had never thought of Antonia as growing older.

Today was a day when she looked younger;—yes, she had reached that stage known to invalids who are not going to recover; and had her good days and her bad days, for age had set in like a turning tide and now the years when a night of deep sleep or three hours in the open air would restore the look of youth, had gone for ever. The tide was going out.

As he stood pouring and mixing at the table, he studied her for a long moment. Yes, today she looked younger; even healthier. Healthy was a word that had never been used of Antonia: her beauty was not of the kind suggesting the word, yet today her cheeks had caught a little glow from the steady sunlight and the careful pallor of her hair was a shade more gold; she did look healthier.

He passed her the glass and lifted his own, and they sipped.

"Good." She put down her glass, and stretched, "Oh, that was a nice walk, wasn't it, darling? I feel full of good air and I didn't think what they were doing at Rooth's without me, all the afternoon . . . at least, I didn't often think. It's ages since I've been for a walk; I'd forgotten what fun it is. We must go again soon." She looked across at him, "You liked it, didn't you?" she asked uncertainly, holding out her hand.

He leant forward and took it. "Very much."

"Didn't find me a shocking bore after all these years?"

"No, darling, I did not."

"Well—" Antonia settled herself more comfortably in her chair, "I think I've been a bore lately. I've only been able to talk about one thing, and that's being a bore, isn't it? But—I don't know—I think I'm beginning to feel better, somehow."

Clive was listening with every muscle in his face effortlessly conveying sympathy. While she talked, he gently held her hand as if it were something precious, and she felt soothed, as if she were standing under a soft rain of scented water.

138

Clive's my Old Faithful, she had sometimes thought, and then accused herself of unkindness and decided that the honour belonged rather to Peter. Clive had been there for longer: in fact he had known him for twenty-five years, but it seemed as if she had always known him . . . and they had been drifting on sweetly until the holiday in Italy, all those years ago.

It had rained. You do not expect rain in Italy, if you are an ordinary person and go there in June. It had poured in Venice; so hard that drops from the rain-smitten Grand Canal had bounced up into the gondola. "The bee's kiss, now . . ." there was some poem he had quoted . . . and it had rained . . . and gone on raining . . . and she had known from the first that it was not going to work, and of course it hadn't worked . . . and now one avoided the subject of Italy when one was talking with him; Clive, dearest of friends, failed lover.

But it was she who had failed.

It was all nothing but a messy, depressing bore. And no one likes being a freak . . .

" . . . so that's what I'm going to do, just ease myself out. Nigel will soon see what I'm doing, of course. You can't hope to deceive Nigel, but I think he'll be grateful to me for going gracefully."

"He'll come crawling to you, in a year or two."

"Oh, yes, that would be fab! I'm a swine to want it, I know, but wouldn't it be fab! But he never would, Clive. When he's run through Ferenc—and at my worst moments I've never thought Ferenc would last, he hasn't any basic talent—he'll find someone else of the same kind . . ."

And so on, for the half-hour that Clive had to give before going to the theatre.

.   .   .

Mrs. Traill was still searching for Chinese lanterns.

It was partly with the celebration of Clive's first night in mind, but it was more that she had now become obsessed with them.

"I must have them and I'm going to have them," she declared in a grim tone one evening at supper. They're somewhere in London and have them I will."

"Haven't seen a Chinese lantern in years," observed James Meredith, conscious that his interest in England's agonizing situation in the Test Match had been taking up his attention to the verge of discourtesy. "Probably those blighters have stopped making 'em—now."

"For pity's sake," Antonia muttered aside, "don't say that. . . ."

"Oh, I'm sure not." Mrs. Traill turned distressed eyes on him. "I saw some as recently as last month. In quite a small shop somewhere. In Catford, I think it was."

"What in the name of all that's unlikely," demanded Diana, "were you doing at Catford?"

"Someone told me there was a row of little Edwardian houses there, quite unspoiled, tucked away at the side of a great new block of offices. I went down there to draw them as background."

"Couldn't you have imagined them—gables, and those coloured-glass panels in the front-doors? Easy enough, and it would have saved you the sweat," said Diana.

Mrs. Traill shook her head. "You know that's not the way I work. If you try to imagine a thing that's *real*, you always miss something—perhaps just one thing—you never *could* have imagined, which would make your drawing just that bit better. You must always go and look at the thing."

"That's beyond me," Diana announced.

"It always was, dear, ever since we started this conversation thirty years ago."

Diana shook her head, and Mrs. Traill returned to the subject of Chinese lanterns.

They continued to click and chatter—in the background, so far as Christine was concerned—during the next week. She was busy settling in Mr. Banks.

Antonia's friend had not been able to fulfil the latter's promise of sending a cleaner along the next day, but she guaranteed one for the end of the week; and sure enough on

Friday afternoon Banks arrived, a tall, broad, elderly cockney with a red face, with whom Christine at once felt comfortable.

This was not because Banks did anything to make her feel comfortable; his manner towards her stopped just short of the line between off-handedness and rudeness.

"I know all that," he interrupted her, when she attempted to explain what she wanted done and how to do it. "General clean down and you tell me when there's anything special."

She seemed fated to employ cleaners who 'knew how to do it', and was not to enjoy the pleasure of giving instruction to the domestic arts. But what a relief it was to understand every word that was said, and to see a white face—well, plum-colour, if you must be particular—instead of a black one, and not have to be extra nice because of him being coloured, to say nothing of not hearing funny remarks about the house saying things; and to learn, flung off as a comment upon the difficulty of getting up to the Village, that he had lived in the neighbourhood for all of his seventy-odd years.

"Laying aside the years I was in the Army," he amended.

"You're ex-Service, then?" said Christine.

" I suppose you may say so," said Banks, not encouragingly.

He then seemed to unbend a little, and slapped the left leg that moved with a slight dragging motion when he walked. "Somme, I got that. 1916." He rolled up his sleeve and indicated a rather horrifying, though small, blue-ridged pit in his forearm. "Warden. 1940. Shrapnel, that was."

Christine found nothing to say. But she liked Banks, with his Tunes of Glory marching faintly in his background, and saw to it that he did not leave Pemberton Hall without being at least offered the cup of tea which he never seemed to want or to appreciate when he had it.

"If you're making," he would say. Once he added, "I'm not one for drowning meself in slops."

The only thing she did not like about him were his ironical glances. She would pass him in the hall or working on the stairs—and he did not bang the brush against the banisters—and his eye, bloodshot, small and grey, would be moving around, taking in the space and the comfort and the beauty of it all.

"Plenty of room round 'ere," he once observed, looking at her over his cup while drinking one of the slops at the kitchen table, and it was surprising what volumes—she did not care to think what *of*—he could convey in five words.

But he had not said it again, and she was well satisfied with him at the end of the week.

It was pleasant to be able to forget the stairs and banisters and the kitchen floor and the outside work until the next Monday or Friday came round. Banks did his work thoroughly and tacitly, rolled and smoked a cigarette, and left dead on the minute. The dreaded spirit of Mrs. Benson retreated from Pemberton Hall as though she had never threatened it.

Suddenly, the background pother about Chinese lanterns died away.

One afternoon Mrs. Traill returned by taxi from one of her grim excursions into London with fifteen of them; large and small, bulbous, instantaneously festive, in softest shades of orange and pink, fascinatingly pleated, and adorned with cherry blossom, and little temples, and almond-faced ladies in trailing robes, and storks and cranes and tiny crookback bridges.

She was calmly triumphant.

"Oh, I knew they were *there* all right," she said as if someone had been devoting the last week to hiding the lanterns in some peculiarly inaccessible place. "It was just a question of sticking to the search and ferreting them out. Aren't they angels?" holding up the smallest, which had a design of monkeys at play in a fir-tree. "I can't wait to see them alight."

Chapter 16

"Can you be in this evening? That child is coming up to fetch her dress. I brought it home this afternoon and I'd like your verdict," said Antonia abruptly.

"I can. I was going to the Music Club. But they've replaced those enchanting early water-colours of Hampstead by contemporary stuff and it looks so wildly wrong in the house where they have the concerts that I really can't face it."

"Oh . . . Well, can you be in?" Mrs. Traill nodded.

Christine overheard these remarks as the two ladies were going upstairs after the evening meal. The Merediths were out to dinner, and Clive Lennox at rehearsal; the rehearsals had increased in frequency and fierceness as the first night drew near and Clive was looking tired; no wonder, and him no chicken, nice though he is, thought Christine. But there—*better to wear out than rust out.*

This was an adage sometimes quoted at Mortimer Road, small though the likelihood of any inhabitant there wearing themselves out might be. Buried deeper than Ariel's corals, dodged around with a skill greater than that of the most spectacular of centre-forwards, swathed in layers of protective cosiness beside which the mufflings of atomic reactors would seem mere drifts of down, were all the feelings that might lead any Mortimer Roadite to wear him or herself out.

Christine hoped that she might be asked to give *her* 'verdict' on Glynis Lennox's dress. But she was not; and never even saw it; though fortunately the ladies kept the door of Antonia's living-room open and Christine, calmly propping that of her own ajar, could hear most of what was being said, and imagine what was being done, while she sat by the window with her magazine.

She did see 'that child' arrive, bounding lithely up the stairs in stained jeans and the leather jacket with her mane flying. But it had been brushed; well-brushed. Christine, peeping over the banisters, could tell that it had.

"Hullo, hullo, come on in," she heard Miss Marriott call, with youthful energy and brightness. "Well, now, here it is." Pause, while the dress was evidently being held out for inspection. "Like it?"

Christine, lingering on the landing, almost pressed her hands together in the fervency of her hope that Glynis would.

"Beautiful colour," said Glynis at last, coolly. "It looks a bit queer, a funny shape or something . . . . "

"That's because it fits, sweetie. Your eye is used to clothes in chunks and blocks. Those seams make it *fit*."

"I rather . . . like that ruffle. Ruffles are being worn, aren't they? One of the girls I share with is clothes-mad. She spends all her money on them and starves. I couldn't do that. She bought a dress with a ruffle the other day."

"This isn't just a ruffle. Look—it goes down at the back and you can wear it like a boa."

"A what?"

"A boa. They were called feather-boas—I suppose because it's like a boa-constrictor.'

"What is, or was, a boa? I mean, what was it that was constricted originally?" put in Mrs. Traill earnestly; Christine imagined her as sprawling on Antonia's sofa, "By the constrictor, I mean?"

"Oh, *God*," Miss Marriott exploded, "*will no one ever* give their *full* attention to clothes? Put it on, Glynis—how *extra-ordinary* you are, Fabia—a Nigel Rooth model, and you go on like Webster's Dic . . .You're the original . . . bore . . . Here, let me help . . . "

Another pause. Christine had given up her pretence with chair and magazine by the window. She imagined Glynis wriggling into the dress, guided by the expert hands of Antonia. The pause lengthened.

"There." She heard the excitement and triumph in Antonia's voice; she must have led Glynis up to the long mirror. The pause lengthened.

"I look absolutely different," Glynis pronounced at last. "I . . . I say, I do look different, don't I? I didn't think I could look so different, I haven't worn costume yet."

"You look absolutely fab," said Antonia shrilly. "Doesn't she look fab, Fabia?"

"Yes, she does. She really does. I wish Clive could see her— he'd be proud of his beautiful daughter," said Mrs. Traill; in the straightforward, kind way she sometimes had.

"Now pull the boa round your shoulders, that's right, now up round your neck—delicious! Doesn't it make you feel good, Glynis?" Antonia persisted, like an adult coaxing a child to express its pleasure in a present and thus increase the pleasure of the giver.

"I don't feel like me," said Glynis, and laughed suddenly.

"Well, you'll have to get used to that, won't you, if you're going to act?" observed Mrs. Traill. "She'll need shoes, Antonia."

"Yes . . . white satin . . . medium heel . . . you're tall enough . . . I'll give you a bit of the stuff and you can take it along to a shop where they'll dye it to match; and be sure they do, Glynis. If they don't, you must take it back and have it done again more than once if necessary, until it's *right*."

"Oh, all right—but what a fuss . . . and I'm having a work-crisis; I'm a slow study, worse luck; I have to study parts longer than most people . . . Won't all this take ages?"

"Think of it as a stage costume that's got to be just right," Mrs. Traill said soothingly. "Here, let me help."

Swish, swish, a gentle, careful sound, as Miss Marriott folded away the dress into its box. She evidently thought this was the occasion for a small lecture, for Christine heard her begin—

"These details are very important, you know. Some writer— I think it was Nancy Mitford, my memory is getting simply awful—said that the entire standard of the *luxe* trades in Paris was kept up by a group of old women who *will* not accept anything but the *best* from the Houses they deal with . . . I wish to heaven we had something like that over here, but all that Englishwomen seem to care about is their dogs and their blasted gardens. Their flowers are divine, but their clothes simply make you want to die on the spot and, as for hair or scent, they never think about it. One duchess who comes to us told Nigel she 'always forgot' to use scent. What can you do with such women? You make up your little mind not to be like that, Glynis."

"Someone did give me a bottle of some stuff for Christmas, and I'm always meaning to use it and I do forget," said Glynis, laughing.

"There you are, you see." Antonia was laughing too. "But it isn't too late for you to reform . . . Now will you be all right with this?" Christine imagined her holding up the box.

" Will it be all right with me, you mean? Oh, yes, someone's driving me down; I shan't leave it on a bus."

Christine was now so absorbed in what was going on that she did not hesitate to look out of her window for a glimpse of 'someone', and in a few minutes saw Glynis, re-armoured in jeans and funereal leather, run across the square to a disreputable, rakishly-glamorous vintage car, sitting high on its big wheels, and already looking as if one could say that it 'belongs to the ages'. A beard was in the driver's seat, and started into life at sight of Glynis, and Christine lingered to see the box, severely plain but wearing Rooth's famous summer-sky blue, bestowed in the back seat. And let's hope oil doesn't get on to it, for that thing looks as if it would fall to pieces for two pins, she thought, moving away from the window.

Conversation, loud and careless, was still coming up from the flat below, and this time Christine Smith did hesitate about continuing to listen. The presence of youth, and the cheerful, almost public manner of the fitting, had seemed to justify her former eavesdropping by some unstated theory that could not be applied to talk going on between two friends thinking themselves unheard.

Nevertheless, after a moment's hesitation, she did not shut her door and pick up her magazine. The fact was that her months at Pemberton Hall had given her a deep curiosity, not by any means pure, in the lives and situations of her employers. It was not pure because it was warmed by affection and the

146

protective instinct, and the strong wish felt by old-fashioned televiewers and readers and cinema-goers for a 'happy ending'.

She did very much want to see Miss Marriott safely out of the muddle at Nigel Rooth's; she earnestly hoped Mrs. Meredith's pottery would be bought for many 'pennies'; she wanted Mrs. Traill's drawings to sell to discerning editors and Mr. Lennox's show to be a 'smash hit'.

There were also interesting side developments . . .

"Oh, she means to have him," Miss Marriott was saying. "You see, that would mean she needn't worry about me so much."

"Does she worry about you?" Mrs. Traill's tone was sceptical.

"Of course she does. It's never been fair on her, poor Mummy. First Daddy leaving us so poor—you know how she had to scrape to send me to Claregates—and I loathed it anyway—and then my breaking off *three* engagements and then, when she isn't even middle-aged any more, all this business starts at Nigel's, and she has to wonder what'll happen to me in my old age."

"What good does she think marrying that old man will do? He must be eighty," Mrs. Traill said—severely, this time.

"He's over eighty. But he has got some money, and if she were Lady Belsize she could help me from time to time if I needed it. And her mind would be at rest."

Christine was trying to imagine Mrs. Traill's face. She felt sure that it expressed disbelief in Mrs Marriott's having the kind of mind that needed to be, or could be, at rest.

"It would be fun for her, too," her daughter went on. "She would love it. And he does need a wife; he's so old, and he *will* drag round London to everything that's on, until he's utterly worn out and has a stroke. Then he gets better and starts all over again. Mummy wouldn't let him."

"But if he *likes* doing it, Antonia . . . "

"But he doesn't. When he has a stroke, he's always saying how nice it is to be in bed and read James Bond . . . but people will ask him to things and he can't say 'no'. And Mummy could give up her work, then. I think it's a good idea."

147

"And you could marry Clive," Mrs. Traill said. She must have been waiting to get that in.

Silence: dead silence, with a quality in it that was different from the former laughing pauses. Then Miss Marriott said—

"I don't want to talk about it, Fabia."

"That's just your trouble and always has been, not talking about things. You can't or won't see that your mind needs the relief of talking. Sometimes I've thought of recommending a good analyst—"

"Thank you. I'm not going dotty."

"Oh, don't be childish. No one's talking about going dotty, if you could only face up to that business in Italy, drag it out, and look at it—"

"I've told you, I don't want to talk about it." Christine heard repeated nervous clickings of Miss Marriott's *luxe* little gold lighter.

"I'm telling you for your own good . . . "

"Oh, please don't, please shut up. I do try to think about it sometimes, but I still feel so awful about it. I always loathed the idea of being married. I'm a freak or something. Do you think I don't know I'm a freak, a kind of joke? That's why I try not to think about it." Her voice had grown shriller as the sentences went on, and Christine, listening with slightly open mouth, shook her head. *Least said, soonest mended.*

"But it's natural, Antonia . . . " Mrs. Traill began kindly.

"I know it's natural. I'm not twelve years old, Fabia. I hate it,"—and then, as if suddenly recalling the theory that the best method of defence is attack—"That button! Really, you are quite extraordinary. I simply do not know where you get your things. I believe you get someone to *mould* them for you in some cellar somewhere."

"It's a set. I designed them and Kupetsky carved them for me. It's Japanese cedar. I brought a lump back with me, I adore that smooth grain and the honey colour."

"It's—it's distorted-looking."

"I meant them to have a Japanese feeling."

"Well, it certainly has something . . . I wouldn't care to say

148

what . . . For God's sake shall we go to a cinema? You've made me feel awful."

The murmurs that followed were presumably concerned, accompanied as they were by rustlings of a newspaper, with making arrangements for the excursion, and in a moment Christine heard the pair going downstairs—looking, she thought inevitably, like the Long and Short of It. As they passed out of earshot, she heard Miss Marriott say, in a pensive and confidential tone, "You know, it's funny, but I can talk to Clive. About *anything* else, I mean." To which Mrs. Traill replied oracularly, "There you are, you see," before they shut the front door on themselves.

Christine returned to her agreeable pottering about. Though her imagination made no attempt to carry her beyond the flat statement of detestation made by Miss Marriott, she vaguely linked it with her own picture of marriage as being a bother and a nuisance, and she sympathized. People, thought Christine, were always on at you about something. Why couldn't they leave each other alone?

The enormous question faltered, and died out on the quiet air of her room.

Chapter 17

It had been arranged that Christine should meet Tom at the end of Avalon Road, and, precisely at four o'clock, she was crossing the road leading down into it by the pillar-box, as he had recommended, when she saw him strolling towards her.

He was hatless, as usual, and wearing a more domestic air than commonly because of an old green tweed jacket with bits of leather on its elbows. And his trousers seriously needed pressing and his hair was standing on end, and it could not be called a good beginning to the festivities that Christine's immediate thought was that he looked a regular sight.

The relaxed mood of Sunday afternoon had not been permitted to touch herself; a polished cotton two-piece *had* been pressed, and a coffee stain almost successfully removed with a patent fluid, and the second pair of white gloves was on duty.

"Hul-lo!" exclaimed Tom, smiling so kindly and with such pleasure at the sight of her that she felt a little ashamed. "Why, Chris, you do look smart. I like all those strong clear colours. You make me think of a Gauguin."

Christine smiled, pleased, as they walked on together; she had an idea that a Gauguin was some kind of foreign bird, but the open admiration was welcome. No, she was not nervous, she knew that she looked her best, and if old Moira didn't like her, she could do the other thing. They talked animatedly, as they approached the gate of Number Twenty-Four.

This was the old part of the widening, ever-developing suburb; three or four streets of two-storey smallish houses built in a dark brown brick, with white quoins and gables shaded by sycamores, and separated from one another by enough space to give just a little of the dignity of privacy. It was all very Smith; these houses were like smaller versions of Number Forty-Five, and, almost against her will, Christine began to feel on her guard. She deliberately began to think about the space and airy silence and beauty of Pemberton Hall.

But when Tom stopped at the shabby green gate, being guarded—and Pemberton Hall—slipped completely from her mind. For here, in a plot of ground some eighteen feet by fifteen, were two solid sheets of cream snapdragons and an old, gnarled, knotted jasmine wrapping and shading the walls of the house with its lacy foliage and white stars. There was no grass plot, no other colours.

Christine lingered, staring, but all she could find to say was: "What an effective garden. Quite original . . ."

"Ah, I thought you'd like that; that's old Frank's fine Italian hand. He's a great gardener. You must tell him you approve, it'll quite win his heart."

I don't want to win it, thought Christine, determined not to be sucked back into the strong Mortimer Road atmosphere; and, a figure at that moment opening the front-door who must be Moira, it was instantly eclipsed by a large clean boy in a large clean shirt, who darrted out in front of it shouting, "Hullo, Uncle Tom, hullo Chris, I can't stop, I'm sorry," and, precipitating himself upon a moped leaning against the hedge, shot away.

Tom was still muttering, "Noisy young beggar," as Moira came towards them, smiling and saying, "Hullo, Chris, You don't mind me calling you, Chris, do you—I've heard so much about you."

Moira was not like what Christine had expected.

The bustle and high colour and loud managing voice which she associated with a three-day cake-baker were notably absent; Moira was small, with an ordinary figure and wearing the usual flowered summer dress; she had a round, reddish, unlined face surrounded by coarse, drooping grey curls, and her eyes looked large and light behind thick lenses. Christine was again slightly thrown off her guard. She shook hands and said, "I've heard a lot about you, too," and smiled, but felt that her armour for getting through the afternoon must be redoubled; she followed Moira and Tom into a room at the back of the house overlooking the garden in some confusion.

The room was another surprise. Its shady length ended in French windows curtained in a soothing rose-coloured and grey chintz, and there were many flowers: it was an unexpected kind of room to find in such a Mortimer Road kind of house, and it increased her bewilderment. But—

"What a pretty room," she said at once, looking admiringly around.

"Ah, that's Moira." Tom glanced at his sister. "She took a course in Home Decoration last year, one of those Evening School affairs."

"But you'd better tell Chris that I walked out after the third lesson. It was all too cut-and-dried for me; I like to choose things that *I* like. But I did pick up a few hints. And the teacher was very nice."

She laughed; a longer and a lighter laugh than Christine was accustomed to hear at Pemberton Hall, where people tended either to be lengthily convulsed over some communal private joke or not to laugh at all. Moira was one of those people who often laugh, as Christine found out during her visit: she laughed again when, excusing herself to go and get the tea because Christine, she knew, must be ready for a cup after that long journey, she indicated a distant figure at work in the garden.

"That's Frank," she said. "My husband. You'll have to excuse him, Chris. He never comes in to Sunday tea; he likes to be in the garden all day Sunday. I even take his lunch out to him. Now you make yourself at home, I shan't be a tick."

Christine sat rather far forward on her chair, trying to imagine what would have happened had anyone at Mortimer Road suggested Father's having Sunday lunch in the garden—but the newly-developing faculty failed her and she turned to wondering if certain undecided gestures being made by the form in the greenhouse were intended for gestures of greeting to herself? Presently, doubt was set at rest.

"Old Frank's waving to you," said Tom, who had collapsed on to a sofa, and looked, in this setting, decidedly scruffy.

"Oh," Christine firmly returned the wave, in a hand holding a white glove; she had just been slipping them into her bag, and, instantly, all signs of communication from the other figure ceased.

"He must be quite a character," she ventured at last, "having Sunday lunch in the garden."

"No," said Tom, after a pause, "no, I wouldn't say a character. He likes his own way, though."

Christine allowed her eyes to dwell pensively upon Tom. It seemed ages since he had been Mr. Richards and those shoes were past a joke, and he, too, she suspected, liked his own way. She preferred him as he had seemed to her in the old days. That, she was quite certain about.

"Tom," called Moira's voice, "open the door, please." But even as Tom began to rise reluctantly, the door was opened and round it came Moira carrying the teapot and a rangy brown girl of about fourteen, with lank hair confined by a white bandeau, and a white tennis-frock short and pretty as a ballerina's, pushing a laden trolley.

"It's all right—Anne to the rescue. Chris, meet Anne—our other teenager. That was Michael, who went out just now. He thinks of nothing but that moped of his. It took him eighteen months to save up for it, even third-hand from a friend. Dad and I helped a bit, of course. He's only just got it—"

"He did say 'good-afternoon'," Christine interrupted the purling chatter.

"I'm sure I'm glad to hear it—"

"He said 'Hullo'," put in Tom, who was now helping his niece hand round plates and put them on various little tables.

Christine had never had tea, until she left home, except at a large table, ready, at some unannounced moment, to blossom with knives, forks, and cold ham. Yet this was definitely a Mortimer Road house; it reminded her, in some ways, of home.

"Mum's famous cake. It's turned out all right, hasn't it, Mum?" muttered Anne, who after a shy smile at Christine had retreated as far as possible behind her hair.

Moira took a bite, tasted, paused critically.

"Not one of your successes," pronounced Tom.

153

"No, I can do better. But it'll pass. Life's too short for cake-fussing . . . Do you like cooking, Chris?"

Christine explained about her cooking, and they had some pleasant talk about cookery.

But she was thinking while she chatted, of Moira's remark about life being too short for cake-fussing, it had been just to her taste . . . yes! cake-fussing, electric-iron-fussing, electric-blanket-fussing, while somewhere miles away the sea thundered softly and the woods waved in spring and you never thought about them, much less saw them, and the years glided on.

He eye was caught by a large hole in Tom's sock . . . Of course, that would be another thing, sock darning.

Second cups of tea—third, in Tom's case—had been reached when a kind of impression of movement, too subdued to be called agitation, began to emanate from the corner where Anne had poked herself, and presently murmurs—"Yes, I will. Yes. Yes, Mum . . . can I go, now, then?" and then a kind of inclusive smile, with chin-well-ducked into her chest, and a sidling exit.

"First date," said Moira, when the door had been shut for a full minute, "a nice boy. Local. They're going to play tennis." Her voice sounded soft and proud.

"You don't want her getting married too young, Moira," Tom said, in such a tone as to draw a look from Christine.

"Married! He's sixteen-and-a-half," said Moira, rippling off into a laugh with a sidelong glance, like a freshet from the mainstream, at the guest.

"I know all about that, but they start young nowadays—seventeen, eighteen. I ought to know about young marriages, if anyone does." There was a pause. "I think I'll go and take a look at old Frank," said Tom, and got up and went out into the garden.

Both women were conscious that old Frank would not want to be looked at, and they smiled at one another.

"Poor Tom," said Moira. "He was twenty when he married Dorothy—that was my sister-in-law. She wasn't at all a nice woman, I'm afraid. Discontented, and always on at him to make more money. It sounds a dreadful thing to say but I was quite relieved when she died, and he wasn't all that heart-broken, either . . . funny, isn't it? If Frank died, I would want to die too."

"If I'd ever got married," Christine said, colouring, and after another pause, "that's how I'd like to feel—how I'd like to have felt, I mean."

"Yes . . . " Moira's eyes turned to her face and lingered with a thoughtful look. "That's how it is, for some people. I should have thought you'd be like that—our kind has to be careful."

Neither said any more. But, as she finished her cup of tea, Christine was wondering what Moira had meant, by telling her about Tom's first marriage? Was she letting her know that there were no happy memories she need feel jealous of? Or was she what Christine thought of as 'hinting', telling her that she was not likely to be happy with him in that special way, that way which would make you want to die, too, if the other person died? *Our kind has to be careful*—yes, careful not to marry anyone but the right person.

She suddenly wished that it might have been an ordinary visit, without this business about Tom. It had not spoiled the afternoon, which was being more enjoyable than she had expected, but she was conscious of it all the time; all Moira's remarks, interesting and even helpful as they were, had reminded her that a proposal was hanging over her, with its attendant discomforts and embarrassments.

She glanced out of the window

"I do admire your garden. I never saw so many flowers. Do you do it all yourselves?"

"I don't do it at all; it's Frank's baby. Come out and look at it. I know it seems rude, him not coming in to tea," as she led the way through the French windows, "but he works so hard at the office all the week and I do like him to have his garden on Sundays. Come on—he loves showing it to friends."

She has a nice way of putting things, Christine thought.

They stepped out into the plot, which was given depth and length because the opposing garden was separated from it by a golden privet hedge and a screen of young beeches.

Christine was now reflecting that her impression of Moira being inquisitive about Pemberton Hall and its inmates must have been wrong. She had shown not a trace of it during the afternoon, and perhaps—Christine did just wonder—if Tom himself was inquisitive about them, and if he had been—I am afraid the words *noseying about* occurred to her—in order to gratify his own curiosity, not his sister's? Pretending Moira wanted to know, Moira asked this and that—I'm sure she never did, Christine decided indignantly.

Reflections about one more nail in someone's coffin, however, were now dispelled.

The miniature beauty of the garden waylaid her; it was impossible to think about anything disagreeable in the midst of these crimson bells, these lilac clusters, these white and brown butterflies drowsing on long purple blooms, all bathed in the low light of the evening sun. Rounded cushions of blossom flowed on to the bricks of the tiny paths that had been painstakingly set by an amateur hand, looking as if they were sculptured from some marvellous soft blue stone.

"It's a picture, a perfect picture," Christine said again and again, while Frank, a tall thin man with a face that at first sight suggested the word *glum*, assured her, over every clump, that she ought to have seen it last year.

He also pressed on her a sizeable packet of foxglove seeds which he took from a kind of seed-library in the greenhouse, trying to make her promise to scatter them over Hampstead Heath.

"Now, Frank, Chris won't want to be bothered doing that," said Moira, laughing long, then, turning to Christine with a change of expression, "or—I don't know—perhaps you might. It's a pretty idea, isn't it? Foxgloves. 'Folk's gloves', it means, really, you know. 'The folk' was the old name for fairies."

"Well, I'm sure you can easily imagine fairies in Mr. Rusting's garden," blurted Christine, anxious to say the prettiest thing she could, and was rewarded by a kind look from Moira and not the faintest sign of acknowledgement from Frank, beyond the dismaying one of his beginning to look for another packet of foxglove seeds which he found, and silently presented to her.

"At the *bottom* of the garden—eh, Chris?" exploded Tom, seizing her unresponsive arm with a laugh.

"I didn't mean that. I meant it was pretty," Christine said firmly, and Frank said that it would be better next year or he would know the reason why. After another slow stroll, back to the greenhouse this time, and a leisurely inspection of its beauties, murmurs began to come from Christine about making a move.

Frank found a rather small specimen of a pink rose hiding itself away in the only corner of the garden that could by any effort of imagination be called shady or remote and, having explained that this particular bush had been "checked in its first season," he presented the lone bloom to Christine. Moira caught her eye and winked.

"I'm sorry I couldn't give you a good big bunch, I'd have loved to," she whispered as they parted at the gate. "Frank's really shocking about that. He never will let me give a thing to anyone, so you'll just have to forgive him. And come in whenever you feel like it—I'm nearly always here—never mind that old journey!"

She suddenly gave Christine's cheek a warm, gentle kiss.

"There," she said. "Lovely to have seen you at last. Bye-bye."

"Well, what did you think of them?" began Tom at once, when they were walking down the road.

"Very nice," said Christine.

"No—but really?" He had taken her arm, and now he pressed it and peered into her face.

"They're nice people, very nice people, of course I liked them, anybody would," Christine said, a little crossly; in another, and a less-controlled woman it might have been a little wildly.

"Well, don't take it like that . . . I only wanted to know." He pressed her arm again. "You know why, don't you, Chris?"

"Why what?" Christine fumbled in her opened bag for a handkerchief, for she felt disagreeably and unbecomingly hot.

157

"Why I want to know if you like them."

"Good gracious, Tom, *I* don't know—don't keep *on* so about it, I've said I like them. I do like them, very much. Isn't that enough?"

"I can see you aren't feeling up to the mark, dear. I expect it's the heat, so I won't say any more," said Tom, keeping firm hold of her arm. "Feel like doing a film this evening?"

"Oh, *good heavens*, no!" exclaimed Christine quite loudly and before she could prevent herself. "I've got all that mending to do and—and I think Mrs. Traill did say something about—about clearing up the garden."

Her voice became calmer as she enlarged upon this subject, and Tom took his cue from her and did not return, even circuitously, to the subject whose approach she was beginning to dread. He read her a lecture, all the way to the bus-stop, on the necessity of not letting herself be exploited by *those people*.

He was kind, he was nice, and Moira was unexpectedly nice, and the kids were nice, Frank was a bit of a bore but nice too and the garden was ever so pretty, but it was with Oh! such a great, shaking sigh of relief that Christine at last sank on to the hard seat on top of the bus and was borne away from all the Richards—so she collectively thought of them—through the impersonal sunny breezes of the evening.

And, thinking of Tom's kindness, and his attempt to understand how she felt, and his avoidance of any return to that subject which plainly caused her distress, surprising tears suddenly rushed up into her eyes and she thought, it's all too late. Too late, that's what it is. I've spent the best years of my life on *them*, and I've got nothing to show for it, and oh, if this had only come when I was twenty-five!

But they had not been the best years of her life.

Chapter 18

THE WHEEL HAD ARRIVED. IT WAS CARRIED INTO MRS. MEREDITH'S shed one morning by three men, and they set it up. Permission had been obtained from the necessary official body, electricity had been installed there by a cable running through the wall of the house and along the wall behind the shed, and Mrs. Meredith had brought in three rolls of ready 'pugged' clay and had arranged them, wrapped in damp cloths, in a box specially made to retain moisture.

"Don't you have to bake it?" asked Christine, who could not resist looking into the shed from time to time.

"Of course. A place down in London will do that for me; would be more fun to have my own kiln but that's looking some way ahead. I shall, one of these days."

"And will the pots be those lovely colours, like those dinner services, I mean?"

"Oh, mercy, give me a chance, I shall start on ordinary pots and vases with a brown glaze or some ordinary colour, it'll take me some time to get my hand in again." She turned down a switch, and a low dreamy humming crept out on the air.

"Well, I won't intrude, Mrs. Meredith," and Christine went on her way. Diana did not look up; she was standing with bent head, listening, a quiet expression on her usually alert face.

In the evening they all strolled down to have a look. Mrs. Traill shook her head when she heard that Diana hoped to have some pots to show to the guests at the party in a fortnight's time.

"I really wouldn't try, Diana—"

"I daresay you wouldn't. I'm a quick worker. I shall soon get my hand in." With square-nailed brown fingers she lightly touched the rough surface of the wheel. "No one will expect miracles. But I must have something to show."

"Can you make me some bulb-bowls?" Miss Marriott asked, pausing on her way out to dinner with some man. "I really adore Chinese bowls, but they cost the earth and you have to hunt for them; there are only those plastic things in most of the shops. Could you make me six? Have you got an order-book?"

This was evidently a prearranged question, for she produced from behind her nylon-draped back a ledger bound in crimson and gold. "There. It's got your name on. Look."

"You are a duck, Antonia. No one but you would have thought of that; thank you lots," said Diana, examining it. And then Mrs. Traill fished behind a convenient bush and brought up a beautifully-lettered gilt sign on a square board.

PEMBERTON POTTERIES
D. Meredith. Prop.

In one corner was painted a tiny classic pot, in Diana's favourite shade of purple.

"All ready to hang up," said Mrs. Traill, displaying its neat chains and pointing to the nails she had hammered into the shed. Diana threw her arms round her and bestowed an impulsive kiss; it struck Christine, hovering on the edge of the group, that a little more kindness and the hard turquoise eye would film over.

Mrs. Traill was hanging the sign, and Diana was making the wheel's drone now loud, now quieter; Antonia gave her a quick kiss and hastened away with the skirts of her evening-coat flying, and James Meredith looked with quiet satisfaction on the scene.

"Now," said Mrs. Traill contentedly. "we must start arranging the party. Thank goodness," to Diana, "she didn't start going on about *Chinese bowls.* I've had such a time looking for my lanterns, I never want to hear about anything Chinese again."

At the moment just before the first guest was due, Christine stood at one of the windows looking down on the garden, feeling full of gratitude that Mrs. Benson could not see it.

The Chinese lanterns—it had been worth all that trouble finding them, Mrs. Traill had been right—bloomed from the leafy branches like Oriental fruits, rounded and serene, in their gentle pink and orange light. The long *buffet* with its gay china and festive bottles glimmered in the middle of the lawn; little tables set with little gilt chairs stood about; the air was so still that the flames of their candles burned upwards without a flicker. And, as background to this dewy twilight and calmly shining lanterns and dim trees, there was London; sparkling and glittering like the malicious old fairy she was, far, far below.

The scene was unprofaned by activities on the part of the waiters, who, having seen to the last details, were standing about in their white jackets, motionless and in relaxed attitudes, sometimes exchanging a quiet remark, as if even they had been slightly entranced by the surroundings.

Lovely, thought Christine, leaning against the frame of the open window, really lovely. Oh, I am glad she can't see it; she'd say something about being glad she hadn't to wash all that lot up. I can never be thankful enough for living with nice people.

It also occurred to her, before she turned away from the fairy scene, that Banks would say there was plenty of room, wasn't there? But she put him out of her mind.

Soon the cars began coming up, and the voices and greetings, and the affectionate kissing of wrinkled and familar faces began. The waiters started their professional gliding and darting like so many white-winged birds, and Christine was kept fully-occupied showing ladies upstairs and where to leave their fur coats.

She was standing in the hall, waiting for the bell to ring again; when it did, she opened it to Mrs. Marriot, in one of the fur coats, and accompanied by a stout old gentleman with a white moustache.

"Good-evening, Miss Smith," Mrs. Marriott said clearly, "what beautiful weather for the party. Will you take Lord Belsize's muffler? Percy, I will see you in the garden."

Lord Belsize, who gave the impression of being

> '. . . a creature
> Moving about in worlds not realised'

silently handed a dingy strip of wool to Christine and then
made a slight movement indicating that he was ready to follow
where she led.

She took him through the house to the iron steps that descended to the garden. They were narrow and dangerous and
the biggest of the lanterns, hanging from the tree over-shading
them, gave a light picturesque rather than sufficient. She wondered if she should utter a word of warning?

"Damned unsafe," observed Lord Belsize in a melancholy
mutter. "Can't see. Take my time, you go on in, thank you."

He began a descent so cautious as to arouse real apprehen-
sion in Christine, who lingered. A nice thing it would be if a
lord fell down the iron stairs. Upset everything, and *she* would
no doubt be blamed by that Mrs. Marriott, who, she was certain, did not like her, and 'looked down' on her.

"Go on in, hanging about, perfectly all right," said Lord
Belsize irritably, halfway down the steps, and at that moment
Mrs. Marriott appeared at the top of them, crisp in taffetas,
and, saying distinctly, "I am here, Percy," marched past Christine and led him safely to the lawn.

Christine did not obey his lordship. She lingered by the open
French windows for a moment, enjoying the scene, now illu-
mined by candlelight, the very last gleam of day, and the first
broad beams of a great moon rolling up over the city.

She felt that they could have managed nicely without Mrs.
Marriott. Still, it was interesting to see the old lord she was
intending to marry.

She was turning back into the twilit passage, when she
saw a beautiful young lady coming down it towards her, ad-
vancing over the polished floor with a faint rustle of dragging,
slender, skirt and a scent of flowers breathing from dark hair
spread about bare shoulders. It was as much her transformed
appearance as the faintness of the light that at first made Christine fail to recognise her, then, as she smiled and said with a

kind of deliberate sweetness, "Good-evening, Miss Smith," and swung the great ruffle about her neck, she saw who it was.

"Oh . . . good-evening . . . Miss Lennox."

The transformation was so complete—beatnik into belle—that Christine was almost astonished into commenting on it. But at that moment Mrs. Marriott came up the steps again, calling reassuringly to Lord Belsize, who stood in some distress at the bottom of them, that she would be back in a moment—she had some in her coat pocket—and saw Glynis.

"Why, my dear," she said briskly, her bright eye seeming to take in dress, hair, scent and manner in one blink, "how nice you look. I hardly recognized you."

"Oh, I recognized you at once, Mrs. Marriott," Glynis retorted, the deliberately-sweet style replaced by a steely one. "Two months older, of course. But otherwise just the same. Did you have a good holiday in Bermuda?"

"Very pleasant, thank you. So nice to be out of our tiresome east winds . . . Will you go down and talk to Lord Belsize for me? He doesn't like my leaving him."

Having thus shown Glynis that she had no fear of exposing her old nobleman to the charms of a girl, and that he was lost without her, Mrs. Marriott went composedly up the stairs, leaving Glynis to proceed slowly down them to Lord Belsize and, with a return of the glucose manner, present herself and entertain him with chat about what she was doing and where.

It appeared that Lord Belsize had a great-nephew, one Harry, who had some idea of making himself into an actor and was attending the Academy where Glynis herself was studying. When Mrs. Marriott returned with the tissues of which she had been in search, she found the two in something like conversation, and looked slightly annoyed.

". . . shocking life, I should think," Lord Belsize was mumbling, gazing haggardly at the vision of warm youth before him, "and very overcrowded, so they say. I can't make it out, his father was in some sort of bank and did very well, liked it, cash coming in regularly, and this acting's very precarious, they say. Of course I suppose it's all right for that chap Olivier and that sort of chap . . . must make quite a packet. But it takes time, getting up there. Harry's not twenty yet. You know Harry? Harry Aldenham. Come across him at all?"

Glynis now recollected a gangling youth with a fiercely-melancholy expression who had made a set at her during a recent social occasion at the Academy, and indicated that she had not. She foresaw nothing but dead tedium in any Belsize-Aldenham connection.

"Ah, . . . large premises, no doubt, Well, here's Nellie . . . good luck with the acting. We'll be seein' you in *The Mouse-trap* in a couple of years, eh?" And Lord Belsize, temporarily resuscitated by the presence of glowing seventeen and crowing feebly at his small jest, was borne away into the crowd by Mrs. Marriott.

It was not an encouraging beginning to the evening.

Glynis stood by the steps, studying the scene, which made her think of the first act of an old-fashioned musical, and decid-ing that the average age at the party must be between two hun-dred and two hundred and seventy. She wondered why she had been so crazy as to fall in with her father's casual suggestion that she should look in for an hour: she had wanted to try out the effect of her dress, and also to test her acting powers in the part of an ardent and sweet young girl, but she had not reckoned with *quite* so much grey hair and eld.

I'm ardent all right but anything but sweet, she reflected. Nevertheless, the dim grass shadowed by trees where lanterns bloomed, and the stilly flames of the candles spiring, as though painted, into the unstirring air, and the moonlight—warm, flooding, magic, all the old words for moonlight—began to affect her senses. Hell, thought Glynis fashionably, they'd call it corny—'they' were her friends—but it's romantic. No one, she thought, looking seriously across the garden at the moon's colossal disc floating above the mad glitter of the city, no one could say it isn't romantic.

The music must have begun to steal out on to the air before she heard it, and at first, when she did hear it, she thought it was someone up in the Long Room playing and singing *Lost Moonlight*. Then, she realized that the song was gay, without a touch of the nostalgia in that song of her father's: the accompanying chords were firm and strong, and the air seemed to be mounting in triumph. Now a voice—a man's—was singing, and she could distinguish words through the chatter of elderly tongues muffled by the canopy of leaves

"In spring for sheer delight I set the lanterns swinging
    through the trees,
Bright as the myriad argosies of night that ride the
    clouded billows of the sky."

A pause, while soft chords in the bass throbbed like drums.

Red dragons leap and plunge in gold and silver seas,
    in gold and silver seas."

Then a sudden change of pace, bringing a thrilling joy that ran unstumbling up to the last triumphant note—

"And oh my garden gleaming cold and white
Thou hast outshone the far faint moon on high.
In spring—for sheer delight—
I set the lanterns swinging through the trees—
For sheer delight!"

The chords mounted, soared, throbbed—then ceased. A man singing, she thought: beautiful. For sheer delight!

She noticed the chancy light of candle and moon on cheeks deeply scored with lines, grey heads and bald heads, bodies stiffly thin or bulgingly fat, and although everyone was pleasingly dressed, and their voices softed by the open air to notes that did not affront the stillness, she suddenly felt that not for one moment longer could she endure being there.

There was the voice again—

"Red dragons leap and plunge in gold and silver seas,
    in gold and silver seas—"

It was soaring among the lanterns and leaves, hovering above them in showers of dancing chords—

"For sheer delight I set the lanterns swinging through
    the trees,
For sheer delight!"

She turned quickly away, and ran lightly up the steps and through the house, dodging surprised groups, snatching up her cloak from the hall as she ran.

"Not going, Miss Lennox?" actually cried out Christine, who was lingering in the hall in case of late arrivals, "Why, you've only just come!"

"Oh yes . . . I simply must . . . it's a lovely party but I've got a date . . . 'for sheer delight!' "

Laughing, she ran down the steps, and Christine stood at the door, smiling sympathetically as she watched her hail a cruising taxi and scramble into it and be borne away.

Really, she looked so nice it was a pleasure to see her. What a pity she didn't always take the trouble, thought Christine, with some complacency smoothing the jacket of her polished cotton burgeoning with its orange and purple flowers.

A moment later, Antonia Marriott came into the hall.

Her movements were never truly hurried, but she came towards Christine in such agitation that her dress, of black chiffon that in its clinging lines and wraith-like drifting panels was almost a parody of current modishness, seemed to swirl about her like smoke from some miniature explosion: the loops of ash-blonde hair drooping from her lovely head seemed about to cascade down in disorder.

"Oh . . . Christine . . . what . . . did you see anyone go out just now—just this minute?"

"Only Miss Lennox. She just went off, by taxi. Said she had a date. I was surprised; she'd only just . . . "

"No—no—a man . . . "

"Nobody went out except her, Miss Marriott." Christine was already imagining burglary, an inclusive haul of all those fur coats, for Antonia's manner was agitated enough to suggest headlines in next morning's papers.

They stood looking at one another. Miss Marriott's heart-beats were shaking the chiffon covering her breast; Christine could see it trembling, and suddenly she glanced wildly up the staircase to the landing, where under Mrs. Traill's instructions the electric light had been replaced by a solitary tall candle burning in an old pottery sconce on her little brass-rimmed table, in front of an open window where the moon was shining through.

"Did you hear anyone singing? she demanded. "A . . . a man's voice?"

Christine shook her head. Irritation began to replace alarm.

"I never heard anything, Miss Marriott, and there was only Miss Lennox . . . I told you. I'm sure I should have seen anyone go out. I haven't left the hall this evening except just to see his lordship—" Christine, not having had occasion to use these words before in their proper context brought them out with satisfaction, though they did remind her of the unsatisfactory Smith nephew always thus referred to—"down the steps, and I was ever so careful to shut the door after anyone came in . . . has anything been missed, then?"

Antonia laughed hysterically.

"Of course not. It . . ." she hesitated, and went on with more her usual manner, "it isn't that kind of thing at all . . . Has anyone been up in the Long Room, do you know?"

They were both looking up the staircase now, at the stilly-burning flame of the candle, blue and yellow as the ancient glass in some cathedral window, and the motionless folds of the curtain behind it, and the whitening moon floating out there in the remote sky. It all looked so peaceful. Christine's heart grew calmer as she watched it. She shook her head.

"I don't think so, Miss Marriott." Her eyes were fixed— kindly now—on Miss Marriott's white face. "I should have seen them, if they had . . ."

"Will you come up there with me?" Antonia said suddenly; in a pleading tone like a child's, "I . . . I just want to look at something . . . it won't take a minute . . ."

"Of course!" Christine Smith said sturdily. "It's always best to have a look . . . and there's plenty of men in the garden." Recollecting the years of most of the guests, she added, "Those waiters, too . . . shall I just nip out and ask two of them to come along with us?"

"Oh, no . . . no . . ." Antonia was already poised on the stairs. Christine glanced towards the corner where Clive and James kept the sticks they took with them on their walks, but, in response to a distracted shake of Antonia's head, gave up any idea of arms, and silently followed. Miss Marriott suddenly turned and smiled tremulously at her and said, "Don't be frightened, Christine, there's nothing to be frightened of, really . . . You're sure you're all right?"

Christine could only smile and shake her head. *She* was all right; she was more concerned about Miss Marriott than anything that might be in the Long Room. Only, as she opened its door, she did for a second wish that one of those waiters, the stout one with the thick neck, was standing behind her. Surprised, she felt chilly fingers steal into her own; Antonia was holding her hand.

The room was empty, of course. It was lit by candles, like all the house that evening, and it looked peaceful and charming and not even lonely, and of course it was empty. It looked just as it had two hours ago, when Christine had shut its door, with the satisfactory thought that it was quite ready for company.

Yet something was different; just a little different. They stood, Christine slightly in advance of Antonia with the latter peering over her shoulder, and Christine, her senses made more perceptive, perhaps, by her months in Pemberton Hall did feel that something was different . . .

"The piano . . ." Antonia said in a low voice. Christine could feel her fingers trembling, as she pointed with the other hand. "Didn't you leave it shut?"

"Oh, no, Miss Marriott." Christine glanced at her over her shoulder in a little mild surprise. "I did want to. I thought it looked tidier, but Mrs. Traill said to leave it open, and she put out some music in case anyone should want to play."

Antonia dropped her hand and went slowly, draggingly, across to the piano and began to turn over the music stacked there. Christine stood by the door, watching. The room had felt different, she decided, because there was a feeling someone had just been there . . . a second before they came in. But how could you tell? The other feeling had gone before you had time to make up your mind that it was really there.

"It's here." Antonia looked across at her and spoke in the same rather low voice.

"The song . . . he . . . was singing. 'A Feast of Lanterns'. It was one of . . . I thought I heard it . . . perhaps I imagined the whole thing . . . I don't know." She turned away from the scattered music, "Let's go back, shall we? And I could use a drink . . . couldn't you?"

"I would like some of that cup, Miss Marriott. I made it, so I know it's good." Christine laughed as she shut the door.

"Well, let's . . . " Miss Marriott put her hands up to her hair. "Mercy, what's happening . . . I must look an utter mess, I'll go and fix myself . . . I'm sorry about all this, Christine. I must have been dreaming . . . Oh, I wish . . . Mr. Lennox were here . . . " She drifted away, towards her own flat.

Christine marched down to the hall. The thought of that cup had suddenly become more attractive. Miss Marriott ought to get a good tonic; it must be all the worry at that place that had upset her nerves—and even now, when all the fuss seemed to be over, Christine had not a real clue as to what it had been about. Some man singing a song in the Long Room . . . ?

She turned back, prompted by some instinct which she did not think about, for a last look at the landing. The candle burned on, the far moon sailed, the curtains hung straight and full. Suddenly, the one on the left floated straight out, hung there a second revealing the empty sill behind it, and subsided again just as if a hand had given it a quick, impudent flick. Funny, thought Christine, smiling; you had to smile, it was only a breeze but it was just as if someone was teasing . . . can't catch me . . . had you that time . . . but all in good nature, as it were. Well, we couldn't have had better weather for our party, could we?

Silly of me, just as if I was asking someone, she thought; I suppose I'd better go and find that cup.

Chapter 19

SOMETIME IN THE SMALL HOURS, CLIVE LENNOX'S LITTLE CAR
drove into the Square and stopped outside the iron gates. Hell,
he thought, glancing at the lighted windows, they're still at
it—though he had expected them to be. He locked the car and
pushed open the gates and went, rather slowly, up the steps.

The door opened before he could put in his key.

"Darling . . ." Antonia said agitatedly, standing there alone,
and almost on tiptoe in her smoky draperies . . . "Thank God
you're here . . ."

"Something wrong?" with a tired smile.

"Not wrong, really, but . . . Oh, Clive . . . I heard Maurice
singing."

"Maurice?"

"Well, a voice so like his I could have sworn . . . in the Long
Room . . . and it . . . he . . . was singing . . . Oh, darling . . . he
was singing 'A Feast of Lanterns'."

He took her by the elbow and steered her down the passage.

"Let's get a drink . . . then you can tell me *all* about it."

The 'all' held the note he would have used to a child, but
when they were almost at the door of the room overlooking
the garden, in which most of what was left of the party had
collected, he burst out, "My God, Antonia, you are extraordinary . . . don't you want to know how it went?"

"Of course, darling," looking back at him contritely over her
shoulder, "how awful of me . . . only I've been in such a state
. . . how did it go?"

"Oh, like a bomb . . . ten curtain-calls . . . I got four and some
of them were still shouting for me when they brought Max
out in front . . . I think we've got a smash hit . . . and I had an
encore . . ."

"Fab, darling," she said with her Christmas-card angel's smile.

"Darling! Well, how did it go?" Mrs. Traill disengaged herself from four men to totter up to her old friend and peer into his face.

"Oh, marvellously ... I got an encore ... bless you ... " he ended suddenly, stooping to kiss her.

Mrs. Traill was always ready to be kissed and she returned his with warmth. People came up, questioning and eager; James Meredith clapped him on the back with the hand that wasn't holding the bottle he had been carrying around since midnight, repairing oversights on the part of the drowsy waiters; Diana Meredith started a small burst of clapping; and Clive's spirits, which had dropped on the homeward drive because he was in his sixth decade, began to climb up like a column of mercury.

"Now you're here—" said someone, "couldn't we go to that Long Room—"

"Clive, won't you sing for us?"

"Oh, yes, do."

"Sing the thing you had to encore ... what is it? ..."

" 'Me and My Ego' ... "

"Yes ... yes ... 'Me and My Ego' ... "

"No, no," Antonia called lightly, taking him by the fingers, "we're going to sit in the garden. He doesn't want to sing any more, do you, sweetie-pie, and he must be starving"—

"Starving! Don't anyone mention food for days—he gave us a party at the 'Yellow Bird'. But drink is another story ..."

'He' must be Mr. Noël Coward, Christine thought, watching the pair—so tall, so romantic—going down the iron steps. She was very pleased that the first night had been a success. Dear Mr. Lennox, thought Christine.

" 'Me and My Ego' ... is that one of Noël's?"

"I don't think so ... " The voices began to fade into the distance.

Antonia led Clive to a table beside a syringa bush in flower, where a solitary candle burned. While he went to find them some drink, she sat upright on the edge of her chair, staring straight ahead, with hands tightly clasped, and when he came back with a bottle of champagne she impatiently waved away him and his glass and his question as she burst out—

"Oh, do let me tell you . . . I'm dying to . . . " and began at once on the story.

Clive sat listening. He was very tired; his throat was taut; his eyes were stinging; he felt as if the sixty-year-old machine that housed him were rattling like a vintage car at the end of the run to Brighton; and the story was just absurd enough—told in Antonia's little-girl voice with her enormous eyes silly with wonder—to irritate him; there was pain, too; of several kinds.

"Nonsense," he said flatly, when she had finished.

"I had a feeling you'd say that. I do know it *sounds* like nonsense . . . Open that, will you?" indicating the neglected bottle.

"I don't know what to say, Antonia. I'm damned tired and . . . I don't know what to say." He untwisted the last wire and began cautiously to ease out the cork.

"Well you might say *something* . . . I've been so longing to tell you . . . I was . . . oh, thrilled and scared and so excited, and I thought Clive's the person to share this with . . . You were so fond of him . . . You were such friends."

"Can't you see . . . " he paused while he deftly steered the wine into their glasses " . . . it's just because of that that I can't take it quite as you do . . . You see, darling, I can't feel certain you heard anything at all. Did you ask anyone else if they'd heard it?"

She shook her head. "I thought if I did it would start silly rumours—you know people love that sort of thing—and most of the people here didn't know Maurice well, it would just have been a kind of stunt . . . "

"But Fabia—or Diana or James? Didn't you ask any of them?"

"Fabia's been so high all the evening I thought she'd start telling everyone—and I couldn't get at Diana. She and James have been stuck in that shed showing people her wretched pots and twizzling that wheel round . . . I did ask Christine . . . "

"And what did she say? That was sensible of you, she'd have heard anything—if there was anything to hear . . ."

"Oh, I don't agree at all. She's the last person—about as psychic as a teapot, I should think—but she *was* in the hall all the first part of the evening and she must have heard it if . . ."

"There you are, you see." The comment ended the sentence for her.

"But *not at all*, Clive! It doesn't follow that if she didn't hear it . . . If she was there she must have . . . Only of course if she isn't in the least psychic . . . Oh, yes. I see what you mean. Oh, dear." And Antonia sank her face dejectedly onto her hands. "I can't make you believe I heard it."

"Darling, I do believe you *think* you heard it. I can't imagine why. But I certainly don't believe it—the voice—whatever it was you heard—was Maurice."

"Why not?"

Clive shrugged, and there was a silence.

The softly-burning Chinese lanterns and the newly-lit candles on the tables seemed to make no sensible inroad on the thin, balmy darkness that comes just before dawn in the months of summer; it pressed close upon their auras of painted gold, bringing a sense of night and sleep; hushing voices and summoning up memories. The spirit had crept into the room at the top of the stairs, where, by the dim light, people were gossiping smilingly about the past.

But champagne was at work again in Clive and Antonia; she began to remember the gaiety of the song heard, or imagined, in the Long Room, and, gazing at the lanterns through a haze, began to hum it.

" 'For sheer delight!' " she carolled softly, "—Isn't it delicious? I'm sorry I pounced on you, honey, . . . Now here's something you will enjoy. Your daughter has been the belle of the ball."

"What?" Clive roused himself. "Glynis, How?"

Antonia gleefully described Glynis's arrival in the red dress, and her conversing with Lord Belsize at the foot of the stairs. It appeared that a lot of people had noticed her—she being the only young creature there—and asked who she was, and had admired her looks and been interested to hear she was Clive's daughter: and Lord Belsize had kept on about her until Mummy was quite annoyed. "She doesn't like him to be a silly old man."

Clive laughed. "But tell me about Glynis. She'd actually been to work with a hairbrush?"

"Oh, yes. And scent—Lord Belsize particularly noticed the scent—the works. I couldn't be more pleased." She smiled hazily, ghosts and tensions forgotten, twirling the stem of her glass. "I hoped that dress would do something for her."

"It's sweet of you to take an interest," Clive said after a pause. "No, it is, darling, I mean it."

"But I *would*, Clive, wouldn't I? It's a question of clothes—and she is your daughter."

Yes: but in her answer clothes had come, as they always did, first. She would have done as much, and been as interested, if any other young girl with whom no dress-sense had been involved. Clive was touched; but it was a detached emotion. Poor Antonia—and the cruel word *cripple* just glided through his mind and was instantly banished. Oh, so much was left, unfortunately; tenderness, companionship, delight in her delicate beauty—but it was all spoiled by this over-riding pathos and sense of failure.

He had once or twice thought of suggesting that they should try again. But was what had failed in youth likely to succeed in—age?

Ugly word . . . he never thought about it unless he were low in spirits.

"How ghostly that looks—those lights down in the city . . . just those few," she was saying, and then, in surprise—"Oh—it's getting light."

He glanced round. While they were talking the leaves and grass had crept into view, all bathed in eerie silver-grey, and suddenly a bird chirrupped impudently. Antonia said "Listen to that darling thing," and shivered.

"You're cold, we'll go in."

"No, no, I'm not. Let's stay and see the sunrise, I've never seen that."

"Never seen the sunrise?" Another bird called, an astoundingly fresh sound, as if newly-made. Now the candles and the Chinese lanterns were beginning to look more coloured than alight. "I've seen it often in the wars—worse luck—and I can tell you one thing, it takes a jolly sight longer to come up than you think it will."

"Oh, do let's stay."

"All right . . . Fabia's trying not to look at us out of the window." Antonia giggled.

"Let's go down to the wall. We can see it better from there."

"What a child you are." He put his arm round her and drew her close to him as they strolled across the lawn, gently crushing the smoky chiffon she had drawn for warmth round her head and shoulders, "Aren't you?"

Antonia did not reply. If she could have put her feelings into a murmur, it would have been to the effect that she did so wish that time in Italy could have worked: the pressure of his arm about her shoulders gave her the sense of being protected that she was always, consciously or unconsciously, seeking . . . No one like my Clive, she thought.

They stood in silence, looking out over the delicate grey mass of the city—where a few green lights glittered—conveying an impression of evil which was erroneous, as they were hardworking ones on the railways.

"I warned you," said Clive, after they had been standing there some time. "You think it's never coming."

"But it's all right really—you know it will—it always has—it always does," she babbled.

"Until this morning, yes. But there was something on the late-news bulletin—they interrupted the music at 'The Yellow Bird' to tell us—I expect you missed it, I'm trying to break it gently—"

"Oh, don't—" shaking his arm, "No, please, it's horrid— let's just be quiet. It's so lovely and peaceful."

But the birds were carolling as if demented; joyous shrieks, piercing jets of tiny sound so shrill they seemed to burn the ears like showers of glacial water. The miniature screams hopped from leaf to leaf, far and near, tearing the grey air that was changing, at a snail's rate, to yellow and rose. Gradually the slow east streamed and flooded with fire.

"Oh, there he is! Oh, isn't he gorgeous!"

Up he came, majestic and ordinary, and every dew-wet roof gleamed argent to meet him.

"Beautifully produced," said Clive. "The lighting effects especially worthy of mention."

"There—he did come, you see, I knew he would. Let's go in now, and see what the others are up to."

Clive had been about to suggest bed. But it was a word which, absurdly, he found himself hesitating to use. He followed her into the house, leaving the sunrise strictly to the birds.

Mrs. Traill had been hoping that he was proposing. Not exactly proposing marriage; marriage was something which, on the blurred map of Mrs. Traill's own matrimonial experiences, was an afterthought; something you arranged when everything else was working satisfactorily. Her tactful glances through the French windows had been in hope of seeing some conclusive embrace, and it was with hope that she studied their faces as they came into the room. But all she saw was what a less romantic type might expect to see on two faces, long past youth, that had been up all night.

The few stalwarts who were left now exclaimed in horror at the spectacle of dawn. Ones with cars began to arrange to ferry those who were carless back to their homes. A little crowd wandered out into the hall, coats and furs were donned, cars began to drive away.

"Christine must have brought them down," Diana Meredith said, yawning, as she indicated the row of visitors' garments carefully arranged in a row along a wooden chest, "She really is rather a gem, you know. She drives me up the wall sometimes but she brought 'em down to save us the sweat of going up for them . . . lose her? Oh, she'd never leave of her own accord; she adores us. But we might want her flat, one day, for Dick and Amanda."

In fact, Christine had been overcome by champagne and sleep about two o'clock. She had wondered for some time

176

whether she was expected to sit up; those waiters seemed decent enough to leave without stealing anything; she would have liked to stay up to see Mr. Lennox come in and hear how his show had gone, but really she could hardly keep her eyes open. So she had arranged the company's coats, and crept off.

The lanterns were still burning; she took a last glance out at the garden through her window before she got into bed. And then, just as her eyes shut themselves, if someone hadn't started playing the piano in the Long Room! At this hour in the morning—well, it was the morning now, wasn't it?—a nice tune, though, kind of gay, and exciting.

Singing, now. One of the gentlemen. She hoped that it would not keep her awake, and it didn't.

Chapter 20

SHE DID NOT AWAKEN UNTIL ELEVEN O'CLOCK, AND NEVER
remembered either having done such a thing in her life before,
or feeling as she did when she opened her eyes. She wondered
if she had caught the flu somewhere.

But quiet attention to dressing steadied her head and les-
sened its ache, and by half-past eleven she was in the kitchen,
making tea.

The house was absolutely silent. Bells had rung from the
church almost next door to Pemberton Hall; rung again half-
an-hour or so later; sunlight was reflected sudbuedly into the
kitchen; Sunday life was going on as usual in the Square.
Christine collected the papers from the front step and ventured to glance through the pages of her own favourite to
see what it thought of Mr. Lennox's—well, Mr. Coward's
really—show. Here it was . . . Oh, dear.

Well, *really!* Quite insulting.

Still, he did say that his remarks woud make no difference
to the theatre-going public who enjoyed musicals; *they* would
flock to Mr. Coward's latest effort in their tens of thousands.
So that was all right; I'm glad he's got the face to admit it,
thought Christine, sipping tea.

The door was slowly opened and, accompanied by a low
complaining sound, Mrs. Traill tottered in.

"Hullo," she moaned, "is there any coffee?"

"I'll have it for you in a minute, Mrs. Traill. I say, please
don't mind me saying so, but you do look bad. Hadn't you
better see the doctor? It must be some germ about; I had ever
such a headache when I woke up and felt all shaky."

Mrs. Traill had seated herself at the table with her freckled
arms extended on it at full length as if they must have support;

and was looking wanly at her wrist, manacled by an enormous bracelet of yellow pottery which suggested a variation on the marital neck-ring, introduced by some experimental Ostrogoth. She now uttered a short laugh.

"That's a hangover, my dear woman. What I've got."

"Oh." Christine turned her attention to the coffee. She was certain that it was no such thing. Mrs. Traill might have one; Christine Smith was not the kind that had hangovers. "There." She handed the sufferer a brimming cup, ebony and scalding.

"Thank God," said Mrs. Traill, shutting her eyes and beginning to sip. "Oh, damn this thing—" as the bracelet slid clumsily down her wrist and threatened to break the cup.

"It's very original," Christine said, eyeing the monstrosity.

"I got it in Chile." Mrs. Traill could always be revived by admiration. "The Indians make them. I thought it looked so primitive and honest."

Christine had suspected that the feeble scratchings of pattern on the thing's surface could scarcely have been made by any civilised hand, but, having spoken half of her thoughts, said no more. Mrs. Traill droned on—

" . . . when we lived in Spain we had a wonderful all-night party, on the shore, the gipsies came and sang for us, and we all went swimming at sunrise. Naked."

Christine poured herself some more tea, her face expressing nothing.

"Last night was a bit bourgeois, I thought . . . just what I expected . . . That's Antonia and Diana, of course . . . But I did think Clive might have wanted something a bit livelier . . . If it hadn't been for my lanterns it would have been *utterly* ordinary . . ." Pause, and more sipping with shut eyes.

"I thought they were all such old friends of yours and Mrs. Meredith's and Miss—"

"Oh, yes, well, they were, of course. But I do think a few young faces . . . I met a charming boy in Paris in April, an Armenian. I tried 'phoning him. He's been living in London, but he must have moved . . . I thought Glynis looked very conventional, didn't you?"

"Oh, Mrs. Traill, I thought she looked simply lovely!"

"Yes, but rather like an advertisement for dress-hire, didn't you think? It's so important to work out your own style."

"I thought she looked *lovely*," Christine stubbornly repeated, which caused Mrs. Traill to glance across at her, with a kind of affectionate indulgence. Then, murmuring, "I don't know how it is, I used to be able to drink what I liked and feel like a bird afterwards," she pulled a curiously ugly blue-and-yellow Japanese robe about herself and tottered away.

By this time, Christine was beginning to wonder if they were all feeling like this and would want her to provide lunch? Diana Meredith had appeared, but as she only walked past the open door at the end of the kitchen passage, looking purposeful in one of her new overalls, on her way to the pottery shed, she did not contribute anything towards solving the question. She must have breakfasted, as usual, in their flat.

After another ten minutes, however, Miss Marriott trailed in, followed by Mr. Lennox. They greeted Christine with languid half-smiles and Clive, after muttering something about would she be a sweetie and get them some coffee, continued the sentence Christine had heard coming down the stairs . . .

" . . . congratulated me, calling her a 'lovely child', and said where had I been hiding her all this time? I was a bit took aback, I'm so used to seeing her look all beatnik. Then he said she certainly had the looks for the stage, and when I said Oh, that doesn't count as it did in our day, he said looks were always useful no matter whose day it was, ha ha. So there you are."

"Well, I know Mummy was pleased. She's been really worried about her." Antonia, smiling absently in Christine's direction, groped for a cup of coffee. "Thank you, Christine."

Clive managed to look as if he thought Mrs. Marriott capable of worrying about something beyond invitations to parties, and Antonia went on, fingers thrust in her falling locks and still-drowsy eyes fixed on his face, "Mummy's so *sensible*. I don't usually worry her about my worries but some weeks ago I felt so—well, I did write to her. When she was in Bermuda. Pages and pages, I wrote. And she—"

"And she told you to see your doctor," Clive interrupted,

"and get a good tonic, and buy some new clothes, and keep your eye on United Aluminium or something because they'd gone up threepence ha'penny in the last few days. Am I right?"

"Dead right," she said, laughing, "but it was sensible. I did get a tonic and I did get some new clothes and Herzie made a little bit for me on the United Aluminiums . . . it wasn't Aluminiums, I forgot what it was . . . But Herzie knew."

"Herzie's quite useful, isn't he?"

Out of the corner of her eye, Christine saw Antonia's hand steal across the table to lie over his. "I meant to tell you, darling . . ." she heard, in the most lulling of murmurs, "our walk is off . . . Peter carried on so last night—you know, sitting in the same corner for hours and staring into his drink with a face like a lobster—"

"It always is. (Boy, a saucer of milk for Mr. Lennox.")" Clive moved his hand away to take his cup.

"I know but last night it was like a lobster's that's been crying. So I said I'd go for a drive this afternoon. I couldn't be sorrier; it'll be nothing but a dead loss but what was I to do?"

"I see. Yes. Well. I wasn't quite certain I could make it, and as the boys seem to have got out the black cap in a bunch for that casino bit in our second half, I suppose I'd better contact Max and spend the afternoon on a nice bit of postmorteming."

She was looking at him woefully.

"It's all right. I'll survive," he said, and patted her hand.

"I wanted to talk to you about—you know. What you say I *thought* I heard."

"Then go ahead. Aren't you a bit clearer about things this morning?" He had half-risen from the table but now sat down again, looking patient.

Antonia glanced at Christine, who had been finishing her tea at the other end of the table with eyes fixed immovably on the sheets of a newspaper. Thus, she might with credibility on the part of all be supposed out of earshot. "Christine, you remember my asking you last night if you heard someone singing in the Long Room?" Christine looked up.

"Yes, Miss Marriott. I didn't, I said so . . . we went up and looked . . . Don't . . ." She choked off the sentence which might have suggested that Miss Marriott had had too much drink to remember.

"Yes, of course, I remember. But I do want you to *think hard*. It's most frightfully important." Antonia's enormous eyes were fixed on Christine's calm face, "You see, I thought it was a . . . ghost."

"Oh, Miss Marriott! —you don't believe in all that superstition, do you?"

Clive just stirred in his chair.

"Well, not the sort of ghost with its head under one arm, or chains, and that sort of thing, of course. But . . . a spirit. It, the voice I heard, was so like the voice of that great friend of ours who was killed in the war . . ."

"Mr. Condron, yes," Christine nodded. The name, and the thought of him, were now joined in her mind with those of the others, who lived in the house. In a way it was sometimes as if he lived there too; the thoughts of him, in all their minds, were so friendly and so strong.

"Are you quite sure?" Antonia persisted.

"As a matter of fact I did hear someone singing, after I was in bed, Miss Marriott. A gentleman's voice, it was. I thought someone must have come up to the Long Room . . ."

"It was in the Long Room? You're sure?" Antonia was leaning across the table now.

"I . . . *thought* so," Christine said slowly; for some reason she felt reluctant to admit that she had taken for granted that it was there. "Some song about lanterns, it was. I noticed it particularly, the words, I mean, because of our lanterns in the garden."

Antonia looked at Clive. She said nothing.

"If I whistled it to you," he said slowly, "would you recognize it?"

"I think so, Mr. Lennox. It wasn't an ordinary tune; I remember thinking it was rather original."

Lifting his head slightly, Clive whistled the opening bars of the air.

"That's it," she said, nodding her head in time to the dropping cascade of notes.

"And the words—" Antonia joined in eagerly—"how does it go, Clive? 'In spring for sheer delight m . . . m . . . m . . . lanterns swinging through the trees—'"

"Yes, I heard that, Miss Marriott. About the trees, and the lanterns. I noticed that particularly. It was such a clear voice."

There was silence for a moment. Christine looked from one face to the other. Then Clive got up from the table.

"The music is on the piano, Antonia. Someone might just have . . . or perhaps it was wireless, outside somewhere."

"The Light does go on until two now, Mr. Lennox . . . though who they think'll be listening to it at that time in the morning I don't know," said Christine.

"Well, you were, for one," he said, laughing. "No," putting an arm round Antonia's shoulders. "I'm sorry. I'd like to believe it but I can't. I simply cannot imagine what the explanation is; it's all mixed up with E.S.P., I suspect. . . . I'd like to believe it, very much . . .

"Then believe it," Antonia said. "Darling Maurice was playing his favourite song to us at a party. It's perfectly simple and just what he would do. Isn't it?"

"Yes . . . but . . . "

"Isn't it?"

"Antonia, it's no use . . . I can't. I'm sorry. I must go and call Max," and he went out.

.   .   .

When Miss Marriott, too, had drifted away—having gone so far as to confide sighingly that she supposed she must get dressed, she was being fetched at half-past twelve, it was nothing but a dead loss—Christine sat staring out of the kitchen window.

Last night had been Midsummer Eve; it had said so in one of the papers, with jokes about fairies; and she felt that all the past weeks of sunlight and flowers had been leading up to it, and to their party, and now everything was flat. She was also suffering from a slight reaction against her employers. Their affairs, usually so absorbing to her, were receding this morning before a preoccupation with her own.

It was ten days since she had snubbed Tom's approach to the unwelcome subject, and she had not heard from him.

The shower of cold water had acted more effectively than she had expected it to, and now—although her conception of a husband in her life had gradually taken the form of imagining two large black boots permanently planted in the very middle of the Swedish rug beside her bed—she was missing Tom, her friend, and missing male attention, and she was irritated with herself for not having managed things better, and with him for being so touchy, and her peace of mind was ruffled.

He need not have gone off 'like that'.

The only brightness in the picture glowed about his sister's home.

That house in Avalon Road! She liked the atmosphere there better than that of any other home she had ever visited; but she only knew that it was what she called 'just my style', for the particular kind of courage needed to use the words 'love and contentment' had been unknown at Mortimer Road, and were not in Christine Smith's vocabulary.

But she had felt the presence of that bond, between Moira and Frank Rusting, which she had felt between married pairs glimpsed walking arm in arm in the street or sitting by their own fireside, while she rushed past on the top of a bus. It drew her like a magnet. She didn't want to marry Tom Richards, but she wanted to sun herself in that glow from his sister's happiness, and once or twice she had even thought it might be worth marrying Tom to get inside his family.

Mortimer Road, of course, would say contemptuously that she must be crazy to hesitate. A nice fellow, steady, round about the right age, a widower, she must be out of her mind.

Christine crossly told her old home to 'Oh, shut up'.

Sitting at the table, with hands folded before her in a highly unusual state of idleness, she tried to work it all out.

Mightn't Tom be more like his sister than he seemed to be?

And would this likeness perhaps 'come out' after they were married?

Christine could not believe it.

Tom meant to be kind, and Moira was very kind, but that was all they had in common. He had often criticized his sister's home, saying the youngsters were noisy and old Frank so wrapped up in the garden that he cared about nothing else—"The real world seems to pass him by, somehow, I don't know—" (Recalling various contemporary circumstances Christine could not feel that this mattered much). And he—Tom—made silly, un-understanding jokes.

But—to marry into that family! She had liked them all so much, even Michael of whom there had been only a glimpse: their homely faces, their bulbous communal nose and wide smiles, their playfulness towards each other. They would be a grand crowd to marry into, and Moira would be her sister-in-law.

Nevertheless, the boots with the untidy laces remained immovably present in her mind's eye, and, presently, she thumped the table with both fists, muttered, "Well, this won't buy the baby a new frock," and set to work tidying the kitchen. Those waiters hadn't made too bad a job of it, but, of course, not how you'd do it yourself; people never did.

Chapter 21

BY THE MIDDLE OF AUGUST, SHE HAD NOT HEARD FROM HIM FOR a month. It was as plain as the nose on your face: he had dropped her.

Going on like some boy of nineteen, thought Christine with mingled mortification and regret. Having firmly dealt with his attempts to broaden her mind (Thank you—if that was broadening she'd stay narrow) and stopped him, by mutters and a mulish expression, from going on about coal-miners or that bomb or travelling conditions before the war, and made it quite clear to him what shows she enjoyed and what kind of thing *she* liked talking about—in short, having made him into the kind of man-friend she wanted, he had to turn sulky and cool off.

There was no doubt that Mortimer Road had been right about men: you had to manage them, for your own comfort and their good. But it hadn't been right about there always being other fish in the sea and pebbles on the beach: Christine Smith was left without an admirer.

What else can you expect, Mortimer Road asked, at your age?

But she missed him. Some faint excitement, some sense of self-congratulation at being like everyone else now, had gone out of her life. Perhaps it would be truer to say that she missed these feelings more than she missed the man.

And she felt quite depressed, really worried, you might say, at th idea of never seeing the Rustings, particularly Moira, again. I could have been real friends with her, Christine often thought.

It never seriously occurred to her to write to Tom or telephone him. Deeply wounded feelings and real grief and longing might just have compelled her; pride and irritation and Mortimer Road wouldn't hear of such a thing.

And then Moira wrote to her. Such a surprise—such a nice one! Saying they didn't seem to have seen her for ages and wouldn't she go over to tea there next Tuesday or Wednesday: if Moira didn't hear to the contrary, she would expect her on either of those afternoons, nice and early, say about half-past three.

Just like Moira saying it wouldn't matter which day you went. The invitation reinforced Christine's conviction that Moira was not one of the fussy kind. She sent off an eager post-card saying that she would love to come on Tuesday.

She hoped that Tom would not be in. It was always embarrassing when men started cooling off (women didn't cool off; they had too much to gain—at least in Mortimer Road they had—from staying warm) and during the awkward period it was as well to avoid them.

But no doubt Tom understood this as well as she did, and would take care not to be at home.

.   .   .

The Merediths, it occurred to Christine, were having a spending spree. Diana had been encouraged to go on with her work by some small successes in local exhibitions, and purchases from shops displaying her pots and bowls in Hampstead and Highgate, but it could not be these miniature triumphs and their resultant 'pennies', which were causing both of them to splash their money about.

They had bought a handsome new record-player, to hear the café chantant songs they both enjoyed, and the full scores of some successful musicals, and James was boasting a new set of golf-clubs, which he took up to the Club in a neat new dark-green car.

"We're going it, aren't we," Diana observed to Christine as he drove off one morning in this latest toy. "And talking of going it," she went on, "who do you think I saw in Hampstead the other day? Our late Mr. Johnson."

"No! did you, Mrs. Meredith—not really? Did you—did he speak to you?"

"Yes, he spoke to me. Would you like to hear what he said?"

Christine nodded, though shrinking inwardly from the smooth, controlled tone. She was never easy when Mrs. Meredith and Mr. Johnson were in conjunction.

"He was swaggering down the High Street in tan trousers and a striped Italian shirt and a guitar over his shoulder, with three little boys tagging after him. Bursting with prosperity and cheek. I was going past without stopping, of course. It made me sick, because he used to be a decent boy, as they go, but he stopped me and said, 'Hullo, Mrs. Meredith. Lovely day.' I asked him how he liked his new place—I said 'place' deliberately—and he grinned and ruffled one of the boys' hair and said, 'Oh, I quite one of the family now, dear. Bye-bye—give them all my love over Highgate way.' "

"Well!" Christine compressed her lips. "Just what you always said . . . 'quite one of the family' and 'dear', too! The cheek of it. It just shows you can't give them an inch, doesn't it?"

"Probably the people he's with are stinking rich and think it's smart or amusing or God knows what to dress him up like that and let him roam around with a guitar. If he doesn't murder someone they'll be lucky."

"I wonder what happened to those 'responsibilities' he was always going on about?"

"Dropped them, I should think—if he ever had any."

Diana went on into the house but Christine lingered, looking thoughtfully across the Square.

Mr. Johnson had been disgracefully familiar and it did no good to blacks to pamper them up. All the same, she would have liked to see him; in his striped shirt, with his three little admirers. What harm did it do anyone? It only meant there was one more lucky person in the world, and she was glad that Mr. Johnson, instead of going down down down, had landed neatly on his feet.

She wondered why Mrs. Meredith was so hard on blacks. She seemed to mind being in the same world with them. I suppose, Christine reflected, it's like me and Mrs. Benson. And that explained it perfectly, for her, and she dismissed the matter.

The memory of Mrs. Benson never crossed her mind without leaving its faint disagreeable stain, half detestation, half fear, and it was strange how often she saw her by chance; from the top of a bus, perhaps, or from the other side of a hideously crowded street while she was waiting to cross the road.

Wherever the throb and grind of traffic was most hellish, wherever the glare from the confusion of goods in shop windows was weariest and the stench of petrol fumes most overpowering, there, at the worst moment, she would happen to glance up and see Mrs. Benson.

Sometimes the woman seemed to recognize her; more than once there had been a grin and a wave of a thick hand, a parody of pleasure at the sight of her that surprised and sickened Christine; anyone would have thought that they had been real friends.

She could not always be sure that it was Mrs. Benson, either; those great stout women with dyed hair all looked alike, especially with a cigarette sticking out of their face.

It was a common face, in both senses of the word; moving like some embodiment of the scene through the noise and the sickening smells.

Christine summed up her feelings towards this figure from the past in the thought: *she makes me think of everything I hate most.*

       ·   ·   ·

"Three changes of bus and then that walk to the pillar-box— I always think 'hooray' when I see the pillar-box—yes, it is a difficult journey, I think it's nice of people to come out all this way to see us."

"It's nice when you get here," said Christine, and Moira rippled.

They were standing—of all places—in Tom's bedroom. Tea was over, and, after some comfortable talk, Moira had suggested that Christine might like to see over the house; she herself loved seeing over people's homes; and Christine's acceptance had been more eager because she knew that Tom *was* out. She had half-expected to see The Boots standing by his bed, and told herself not to be silly, and leant forward to look out of his window.

"What's that blue hill you can just see between the trees?"

"Oh—up Mill Hill way—it might be the country, mightn't it, with all the trees."

"And so quiet. I like all these shady roads."

"Oh, so do I. I love living here—never want to go anywhere else. We've been here nearly thirty years—came here before the war."

Christine looked down into Frank's garden. A drowsy scent floated up from its tiny parterres and brick paths, framed in their thick beech hedge and shaded by their laburnum and lilac.

"Anne cut the grass on Sunday. It looks nice, doesn't it?"

Christine admired, then went on to ask how Anne was getting on with her mathematics, over which there had been difficulty. Now there was improvement, Moira said; Michael had been helping her. *He* found *English* difficult. Having been 'set on' being a dentist since he was twelve, he was more interested in 'that kind of thing', and in machinery, than in poetry and essays and *that* kind of thing.

"I don't see why you need poetry to be a dentist," Christine said.

"You don't use it while you're pulling out teeth, you silly girl," said Moira, rippling again. "It's to give you a broad general education. Culture. That's what the Grammar Schools aim at—so I'm told. Oh, I used to love poetry when I was Anne's age. Did you?"

Christine's mother used to say 'you silly girl,' but not in the affectionate tone that Moira had used, and her question about liking poetry had not been put in the form 'didn't you?', which would have implied that all nice people did like it.

"I never read any." At school, Christine remembered, they used to say *You're a poet And don't know it*. And poetry rhymed. Poetry?

"My favourite poem used to be *Sohrab and Rustum*, by Matthew Arnold," said Moira. "I know bits of it by heart. I was always saying them over to myself, I was so crazy about it."

And then and there, sounds began to come out on the shady air of the room above the glowing garden; the blue hill looked between its leaves; the scented air listened; marriages of the ordinary vowels and consonants that Christine heard and used every day, but had never in her life heard used as they sounded now—

> "Oxus, forgetting the bright speed he had
> In his high mountain-cradle in Pamir,
> A foiled circuitous wanderer—till at last
> The long'd-for dash of waves is heard, and wide
> His luminous home of waters opens, bright
> And tranquil, from whose floor the new-bathed stars
> Emerge, and shine upon the Aral Sea."

Moira's coarse-featured face, with its surrounding curls of greying hair, was full of gentle delight. Her eyes were fixed questioningly on Christine's face.

Christine was looking down, pulling slowly at the hem of her jacket. She was so moved that the struggling of the feelings with herself—to escape, to express themselves—to make some sound that should not spoil the sounds she had just heard—was actual pain. Oh, what was it? This something—this world hinting at its own existence but no more than hinting—that could neither be had for the wanting nor would tell you what and where it was? Surely, it had nothing to do with the real world? It hardly seemed to be there at all. It was something you just saw or felt or heard for an instant—and wanted ever afterwards with all your heart and never forgot.

And there was no one to talk to, and Mortimer Road still held her in its dull grip.

"Where's Tom these days?" she asked, looking up at last. "Yes—fancy your remembering all that—I haven't seen him for ages."

The confused sensations of delight and pain showed themselves only in the directness of her question. She didn't care a straw where Tom was, and usually she would have been too conscious of what Tom's sister would think, to ask such a thing. But now she blurted it out without hesitation.

Moira sat down on a chair beside the window, keeping her eyes fixed on Christine's face. Her expression was still gentle, but faintly troubled now. Yet she did not hesitate as she said:

"He's got a girl-friend, much younger than he is. They've been going out every night; she lives just down the road. I think he means to marry her, Christine."

Silence.

"I kept it from you as long as I could, dear—but I feel sure, now, that you don't *really* mind. Not mind in the way you and I were talking about that first afternoon you came here."

Another pause.

"It's all right, I don't mind," Christine said slowly.

"I'm so glad, Chris. I knew you wouldn't, but it's a relief to hear you say so."

Nevertheless, there was yet another silence, during which Moira kept her eyes rather carefully away from Christine's brooding face. A bee flew in from the garden and flung itself against the window and banged about exasperatedly; Moira got up, and steered it, without co-operation on its part, out on to the air again.

Christine was feeling surprised, amid all her other confused, shocked, angry thoughts, that Moira and she had come into the open like that about the situation between herself and Tom.

Moira had spoken right out. She had known, all along, that Christine might be her sister-in-law. Well, Christine had guessed that. But she seemed to have it all so clear in her mind —how, Christine felt, how Tom must be feeling—how she herself felt—all of it; all the feelings and facts that in Christine's old home would have been muddled or ignored. Christine liked this clarity; she hung on to it, through her sensation of shock, with one of comfort. Yes, Moira was a dear.

"I don't *mind*," she suddenly said, "but it's a surprise and I don't mind telling you I feel a bit—annoyed."

"That's only natural, dear," Moira answered pitifully. Her

eyes, moving over the large, still figure leaning against the window-frame, seemed to see all the Christines there had been since Christine had been a child; the cheerful dutiful girl who knew nothing about anything, the uncomplaining slave of electrical devices; the starved spirit slowly led out at last into the wider world. But she said no more.

It would also have been natural if Christine had given way to her strong curiosity and asked some questions about this girl much younger than Tom whom he meant to marry, but pride forbade her. She stared heavily out of the window for a moment longer, then determinedly began on a new subject with—

"I don't know what to do about those foxglove seeds, Moira. I can't go scattering them about anywhere; I should feel so silly."

"It's all right, I always tell people he gives them to to make a forget of it. It's a kind of compliment, really, when he gives them to you."

"Yes, I can see that," Christine said, feeling her way into understanding why this should be so, and relieved to have something else than Tom Richards to think about.

"He thinks you're—you're *worthy* to spread about two million foxgloves round the place," Moira explained. "It means he likes you."

"Does it?"

"Yes, and old Frank doesn't like everybody, believe you me. I tell him he's an old *recluse*. But he does like you, he says you remind him of his favourite sister, the one who died."

Christine meditated this. "Does he come of a large family?"

"Frank? Oh—huge. There were ten of them. They paired up, as kids in big families do, and he and Em were always the ones."

Christine would have enjoyed, even amidst irritation, hearing more about Em. It was this sensation of amplitude, of having within herself stores of information about cosy, funny, nice people, diffused by Moira that was one of the things Christine found attractive in Avalon Road. But she was tingling with shock, and irritation and, behind that, the memory

of that poetry. She wanted to be alone, to think about that—
yes, that was what she wanted.

"*Hush'd Chorasmian waste*," suddenly said Moira.

"What?"

"It's another bit of the poem. I've just remembered it."

"—What was that word? Chorus—something? Say it again."

"*Hush'd Chorasmian waste.* Doesn't it sound beautiful?"

Christine gave a nervous smile, but did not answer. In a moment she said—

"I'm glad Frank likes me. I like him, too."

On this pleasanter note, she was taken up to see the attics; and nothing more of any significance passed until they were in the hall, saying good-bye: she had warned Moira that she would not be able to spend the evening at Avalon Road because she would be needed at home to get supper.

"Well . . . come again soon," Moira said. She was tying up a bunch of stolen flowers with string taken from a drawer in the hall table; Christine was inspecting her hair in the looking-glass above the hat-stand. She hesitated—then went on. "Chris . . . I must say this. *Please* don't let it make any difference to you being friends with us—this business about Tom, I mean. You won't will you? Frank and I like you so much; we don't want to lose you." She smiled, looking up into Christine's slightly surprised face. "You know, you're like one of the family."

"Of course I won't," Christine said emphatically—just stopping herself from saying it would take more than Tom Richards getting married to some bit of a girl to make her drop his sister. She tried to say something more, but failed; by this time she was so choked with unfamiliar thoughts and sensations that nothing would come out, and she could only repeat "*Of course I won't,*" and affectionately return Moira's parting kiss.

On the long, complicated bus-ride back to Highgate, she was so sunk in thought that more than once she was almost carried past the stop where she changed. Over and over again, she thought of that spinster's defence heard so often in Mortimer Road—*I could have been married if I'd wanted to*—and Mortimer Road's unvarying comment, *Oh yes I daresay.* Well, now she, Christine Smith, formerly of Mortimer Road, would never truthfully be able to say it; and she minded; she didn't care a button about Tom Richards—queer to think that he had once been the admired and respected Mr. Richards of Lloyd and Farmer's! —but she would have enjoyed being able to make the spinster's defence and know that it was true. That was only natural, wasn't it?

Gradually, however, bitterish thoughts faded into the background. The spell of Pemberton Hall had worked upon her to such effect that, if her soul may be compared to the keyboard of an organ, its stiff, mute stops had been wooed gently out, and made to give forth a faint music. And when the bus stopped at last outside Golders Green Station, she was actually thinking more of the poetry that Moira had said than of Tom and his new girl friend.

It had been like . . . like a kind of signpost pointing towards That Day: not the feeling itself, but belonging . . . belonging . . . like it, anyway. Like it.

See her giving up the Rustings because of Tom's cooling off! No fear!

All the same, when she finally did get down from the bus, she was still feeling decidedly 'off' men, and when she encountered, by a casual glance, a huge Face on a political poster on a nearby hoarding, looking winningly at her and suggesting that she should Trust herself to it, she felt an instant sense of irritated repudiation.

She seldom thought about politics, and her usual response to any remark about them was the thought, spoken or unspoken—*at it again*—or *always going on about something*, and the wish that They would *shut up and give everybody a bit of peace.* After such an afternoon, the mere sight of this vast countenance was an affront. Soapy, thought Christine.

She got home in a thoroughly unsatisfactory state of mind.

Chapter 22

BEFORE SHE REALISED IT, LATE SUMMER HAD COME AND SOME
leaves were turning among the trees in the Square, and everyone at Pemberton Hall had gone off on holiday.

Mrs. Traill departed with a friend, small, calm and tough
as herself, for Montenegro; the Merediths were paying a round
of visits to friends, returning to the Hall for a few days between
these occasions, Miss Marriott flew off to one of the warm
islands somewhere for three weeks, and Mr. Lennox went to
America, to play on Broadway the part he had played in
London. Christine was left alone in the spacious, sunny house.

She enjoyed this season of idleness and quiet. There had
been kind, if unfussy, enquiries about whether she wouldn't
mind sleeping alone in that great place? Wouldn't she like to
invite a friend to stay? But of course she could! Didn't she
know that?

No, Christine didn't want a friend to stay, and she wouldn't
be nervous.

So they all went away, and Pemberton Hall and Christine
were left to entertain one another.

It was a quiet, busy time. She experimented with some
elaborate cooking, concentrating on what might be described
as Famous Cakes of The Western World, and trying her hand
at Maids of Honour and even Lady Baltimore, which—quite
unknown to Christine—is the only cake ever to have given its
name to a novel. But this failed, in her opinion, because she
couldn't buy pecan nuts anywhere, not even at some of the
grand London shops patronized by Diana Meredith.

But when they were made there was no one there to show
them to and eat them with. She invited Moira over to tea every
week, and that was very enjoyable, only—only—after Moira
had gone, the house seemed larger, and quieter than ever.

Still beautiful, still offering that 'happy welcome' once detected by Mr. Johnson. But that wasn't enough.

You needed to hear it said in a human voice.

She missed her employers. Their peculiar group-atmosphere of charm, casualness and amusing malice had crept into her veins like some irresistible drug, and there wasn't any denying that the days were long. Pleasant, but long.

Those people across the Square whose wireless was always playing Old Favourites of the Thirties didn't seem to have gone away; for music floated through the Long Room every long, warm, drowsy afternoon while the pigeons cooed and stuffed themselves in the Square and the first leaves sailed down. It might have been in the house itself; gay ripples from a piano, silly, sweet songs in a man's agreeable tenor, occasionally an old music-hall favourite. Christine would hum, or even softly whistle, to herself as she recognized airs popular in her girlhood.

The glamorous atmosphere diffused by her employers, however, was not completely absent; they knew interesting people, as well as being interesting themselves, and sometimes she saw a Name or a familiar face in her favourite newspaper.

For instance, about the middle of the month Mrs. Marriott married Lord Belsize! (Christine felt that it should be announced like this, rather than as "Mrs. Marriott and Lord Belsize were married.") She bought two papers that morning, and there were photographs in both and a paragraph in that 'Londoner's Diary', though it wasn't what you might call interesting, being all about how Lord Belsize used to keep some kind of pig from dying out, up in Yorkshire. Who would want to read about that? And years ago, anyway.

Mrs. Marriott had come out ever so clear, wearing one of those caps, with more petals all over it than Christine had ever seen on one before, and looking more like a Pekinese than ever. Lord Belsize appeared to be shrinking from the camera; at least, his expression suggested it, though his stance was soldierly, as befitted an ex-Guardee. Christine took the papers over to Avalon Road to show to Moira. They both said, poor old man, which was satisfactory.

Then, towards the end of the month, Nigel Rooth's had an early dress show, and Christine marvelled over a photograph of Ferenc Brigg's designs and his hair, which he wore in a fringe and tucked behind his ears. She gave less attention to one of a suit by Miss Marriott, whose lines, classic in their simplicity, yet had just the effortless touches of exaggeration needed to make them beautiful. They seemed dull somehow— to Christine at least—after seeing his. For he had at last designed a suit, just as Antonia had dared him to and feared that he would. It was a trouser-suit, perversely smart.

Early in September, Moira told her, Tom and his Glenda were getting married. He had bought a small house; Christine was relieved to hear that it was at Woking, miles the other side of London. Moira talked quite openly and frequently about his plans, as if taking it for granted that Christine's hard feelings, such as they were, had healed themselves, and this was a fact; they had. All the same, Woking was near enough.

It often seemed queer to her, now, to think that her best friend was Mr. Richards' sister.

.   .   .

Miss Marriott was the first to come home.

She arrived late one afternoon, squired by Peter-whose-other-name-Christine-had-never-heard, and Mr. Herz; they were all in Peter's car.

"Oh, Miss Marriott, I do wish I'd known—I'd have had everything ready for you. Your flat is all dusted; I did it yesterday, but I'd have put some flowers . . ."

"Sweet of you, but it's all right . . . we're going out to dinner almost at once . . . Peter! That's apricot liqueur in there . . . careful!"

They followed her up the steps, Mr. Herz plump and dark and elegant, Peter looking pink and foolish, as usual.

Miss Marriott actually looked plump, too. Why, she must have been a big girl before she started modelling, thought Christine, who knew that this was how Antonia had begun on her career. She could not help staring; she did not know that she was doing it.

"Yes, I know I've got enormous," Antonia said good-naturedly, turning to smile, almost to laugh, at her, as they came into the hall. "I suppose I'll have to start taking it off soon, but it is such bliss not having to worry about dieting on the top of everything else . . . how pretty everything looks . . . bliss to be back, really . . ."

She passed a hand over her hair, paled by the sun, looking less arranged than formerly. Her skin was delicately brown and her eyes glittered as if reflecting the summer seas she had been drowsing beside.

"You do look well, Miss Marriott!"

"Oh, I feel well . . . it's wonderful. Just dump them there, darling . . . Christine will take them up, won't you, Christine . . . Oh, very well . . ." as Peter, smiling at Christine, began to take the cases upstairs.

When he came down, they went out to his car and drove away. Christine stood at the door to watch them go; it was so nice to have one of them home again; She does seem better; perhaps she'll marry someone now, Christine thought. I hope it's Mr. Lennox.

There had been good news of Mr. Lennox; the show had been a success on Broadway. It was only booked for a six-week run, however, because it was not possible to get a theatre for longer, and Christine supposed that then he too would soon be coming home. From her newspaper she gathered that he had had a personal success, as well; the local paper had a column about him, one week-end.

Miss Marriott did not go back to work immediately.

She seemed more relaxed, and spent most of the next few days at home; sleeping late, gossiping for half-hours at a time on the telephone, or wandering out to have things done to her nails and hair; in the evenings she usually sat in the Long Room laughing with Peter, or Mr. Herz, or both, and drinking something Peter had invented which he called "Antonia's Special".

If anything, she continued to put on weight. It was surprisingly becoming to her; Christine once heard Mr. Herz, who seemed to own one of those galleries where paintings are

199

shown off, tell her that if she wasn't careful she would look like a Ray-nwar (which was, Christine supposed, some kind of picture).

Miss Marriott 'took up with' Mr. Lennox's daughter, bringing her back to lunch or supper and going on shopping expeditions with her to buy clothes. They seemed to get on very well together, and Christine thought that this meant Miss Marriott really was thinking of settling down with Glynis's father. They laughed a good deal. She would hear the peals coming down from Antonia's sitting-room: Laugh and grow fat, as they say, thought Christine.

Glynis no longer looked like one of those beatniks. She was working out a style of her own, thought Christine; rather—it was not easy to find a word for it, Christine, not having *poetic* in her vocabulary, had to fall back on *individual*, of which she was rather proud. There was a white tweed cloak, and a little embroidered cap like a fez. Yet it didn't look like fancy-dress.

Miss Marriott took a great interest in all this.

She also lectured Glynis about the way she should dress when she was older; this conversation took place one evening while the three were at supper in the kitchen.

"Fabia's the awful example," Miss Marriott said. "She can't or won't see that you can get away with 1917-trenches colour and no cut until you're forty-five or so, but after that you have to have so much personality that people simply don't notice what you're wearing—and she hasn't got it. After fifty, you just look like one more peculiar arty female."

"Oh I like Mrs. Traill's style, Miss Marriott," Christine said, pausing between table and stove with a summer pudding suspended. "I can see what you mean, in a way, but I do think Mrs. Traill always looks very nice."

"God help us," cried Miss Marriott, darting a sparkle at Glynis which Christine, turning away to get the cream, did not see. "All right, if you really want to see everybody of her age going around in sludge-coloured shopping bags . . ."

"I didn't mean that, Miss Marriott." Christine, smiling indulgently, began spooning out icy heaps of bread soaked in rich blackish-red juice, "I only meant I think it suits Mrs. Traill."

Glynis sat in silence, smiling, while this went on. The long summer seemed to have brought her looks into bloom, as well as revivifying those of Antonia, and she glowed in a dress of white cotton, cut low to show her brown, now full, bosom; skirt and bodice covered in little sprigs of currants, the same dark red as the fruit in the summer pudding.

As she took her place between the two beauties, one in her first pride, the other enjoying a last return of her tide before it went out for ever, Christine experienced a selfless wish that all this beauty and gaiety might be enjoyed by what she thought of as *sweethearts*. It seemed such a waste.

Her regrets were ill-founded. The young girl came to Pemberton Hall between bouts of furious love-making: the elderly one, sailing on this return of the tide of youth, now had her hopes.

Chapter 23

ANOTHER WEEK, AND THE REST OF THEM WERE HOME AGAIN, and found Christine with a pleased welcome but also with a list of things that were Going, or had Gone, Wrong.

It struck her, as the only person in the group who had lived in the same house for more than half a century, that her employers must have been fortunate in where they had lived.

Slates working loose on roofs, outside lead pipes forced out of shape by the battering of garden brooms, electric wiring that had worn itself out over the years—they seemed to have so little experience of these daily misfortunes of the householder that they received her doleful report with incredulity and a little indignation.

There seemed to be an unspoken agreement that Pemberton Hall had in some way let them down.

"Why, it was only done up in April," cried Mrs. Meredith, sunburnt and thinner than ever from sailing with friends on the Broads.

"Yes, but I didn't trust that surveyor, I said at the time I thought he was deeply unsure of himself," said Mrs. Traill.

"That wouldn't stop him giving an honest report."

"It might, Diana. Unsure people have a deep-seated wish to give pleasure."

"So that's why he didn't tell us the whole place would need re-wiring and it would cost five hundred pounds," said Diana. "It's nice to know."

Antonia gave one of her shrieks, but rather lazily.

Mrs. Meredith whistled dolefully and glanced out of the windows as if seeking inspiration from the Faces. They were growing ever more visible as the leaves drifted down from the trees, and everyone at Pemberton Hall had taken to complaining about the forthcoming General Election, which was felt to be creeping up on one, like that figure in the picture in the M. R. James ghost story.

"Yes," said Diana, following his glance, "and that isn't going to make it easier. I can't think of a worse time to find spare cash for house repairs. If those brutes get in, shares will drop like lead."

"Perhaps they won't. The latest poll showed a slight tendency the other way."

'Oh, I know, but do you take much notice of these things?"

"I never take any notice of any of it," said Mrs. Traill, who had returned from Montenegro with perhaps the one ugly tunic embroidered during the last five years by peasants in that interesting region, and was now wearing it over blue jeans. "Why do you have to? You can choose which age you like, and live in it. I saw that somewhere, the other day; some artist said it. Or was it in some novel?"

"Bravo, dear," Diana said absently. "Any news from Clive, Antonia?"

"Not a sound," Antonia said. She had coloured a little.

"Oh well, bless him anyway," Diana leisurely surveyed her friend. "You *do* look well, you know," she pronounced at last. "I haven't seen you look so well for years. What have you been doing?"

Her mocking turquoise eye, fixed on Antonia's face, stated unequivocally what she thought any other woman would have been doing.

"Oh, don't be silly. I don't know—the sun was so gorgeous and Bill and Freda were so sweet to me and it was so heavenly peaceful. I just lay about. I don't know."

"Anyone amusing staying there?"

"Just us, most of the time. I did do one or two designs and posted them off but I slacked disgracefully, really. That poor little boy seemed to have *dropped behind*, somehow. I didn't worry about him and his sparkles." But she sighed as she spoke. "I suppose I must call Nigel tonight. Then back to the grind. I'll look in there tomorrow."

"You haven't got long," said Mrs. Traill, "if the autumn

show's on the twenty-first. No," more energetically, "you haven't, Antonia, if today's the sixth—what is it?"

"It might be the ninth. This morning, actually, it was the twelfth. Does it matter? Fabia, you really are too vague to live. I wonder you haven't 'dropped behind' yourself somewhere, long ago," said Diana.

Mrs. Traill laughed and put her arms behind her silvery head. "Doesn't matter. It's comfortable. You always did fuss."

"Don't stir her up—let her relax," said James kindly, looking at Antonia. "It's true I haven't seen you looking like this for years, Antonia. Congratulations."

"I expect your mother's marriage is a weight off your mind, isn't it? Hasn't he got a house somewhere?—I mean, he doesn't live in hotels, does he?"

"At Esher, yes. Not old, or unique or anything, but about fifteen bedrooms and a nice garden. Just what Mummy likes—you know she can't bear old beautiful places—No," as everyone laughed, "she truly can't, they depress her. She says they're always needing things doing to them, too."

"She's right there," said James. He turned to Christine, "If you'll let me have your little list, I'll see about getting things moving."

"Well, leave me enough cash for a winter coat," said Diana. "And I want one of these leather hats like a space-woman's."

"Oh, God, Diana," mildly said Mrs. Traill.

"I think I could wear one." She looked at her delicate arrogant profile in the long looking-glass across the room. "No specs. yet, no double chin—yes, I'm certain I could."

"I wouldn't, Diana, really, you need to be nineteen to carry one off. Why not get a couple of scarves from the Rumanian shop? Wonderful designs, and so graceful—classic."

"Scarves! You can look like a refugee or a student if you like; I prefer to look my age."

"I don't think she'd take any notice if he did. She's got him rather under her thumb, you know; he relies on her." This remark came from Antonia, who had been discussing her mother's marriage with James. She now glanced at Christine.

"Ducky, could you see to some supper? I'm starving again."

Her new tone towards their housekeeper was very pretty; she had borrowed its easy endearments from Clive's vocabulary.

Christine bustled off willingly, so pleased to have them all home again . . . Mr. Lennox would be back soon, too, and then there might be wedding bells.

. . .

There came a day some weeks later—it happened to be Tom Richards's wedding-day, and Christine was at least trying to regret, for his sake, that it was pouring with rain—when she was standing on the kerb in the Village waiting for a chance to cross the road. The traffic! All you could say was that it didn't, so far, turn on you and chase you down the quieter streets . . .

Under the umbrella she was struggling to hold up against the swooping wind her eye was caught by a placard outside one of the two Village newsagents.

HIGHGATE STAR WEDS IN U.S.

Christine experienced a kind of downward swoop in her stomach, accompanying an awful suspicion. It couldn't be . . . it mustn't . . . Turning again to face the boisterous wind, she hurried across to the shop. It was nonsense, of course, lots of stage and screen people lived in Highgate . . . but Oh, please, don't let it be . . .

But it was.

Disregarding the people in the shop, she stood there holding the paper before her, staring at the paragraph while her umbrella lay dripping and unheeded on the floor. Her eyes swept down the column; Oh, perhaps . . . let there be . . . some mistake . . .

No mistake. Clive Lennox, star in the Noël Coward show now running successfully on Broadway, had married Zetta Dettinger, a dancer. Zetta had starred in musicals and on television in the States. Mr. Lennox lived at Pemberton Hall, in the Square.

Christine slowly folded the paper and stuffed it into her shopping-bag.

No one was looking at her. That was what the world was like: awful things happened, treacheries happened, people's hearts got broken, and no one noticed. No one.

She felt a strong, painful impulse to tell someone, and had to walk out of the shop, carefully putting up her umbrella, so that she should not give way to it. She began to walk briskly homewards through the rain-swept roads, under the bare trees.

Men! Why need there be any?

All they ever seemed to do was to upset things, and women could get on all right without them; of course, you had to have them for other things, like looking at bodies when people were murdered, but if there weren't any men probably no one would get murdered; women weren't always murdering people . . .

Murder? What was she thinking of?

Her thoughts were running wild . . . She deliberately took a hold on herself; she must be ready to face Miss Marriott.

Thank goodness, she thought, she was out today, down at Nigel Rooth's. No one was at home.

Oh this rain . . . 'happy the bride that the sun shines on' . . . poor, poor Miss Marriott . . . and Tom, too . . . Tom was getting married today . . . *I'm getting married in the morning* . . . a pair of them, and both at the church in time. Trust them.

Men.

Christine slammed the front door so forcibly that the noise seemed to shake the house.

Instantly, she was ashamed. Her gesture seemed silly, having nothing to do with the feeling inside the hall. She stood still for a moment, almost listening—and there was the 'happy welcome' as usual, gentle and wooing, laying its silent blessing on heart and spirit and assuring her that anger would pass, but comfort would remain. She went slowly up the stairs.

Chapter 24

SHE SAW NOTHING OF HER EMPLOYERS UNTIL THE EVENING. SHE almost tip-toed about, dreading to be confronted by some distressed face, but the house remained quiet. Then, suddenly, about six o'clock, everyone seemed to come in flourishing newspapers and exclaiming.

"Christine! Have you seen this?" demanded Mrs. Meredith, coming into the kitchen and thrusting the *Evening Standard* at her, eyes sparkling joyfully with excitement and anticipation of more to come. "Isn't it—"

"Yes, Mrs. Meredith. I saw it in the local paper, up in the Village," Christine said, unable, for the life of her, to keep a repressive note out of her voice.

"Well? Isn't it splendid news? She looks a poppet." Mrs. Meredith absorbedly studied the bride, who thrust out her bosom as she stood, flourishing a large knife, beside an equally large cake and her new husband. Mr. Lennox looked much as usual. Christine had somehow expected him to look cowed and remorseful; he ought to, goodness knew.

"She looks like a pretty little frog," Mrs. Meredith pronounced.

"Oh, do you think she's pretty, Mrs. Meredith?"

"By modern standards—very. A *belle laide*—bouncing with vitality and plenty of mouth. Here . . . want it?" She tossed the paper on to the table just as Mrs. Traill glided in.

It was plain to Christine, from the first sight of her, that Mrs. Traill was taking it differently. Even the usual walk had been modified and the paper she held out drooped limply, having got wet in the rain.

"I thought you . . . might . . . like . . . to see this, Christine. It might have come as . . . a bit of a shock. Knowing us all so well," added Mrs. Traill confusedly, as Diana glanced at her in surprise.

"Thank you, Mrs. Traill. It's very nice of you but I had seen it. This afternoon, up in the Village."

"I give it eighteen months," intoned Mrs. Traill, snatching up the other paper and fixing an indignant stare on the wedding group. A descending step on the stair now caused all three, off guard for a second, to exchange lightning glances; the excitement in it was unconscious, but avid as that once greeting the entrance of Christians into the Roman arena.

But it was James.

"Well, what do you think about this?" he demanded of Christine. There is no third evening paper in London now, so at least he could not offer her yet another photograph. "Surprised us all, hasn't he? Last thing I ever thought . . . er . . . pretty little thing, though, don't you think?" He took up Mrs. Traill's paper and studied it.

"I don't admire that style of looks, Mr. Meredith. Piggy little eyes and a huge mouth. I like something more . . . refined," Christine said, rushing biscuits away into a tin.

"She does look very common," Mrs. Meredith said judicially, "but that means nothing nowadays; in fact it's fashionable. God help us all," she added, but without emphasis.

"Sexy," murmured James.

Again, footsteps were heard coming down the stairs, and this time it could only be one person. Her three old friends were temporarily overcome by feelings which, indulged in for thirty years, had become instinctive and quite uncontrollable: malicious interest, and what may be called gossipry, and real affectionate concern, and no one said anything. Christine continued to open packets of biscuits, delivered that afternoon by the grocer, and wedge them recklessly into their tins.

But there was more than one person coming down, and the door opened on Miss Marriott accompanied by the unsurnamed Peter and Mr. Herz. She looked—when Christine dared to glance sideways—radiantly cheerful, and was not yet inside the room before she was carolling—"Well! What news! Our Clivey!" and everybody began babbling at once. James went off to get some drink.

It was all very well for them to make a mock of Peter, but he remembered to pour a glass for Christine and offer it to her so that she could drink to Mr. Lennox's health and happiness. Christine, however, did not join in the chorus of voices saying "Clive!" She took a good sip, feeling she owed it to herself, but in her silence she was drinking a toast to Miss Marriott.

This is how a girl ought to behave when she's been let down, thought Christine. She's behaving like I did when Moira told me about Tom. Of course I took it quieter, I'm not the exciteable type . . . and I expect *her* feelings are hurt, and mine weren't. Poor Miss Marriott—and looking so pretty this evening, really lovely, not like that little frog-face . . . *she* looks like a—well, I know I shouldn't use the word, but she does, really —a tart.

I wouldn't have thought it of Mr. Lennox.

Everyone present 'expected her feelings are hurt', except Peter, who for many years had been mulishly telling himself and all their friends that there was nothing in that old affair between Toni and Clive Lennox (he never suspected that his persistence in calling her 'Toni', in spite of her protests, made it even more impossible for her to think of him as a husband), and who was now congratulating himself, as well as Clive. He, Peter, had been right. The older flame had married a sexy little Yank, and was out of the running. The outsider was drawing ahead. Herzy was nowhere; she'd only known him a year.

But Antonia had said to Mr. Herz: "Benny, I know you'll help me. I do mind. Not lots—my heart isn't broken—but I do mind a bit. And I'm just going to be as madly gay as I can. Everybody'll know I mind, but at least I won't show it. The hell with the lot of them. I adore them but sometimes I wish they weren't all so frantically interested in us all. You'll stand by, won't you, darling?"

Mr. Herz, that clever man, had smiled a little, so that creases came in his soft full dark face, and said, "I will, darling."

It had sounded . . . comforting. Warm, and not too easy. She had glanced at him in a little pleased surprise.

But it did hurt, and she did mind, and she tried not to think about that time they had seen the sun come up over London, and not to think about the pressure of Clive's arm round her shoulders—and, oh!—like a sudden stab from a needle—Italy! *Italy*—when they had both been young!

"Clive!"

She was drinking a great deal of champagne and if tears ran down into it—no, not really, they ran into a hastily-applied handkerchief—well, these were her very old friends, and they would know that a few tears were natural.

In the circumstances.

. . .

The next piece of news was that Mr. Lennox, although the show had closed down in America, was not coming back to Pemberton Hall; he and his bride would live and work in the States.

Christine could understand that he might feel ashamed of himself, and also feel that his little frog-face would not fit in well with his old friends. Still, it was sad news.

Mrs. Traill kept up a steady jeremiad against the Lennox-Dettinger marriage, repeating every time the subject came up that she gave it eighteen months. Everyone said, "Oh come, Fabia," or "Don't be so dreary, darling"—nevertheless, none of them seemed to feel that *such a dreadful thing*, as Christine thought of it, was out of the question.

Glynnis Lennox came sometimes to see Miss Marriott. She had become ever so grown-up, Christine thought; you would take her for twenty-five rather than not yet eighteen, and she might be overheard speaking of her new stepmother as Zetta; what else could you expect, with the girl only a year or so older?

It all seemed *uncomfortable* to Christine: Mortimer Road had its disadvantages and she was thankful to be out of it, but at least, in *these* matters, you knew where you were in it.

Descending the stairs one day, her eye was caught at once

by what looked like a scatter of waste-paper in the hall. She exclaimed in annoyance; surely Mr. Banks hadn't been so careless as to drop a waste-paper basket (it was one of his afternoons for cleaning, she could hear the Hoover going in the Long Room.) Or was it letters?

It was neither; it was no less than twelve postcards, six with one Face on them and six with Another; smaller, local deities as compared with the vast celestial ones that had beamed down over the Square in the late summer.

Elections were like that, Christine thought; they began by reminding you that there was such a thing as politics, with Faces you occasionally saw in the papers, and then they crept up on you, with these other Faces you'd never heard of, much less seen.

But right in your own home—it was too much of a good thing. She slowly stooped and began to gather up the stuff.

"Is that more of their nonsense?" Mrs. Traill asked cheerfully, coming into the hall. "I'm going down—I'll take it."

"Thank you, Mrs. Traill. Who they think's got the time to read through all that, I don't know—as if everybody hadn't something better to do."

"I couldn't agree more . . . Oh, by the way, Christine . . ." she hesitated, then went on, "We're expecting a 'phone call any time, from a Mr. Keiler, an old friend of ours. Would you keep your ears specially open, the next day or so? I've got to be out quite a bit."

"I always do, Mrs. Traill. But I'll do it specially for the next day or two."

"Thank you."

Mrs. Traill wandered away, a slight shade of—compunction, was it?—on her sensitive face. It's a damned shame, she was thinking, it's like laying a mine under a nice baby.

Still, they are two of our oldest friends.

.   .   .

The inhabitants of Pemberton Hall sat up determinedly to listen to the results of the General Election, that is, they sat up until about two in the morning, with drinks and sandwiches, and grilled kippers and coffee in the Long Room at midnight, but as it became plain that their Party was not going to be returned, they gradually lost interest.

James did point out that if the Party they all dreaded did get in, the size of its majority would strongly influence its policy. But this was too technical for the women, who, groaning in chorus, said that if they were in, they were in, and what did their majority matter? The words "the bit between their teeth" were used more than once by the three pretty, elderly creatures crouched yawning beside the log-fire.

"I really can't bear it!" Antonia exclaimed at last, as the impersonal B.B.C. voice proclaimed another victory for the dreaded forces of democracy, "I'm going to bed. Someone can wake me up in the morning and break it gently."

"Talking of breaking things gently, who's going to tackle our Christine?" Diana said, yawning with long arms in silvergrey cashmere stretched behind her head, "I think that will have to be you, ducky," to James.

"All right," was all he said; he was relighting a cigar.

"Well, darling, you are the only one of us who's had to do dirty work officially, sacking people you like personally, I mean. None of us have."

"I always leave it to Nigel," shivered Antonia. "I can't bear hurting people."

"Nor me," said Mrs. Traill, "James, is Clive quite certain he wants to let his flat?"

"Oh, I think so. He hasn't any capital, you know. He was out of work for months before he got this job and he told me just before he did get it that he was down to his last hundred. Of course, he's making a good bit now but you know he never could save—"

Short confirmatory laughs from the women.

"—and I'm prepared to bet he's spending up to the hilt at this very minute. It's a chancy profession, God knows; if he wants to let his flat and keep the proceeds, we can't blame him." James drew peacefully on the cigar, and the delicious azure smoke crept out with aristocratic slowness.

"He won't let it to strangers, for God's sake, will he? Bessy Mendel wants a flat but she hasn't much money either. (Oh do switch that thing off, Antonia, it's giving me the heebie-jeebies,)" said Mrs. Traill. "How much do you think he'll ask?"

Click. The voice announcing a victory for their favoured Party, with an alarmingly reduced majority in a hitherto safe seat, ceased adruptly.

"(Thank God.) She hasn't, you know,"

"Oh, ten guineas, I should think. He'd get that easily from any outsider," said James.

"No garage and not self-contained," Diana pointed out.

"Yes, but we don't want that kind of person, and it wouldn't appeal to them anyway. Situation, and house of character, and congenial professional fellow tenants, and that kind of thing is what we're offering."

"To someone we all know," Diana said emphatically.

"And ten from Dick and Amanda?" suggested Antonia.

"Ha! ha! You're optimistic, aren't you?" Diana scoffed.

"Sh'sh . . . I think I heard Christine's key," said Mrs. Traill.

A moment later the door opened softly, and Christine's face, cheerful in a silk scarf, and with cheeks rosed by the autumn's wind, looked in.

"Good-evening," she said.

"Hullo, Christine . . . nice evening?"

"Yes, thank you, Miss Marriott, I went to see Audrey Hepburn in The Nun's Story with a friend. It was lovely. Rather sad, but lovely, really. What a time those nuns do have! It quite upset me . . . but I did enjoy it."

"I'm glad someone's enjoyed something, this evening," Mrs. Meredith said.

Christine looked enquiringly from one face to another, then smiled.

"Oh . . . the Election. They kept on interrupting the film to tell us . . . My friend and I got so wild. But I suppose you have to know. Difficult to tell who's going to win, isn't it?"

"It's not difficult to tell who's going to lose. It's us," Diana said smartly. "Well . . . goodnight, Christine."

"Good-night, Mrs. Meredith; I have turned down the heating."

"Thanks. Good-night."

"Good night, Christine," murmured the rest of the group, and their housekeeper withdrew. There was silence for a moment.

"It does seem a shame," Mrs. Traill said at last.

"It's a shame all right. And you know, I don't go all that much for Bessy; she flaps and dithers," Diana said. "But, of course, Dick and Amanda . . ."

"Oh, Dick's so amusing," cried Antonia, "I adore him."

"I know, and Bessy's awfully amusing, too, and one can't help liking her," Mrs. Traill loyally said. "Besides, she'd be Clive's tenant, not ours."

"It won't make much difference whose tenant she is—she'd be in and out just the same," James said. "Has she any personal life, do you know?"

"Bessy? A bit too much, I should say. Why?" Diana asked.

"I meant Christine. Friends, family, that kind of thing?"

"Oh, how should I know? Family's a bit unsympathetic, I gather. There is this friend out in the wilds somewhere. The usual voice was asking for her on the telephone the other night. That's 'my friend' I suppose."

"Female?" Antonia demanded.

Mrs. Traill nodded. "Oh, yes. No such luck," was her cryptic answer.

"Well . . ." said James, "if you girls have really made up your minds I'm afraid she's 'for it'."

Chapter 25

THE STORM BROKE: THE PARTY THEY DETESTED WAS IN AND FOR a few days the household at Pemberton Hall went about with noticeably long faces.

But there was also a late spell of fine weather that soothed and lulled, and really it was not possible to feel depressed, under such a sky filled with so much light. Faces shortened, and no one yet cared to tell Christine Smith that the crystalline globe of peace and beauty in which her dear Pemberton Hall seemed to be enclosed was due for shattering.

It was on a Wednesday morning that Mr. Meredith put his head round the door of the Long Room, where she was dusting.

"Can I have a word with you?" he asked.

Christine, who was sliding her duster along the rich black surface of the piano, looked up in a little surprise.

The tone was amiable, he carried *The Times* under one arm as he always did at this hour in the morning. All was as usual—yet a faint foreboding began to creep upon her.

She came towards him, and as she walked down the length of the room, its grace, and the sheen of its old wood floor, and its white walls shaded and lightened by the play of the clouds outside, and its furniture, and the flowers she had chosen for it, held her as if in some delicate casket—Christine Smith, late of Mortimer Road.

"Sit down, won't you." Mr. Meredith just pushed forward an old wing-chair covered in olive brocade, and himself took a seat on the long sofa opposite.

"You don't smoke, do you?" he said, half-getting out his case, then, as she smilingly shook her head, "No, I thought not."

"I did used to, Mr. Meredith, I took it up after my parents

215

died—a kind of wanting to be independent, I suppose—they never liked the idea. But I never really liked it, myself, so I soon gave it up again."

She laughed; she had always liked Mr. Meredith best next to Mr. Lennox. He was her idea of a perfect gentleman; always so easy.

"Very sensible of you. But you're a sensible woman—I've always thought so. Now it won't take long to say what I have to, and the first thing I want to make clear to you is that we've been perfectly satisfied with all you have done for us in the time you've been here—I know you have always done your best, and a very good best it's been. No one—and we're all agreed about this—could have done the job better. We've all become—er—attached to you during the months you've taken such good care of us. Er . . ."

He paused for a second, to tap the ash from his cigarette into a jade ashtray at his elbow. Christine sat upright, hands folded in her lap, her eyes fixed steadily on his stubby, high-bred face—the face she had always thought of as 'kind of sporting'. But the heavy eyelids were cast down; not yet was Mr. Meredith ready to meet Christine Smith's eyes. As she faced him, honest-countenanced and fresh in the soft autumn light, he was actually finding his task a little painful, as well as awkward.

Christine's heart was hammering, for she knew, now, what was coming. If Pemberton Hall and its people had given her an increased sensibility, it had bestowed with the gift an added capacity for suffering, and oh, she guessed what was coming. Beyond his face, the wide, quiet, sunlit room extended indefinitely into light and peace, into a world from which she was being banished.

"We're going to let Mr Lennox's flat to a friend of Mrs. Traill's, and we shall let some old friends have the top flat."

The words came out distinctly; perhaps Mr. Meredith had in mind the old advice, *never explain and never apologize*; he had not called it 'your flat'; there was no play with the cigarette-ash this time, and as he spoke, he looked her full in the eyes: with his own, whose temperate official gaze had sized up many a trembling, weak, stupid, petty criminal in Africa. You must always look them in the eyes.

She was trying to speak. Her lips were moving. He waited, not taking his eyes from her face.

"Take your time," he said. "I expect it has come as a shock. Er—what are your plans?"

Wild thoughts had attacked her like a storm —offer to stay on and work for nothing—what have I done—too bad treating me like this—where will I go—what will I do?

But none of them came out. All the self-respect and courage of the Smiths moved up, in one great silent surge, to the help and support of their far-from-faithful daughter. Offer to stay on? Creep and crawl to them? Traitors! Never.

"It's all right. When would you like me to go?" asked Christine Smith quietly.

.   .   .

It would be stating the case too dramatically to say that she made for Avalon Road like a wounded bird. Indeed, as she hurried through the pelting rain which had inevitably replaced the Lorelei brightness of the morning, the last image suggested by her large raincoat-draped figure was of anything light and winged—and her umbrella was almost blown inside out, and the pavement was all over those wet leaves, so dangerous when you were in a hurry—and—

"Chris! Chris!"

Oh, wasn't that just like Moira? No one but Moira would have been out at the gate with a newspaper over her head in all that rain and her face alight with welcome and affection and concern.

"Come in, dear, I've got the kettle on. You must be soaked. Did you ever see such a change in the weather? Don't trouble to shut the gate!"

Moira's arm was round her, Moira was steering her up to the open front door and into the welcoming hall. "Oh, I've been so worried about you, Chris—and so has Frank. How could they? How could they? But come in, and let's get those wet things off."

217

But Christine had known what was going to happen to her for four hours now, and she had remembered to shut Moira's gate.

She was in outward control of herself—indeed, she had never lost control—not even in the appalling moment when she had stood, alone, in her sitting-room, after she had left Mr. Meredith—and seen her furniture.

She and Moira exchanged a hearty kiss, and then there was bustle and disconnected remarks in the warm kitchen, where the cat got up lazily to welcome her and her raincoat was hung up to drip.

Then—dry, already soothed by the cessation of blustering wind and rain, and sitting by the small open fire Moira had lit in the living-room, she told Moira all about it.

Moira was a most satisfactory confidante. She listened without comment, beyond a faint outward breath or a movement of lids and eyebrows, while Christine explained exactly what had been done to her.

It was not a 'pouring-out'. The story was told without drama or much emphasis, and she did not interrupt herself with condemnations of her employers; a kind of sulky cheerfulness best describes her manner. But Moira thought it kindest not to inflame feelings already wounded and startled to full capacity by any repetition of her first "How *could* they!"

"I don't blame them," Christine ended. "Mr Lennox has got a right to do what he likes with his own flat and . . . and . . . my flat . . . they do want it for some very old friends . . . I've heard them speak of them . . . very old friends . . ." The first gulp came. She was leaning slightly forward in her chair, paler than usual, her hands linked together, staring into Moira's bright little leaping fire. She swallowed painfully, not looking at her friend.

"Nice to see a fire on a day like this," she said in a moment. "You'd think it would be too warm, being so mild outside. But it's just nice."

"Ah, he's a clever boy, my fire," Moira said, gently moving the poker among coal and miniature logs from the prunings of

Frank's apple trees. "He knows when to burn up fiercely and when to just tick over, as they say."

"Of course you don't get the gales here like we do . . . up . . . up . . .our . . . way . . . being so high."

"No. We're nicely sheltered here."

A longish pause followed. But Moira was not merely looking gloomily into the flames; she was thinking, compressing and uncompressing her lips, raising her eyebrows calculatingly, and occasionally a small smile of satisfaction would pass over her face. Presently Christine looked up, and, the lump in her throat having been more or less satisfactorily dealt with, laughed.

"Why are you making all those faces?"

"Was I?" Moira's ready laugh came out too.

"Smiling away—I'm glad someone's got something to smile about. Fact is, I haven't really faced it yet, Moira. What am I going to do? Where can I go? I've got a bit of money, but—"

"Now look, Chris. This was Frank's idea really. You know I've got this back—"

"Yes I do, and very good it must've been for it, you standing out in the rain like that, you crazy monkey. How is it, dear? —I'm sorry, I was so taken up with my own troubles, I never asked."

"It's been bad lately. And Dr. Mason says it isn't going to get much better. He says I've got to learn to live with it (so helpful, but I do know what he means) and I'd sooner do that than be everlastingly dosing myself up with their old tablets and hoping. I must just accept it. You know. But Frank said—when I 'phoned him this morning about you, I was so upset I had to talk to him—he said, right away, why not ask her if she'd come to us? There!"

The twitch of pain that moved her face as she sat upright and looked at Christine with her eyes very wide-open did not affect the eager brightness of her expression. She looked all cheerfulness and hope.

"Do you mean . . . for a visit?" Christine asked—cautiously, but the glow on her friend's face seemed to be already reflected faintly on her own.

"No—no!" Moira shook her head impatiently. "I mean for good. Listen, Chris—" she bent forward, wincing again, in her earnestness, "you could have Tom's room. You remember you did like it, didn't you? It's nearly empty now; he had a lot of his own stuff in it, you know, and he took that of course when he left, and what's left is so old—I vote we send it off to the Old Folks' Home at Martindale, they're just starting and they're voluntary, and appealing for furniture, or it could go to the Church Hall, they're always crying out for stuff—and clear out absolutely *everything*. Curtains and all." (Moira's face appeared actually to shine as she disposed of the curtains.) "Then you could have all your lovely Swedish stuff and those curtains with the ivy. Oh, Chris, wouldn't it be lovely?"

The passionate dark colour that no one at Pemberton Hall had ever noticed had crept up over Christine's face as she stared at Moira, but she said nothing and Moira hurried on—

"We'd love to have you. You know that. But you could be such a help to me, too, Chris. You see—" for the first time her voice faltered in its full, cheerful tide—"Dr. Mason says this back of mine's going to get really bad, some day. I may be bedridden, Chris. While I'm still a comparatively young woman. It'll spread all over me, he says. And I do worry about that with the children just growing up, and Frank not so young as he was. Who's going to take care of them, I keep on thinking—and you know I don't worry as a rule. But—bedridden! . . . You never know what's coming, do you? I never thought I'd be bedridden."

"Well, you aren't—yet," Christine said with sturdiness in her tone; her colour had deepened and deepened during Moira's talk. "But—about this idea, Moira—oh, it *is* kind of you both. It's—I won't ever forget it. I'll always remember what you and Frank said. But—I've only got three hundred pounds. I did mean to save when I went . . . there . . . but somehow—I suppose never having been able to spend my money as I liked and always seeing it having to go on all those electric things, I went a bit wild when I had it all to myself, and I never saved anything. But I'm not in *debt*," Christine ended seriously, fixing her eyes on her friend's face.

"I should think not!" Moira's peal rang out. "The day you get into debt will be the one. But why all this business about money? We—"

"I'd have to pay you something, Moira. Oh yes, I should. It . . . wouldn't be right."

"Well, we could work that out with Frank later. Besides, just until I do get bedridden—and p'raps I mayn't, you never know, you could get a little job somewhere, just locally, not somewhere in London where you'd have to spend shillings and shillings on fares and lunches. I know!" Moira sat upright, as if recharged with energy by the new delightful notion. "Miss Peters at the wool-shop!"

"What—?"

"She was telling me only the other day she wants someone elderly. Her sister got married, of all things, at fifty-six—they'd been running the shop for years, the two of them—and when she went off Miss Peters tried girl after girl and none of them could read or write properly, let alone add up—think how awkward with all those little bills for stockings and needles and elastic all day long—and now she's in despair and going to try for someone elderly. She said she was well on the way to being ruined."

"Oh, but—"

"We'll go round there now, this minute," Moira cried, glancing out at the silvery-wet trees glinting in watery sunlight. "Oh, never mind my back, I'm too excited to think about backs now. Come along. Look, it's stopped raining."

.   .   .

This statement turned out to be a true one for Christine Smith. It had stopped raining.

She was safely in harbour at Avalon Road. Each morning, she made the short walk through the shady streets of Cooper's Green to the shop of Miss Gertrude Peters, where the varying tints of wool, and its different thicknesses, and the perennial misbehaviour of those customers who left deposits on an order and never came back to collect it after it had arrived, were the most moving events in a gently cheerful day.

Antonia finally married Mr. Herz; and six months after she had given him her hand, and was by degrees giving him her heart, the Lennox–Dettinger marriage broke up and Clive came back to England, certain at last that she was the only girl for him.

Alas! alas for Italy, and *Lost Moonlight*!

Bessy Mendel set everyone's teeth on edge by the harsh modernisms of her decorative style in Clive's former flat, and the house resounded to her smart bickering with Dick and Amanda on the top floor; of whom it was customary for the company to say, "Oh, Dick and Amanda have been together for *centuries*." Diana Meredith bought her summer hats and her winter jerseys, and Mrs. Traill's silvery head was still bent dreamily over her drawings.

For some time, life continued at Pemberton Hall almost as formerly.

.   .   .

One Thursday afternoon in late autumn, when the shop closed at one, Christine was again sitting by the fire with Moira Rusting—not yet bedridden, though undeniably less active than formerly.

The sun was setting behind those low ridges of the Home Counties near London, hiding their gentle debauched beauty, and giving to them a long, long-ago country darkness and loneliness; and the clouds were scudding across the sky, and there had already been ominous references to Force Five and Force Nine on the afternoon news flashes, and the first crumpets of the year were buttering in a dish before the fire, and Christine had just returned, as from some foray to a dangerous foreign land, from a shopping expedition to the Archway. She had got Them, in the shops where she thought They would be, and it had been, on all accounts, a satisfactory—a really extraordinarily satisfactory—afternoon.

"And, oh, Moira," she was saying, kneeling beside the sleepily-glowing red fire to add more butter to the already butter-soaked dainty, "I was on a bus . . . I must tell you. Who do you think I saw? No—not anybody from *there*—I don't often think about them now, after all it is nearly three years—yes, doesn't time fly, it is really—and I was on top of this bus going down the hill, and the traffic's worse than ever there; I don't know how anyone ever gets across the road, and oh, the noise . . . and suddenly—it was all like That Day. You remember. I told you."

"Of course I remember, dear."

"But Moira, *everything* was like it—the buses and the terrible traffic and the advertisements and the dirty houses and those great office blocks—*everything*. Everything was beautiful."

The word came out like a bird from a thicket, effortlessly, winged.

"Yes, everything. Just like That Day. And I happened to be looking over the side of the bus when it happened, and I saw her—Mrs. Benson—you know. That woman. And—I know you'll hardly believe it, I can hardly believe it myself, now, and she looked just as she always has, not even a bit older, and—oh, Moira, Mrs. Benson was beautiful."